For the
Love
of Pete

DEBBY MAYNE

A *Bloomfield* Novel

For the Love of Pete

B&H
PUBLISHING GROUP

NASHVILLE, TENNESSEE

978-1-4336-7730-4

Published B&H Publishing Group
Nashville, Tennessee

Dewey Decimal Classification: F
Subject Heading: LOVE STORIES \ CHRISTIAN LIFE—FICTION
\ FEMALE FRIENDSHIP—FICTION

Publisher's Note: The characters and events in this book are fictional, and any resemblance to actual persons or events is coincidental.

1 2 3 4 5 6 7 8 • 18 17 16 15 14

Dedication

This book is dedicated to Gail Sattler, Kathi Macias, Martha Rogers, Trish Perry, Miralee Ferrell, Jenness Walker, and Tracy Bowen. Y'all are the best!

Acknowledgments

Thanks to Tamela Hancock Murray, Julie Gwinn, and Barbara Scott for believing in this project, great editing, and making it happen.

*I don't mind getting older. I just mind
that I have aging children.*

Chapter 1

Bethany Hanahan watched Pete Sprockett pop off the old kitchen faucet and install a new one with little effort. He held up the worn parts. "I'll dispose of these for you."

"Thanks." Warmth flooded her as his smile traveled from his lips to his eyes. That was one of the things she'd always found attractive—the way his entire face showed emotion.

"Anything else . . . any other plumbing work you need while I'm here?"

Bethany inhaled deeply. Pete had awakened some of the feelings she'd buried after her husband's death, and she would love to have him stick around longer. But she knew he had work to do, so she shook her head.

"Then I'd better get going." He gestured toward the front of the house. "Walk me to the door?"

"Sure."

Standing there facing him sent a multitude of feelings surging through her. The warmth of his smile set off shivers as she remembered the crush she'd once had on him—since long before she'd started dating her husband Charlie. Pete's kindness tweaked her heart, and his love for the Lord reminded her that all of his actions were well-intentioned.

"Then c'mon." He started for the front door, and she followed.

As they approached the foyer, Pete hooked his thumbs through his belt loops and glanced around her house, his gaze settling on a collection of knickknacks on the side table. She had always found Pete handsome with his close-cropped brown hair and slim physique that barely offered a hint of the strength that didn't appear to have changed much in the thirty years since they'd graduated from high school.

Pete's expression was unreadable, but Bethany could guess what was on his mind—the same thing that seemed to be on everyone else's. Clutter blanketed her entire house.

She gestured toward the door, but as she took a step back, she tripped over the needlepoint-topped stool her mother-in-law Belva had made. She forgot she'd brought it down from the attic and placed it by the door. Pete caught her by the arm, but he quickly pulled his hand back once she steadied herself.

Bethany's face flamed, as she looked him in the eye. "I appreciate your stopping by and fixing the faucet, Pete. I know I've got a bunch of stuff lying around. Most of it was Charlie's mother's." She stopped herself, realizing she'd fallen into her old habit of explaining too much.

"It's not your stuff I'm worried about." His gaze held hers for a moment before he glanced away, shaking his head.

"I'm fine." Bethany forced a smile. "Really."

"You and Charlie's mom must have gotten along great."

"Yes, we did, but why do you say that?"

He nodded toward the living room. "She loved knickknacks, and it looks like you added to her collections."

Annoyance replaced the warmth she had felt only moments earlier. "And your point is . . . ?"

He visibly swallowed hard and gave her an apologetic look. "So how's Ashley doing in college? Heard from her lately?"

"She called last weekend, and from what she tells me, I gather she's doing quite well." She didn't want to be impolite, but she couldn't help the crispness of her tone.

"That's good. Charlie was so proud of her. Every time I saw him, she was all he talked about."

"I know. They were very close."

Pete chuckled. "I remember her being a mighty spirited young woman. I just hope she doesn't get into a mess like some of those college girls do."

"Why did you say that?" She folded her arms and narrowed her eyes. "Are you trying to worry me?"

"Of course not. Just being realistic."

"Maybe that's your problem." It was time for Pete to leave.

Pete cleared his throat as he walked out onto the porch and turned around to face Bethany. "Let me know if you need anything else."

"You know I will." She stood at the door and watched Pete back his truck out onto the cul-de-sac and take off. Once he was out of sight, she closed the door and let out a deep sigh.

Ever since she moved back to Bloomfield after her husband Charlie passed away two and a half years ago, people had been after her to get rid of the clutter—first her mother Naomi and then a few other garden club members who meant well. But until recently, she didn't see it as clutter. To Bethany, it was all about the memories. Charlie had been a wonderful husband and father before he found out he had advanced stage prostate cancer. After he passed away, her mother had tried to talk her into returning to Bloomfield, but she decided to wait until Ashley finished high school before moving into the modest house Charlie's parents had left them.

Charlie and Pete both worked for their families' businesses part-time during high school, with the understanding they'd eventually go full-time until their parents retired. Bethany and Charlie hung around for a couple of years, but he grew tired of

Bloomfield and the small-town quirkiness. Leaving her family and friends, she moved away with him as soon as he could find a job. She compensated for her homesickness by finding joy in Charlie's happiness.

Bethany once thought they might eventually move back to Bloomfield, but after Ashley was born, that changed. Bethany and Charlie didn't want to pull their daughter away from the church-based social life that kept her busy with so many activities.

Pete had wanted to kick himself a dozen times over during the past few months, but today he wanted to do it with both feet. He had the perfect opportunity to kiss Bethany when she tripped over that silly-looking stool in her foyer, but his old pride and fear of rejection kept him from it. Besides, even if she didn't reject him, that would have been awkward. Bethany had always been the model he'd held up for any girl he dated, and no one ever matched her softness and sweet disposition, making him want to protect her.

Through the years, he even dreamed about her, but when he awoke, his disappointment almost overwhelmed him. So he poured himself into helping his dad with the family plumbing company that seemed to be slipping through his father's un-businesslike fingers.

During Pete's childhood, his parents did the best they could. His mother stayed home with the kids, occasionally taking odd jobs during the holidays to buy gifts. Fortunately, she gave the family a sense of stability, and he never realized back then how difficult it had been for them to make ends meet. His father was always working, which Pete thought might change when he graduated and was able to help out more.

But once Pete took the helm of the family plumbing company, he realized his dad was in over his head with the business and hated facing the family since he felt like such a failure. His dad continued running the business until he got prostate cancer. Pete urged him to take time off, promising to keep the business running until he won the battle with cancer. Then less than a month after he was given the word he was cancer free, Pete's sister gave birth to twins, which kept both of the elder Sprocketts busy helping out with the new grandbabies.

Pete's mom urged him to go out more and find a nice girl. He had watched most of his pals get married, and then he saw how their relationships changed—not only between him and the guys but also between the couples. He cringed as he remembered how girls who'd been all sweet and warm became nagging wives after they had a ring on their fingers.

Bethany was one woman he doubted would ever change. Charlie was the only guy Pete knew who had been just as happy after the wedding as before . . . maybe even happier. Pete was glad Bethany had come back to Bloomfield.

Bethany had leaned on him during Charlie's funeral. Her mother Naomi tried her best to be the strength Bethany needed, but the harder Naomi tried, the more Bethany withdrew. He wished Naomi hadn't been so overbearing—the very thing that had driven away her adult children. Now that Bethany was back, Pete vowed to run interference if he saw even a hint of Naomi trying to change Bethany.

His cell phone rang just as he parked the truck, so he pulled it out of his back pocket and looked at the caller ID. *Naomi McCord.* That woman had some sort of extra sense when it came to timing. It seemed like every time she called, he was thinking about her daughter, but then he'd been thinking about Bethany quite a bit lately.

He pushed the TALK button. "Hey, Naomi, what do you need?"

"I need you to talk some sense into my daughter. You know I kept trying to get her and Charlie to move back to Bloomfield,

God rest his soul. And now that she's here, she's acting like a hermit in that old house." She blew out a breath. "Have you seen what a wreck that place is?" Before he had a chance to reply, she continued. "I know you have 'cause Bethany said you just left there. Can you believe what a mess her house is?" She clicked her tongue. "Clutter everywhere—on the furniture, on the floor . . . everywhere."

"What is it you want me to tell her? She likes her stuff."

"She just thinks she does, but I think she hangs onto it thinking she's somehow showing loyalty to Charlie . . . or because she feels safe hiding behind it."

"There's really nothing I can say—"

"I don't know about that. Her stuff is nothing but junk, and we need to help her get rid of it."

"Bethany has a mind of her own." He sure wished Naomi wouldn't put him in this position.

Naomi chuckled. "Don't I know it. Well, at any rate, maybe you can talk her into getting out more and doing something outside the house."

He wished he hadn't answered the phone. "At least she goes to church."

"Besides church. It took years to get my daughter to move back to Bloomfield, and now that she's here, I'm more worried than ever." Naomi paused for a few seconds. "At least she hasn't started collecting cats."

"Leave it to you to find the bright spot."

"Just call me Suzy Sunshine." The sound of someone talking seemed to pull Naomi away for a moment. "I gotta run. Zumba for Seniors is about to start, and I don't want to be late on account of I'll miss the first part where they teach all the steps. Last time I missed, it took me forever to get the moves right."

"Okay, Naomi."

"Will you at least try to talk to my daughter and get her out of the house more?"

"I'll do what I can."

After he pressed the end button, he shoved the phone into his pocket and got out of the truck. His family business had not only survived his dad's retirement, it had thrived under Pete's direction. As much as he hated to admit anything negative about his own father, the company needed to upgrade the quality of materials and do a better job of training the employees.

Once he came on full-time, he managed to convince his father to at least give it a try. Customers appreciated the higher grade of products and services because they didn't have to call as often. With the smaller workload, the employees enjoyed more time with their families, and that made working for Sprockett Family Plumbing much more pleasant.

He had one more service call to make before calling it a day. Fortunately, this was a simple toy-in-the-toilet issue that he was able to fix in less than ten minutes.

"How much do I owe you?" the harried woman said as her granddaughter pitched a temper tantrum behind her.

Pete lifted his hands and smiled. "This one's on me. Go give your grandbaby the attention she wants. I can let myself out."

"Thank you so mu—" A crashing sound abruptly ended their conversation.

As Pete headed out the door, he chuckled to himself. He'd always enjoyed children, but he wondered how he would have handled his own in a situation like this.

He got back to the office, where his dad stood at the counter chatting with the receptionist.

"Hey, Dad."

"What are you still doing out in the field? You're the CEO now." His dad tilted his head forward and gave him a long look from beneath his thick eyebrows. "You do realize that position comes with certain privileges."

"It also has some responsibilities." The instant those words tumbled from Pete's mouth, he regretted them. "Besides, I like being out in the field. It keeps me humble."

"That's part of your problem, Pete. If you ask me, you're a little too nice. I bet you didn't even charge the folks you helped."

Pete didn't bother responding. "So what brought you to the office today? Getting bored with retirement? Want a job?"

His dad chuckled. "I do need a break from retirement, but working at the plumbing company is the last thing I want to do—unless you need me."

"We can always use another plumber."

"No thanks." His dad grimaced.

"Just thought I'd ask. So what's wrong with retirement?"

"Your mother has me hopping all over the place. First, she wanted me to trim the rose bushes before the garden club makes the rounds for Yard of the Month. As if that wasn't enough, when I got done, I didn't even have time to wash my hands before she shoved some fertilizer in them for the flower beds."

That was probably more manual labor than his dad had done when he worked at the company full time, but Pete would never have come out and said that. He loved both of his parents, but his dad's flaw had been obvious from the moment Pete stepped into the office and taken over. Grandpa had assumed all he had to do was hand the business over to Dad, and everything would come naturally.

"So what is Mom up to today?"

Dad shrugged. "She's all worked up about getting more involved in the garden club again." He chuckled. "I don't know why she'd want to bother with that bunch of busybodies."

Pete thought about Naomi and the president of the club, Pamela Jasper, and laughed. "They mean well, and you have to admit they get things done."

"I know, I know. Those folks are the movers and shakers of Bloomfield, but they still like to stick their noses in everyone else's business."

"I'm sure not all of them are that way." Pete hoped his dad

didn't ask for an example, because he couldn't think of one off the top of his head.

Dad pulled away from the counter where he'd been leaning. "I best be gettin' on home. Your mother just wanted me to stop by and ask you to join us for supper. She said to tell you we're having pot roast."

"Mom will stop at nothing, will she?"

"Especially when she has something up her sleeve."

"Gertie Sprockett is having some friends over for supper, and she wondered if you'd like to join us." Naomi didn't even stop to take a breath before she added, "This is real important to me. I want you to go."

Bethany wished she hadn't answered the phone, and she should have known better when she saw her mother's name and number on the caller ID. "I don't know. I have so much to do."

"Like what?" The tone of impatience in Naomi's voice never failed to back down Bethany, as well as most of the residents of Bloomfield. The only other person Bethany knew who would stand her ground to the bitter end was Pamela, the president of the Bloomfield Garden Club. When Pamela and Naomi disagreed on something, which was frequent, sparks flew, and everyone hunkered down for a long verbal battle that almost always ended with them agreeing and creating a formidable force no one else wanted to deal with. "Now don't go giving me the silent treatment. It's not going to work with me."

"I'm not giving you the silent treatment. I'm just trying to—"

"Think of an excuse? It won't work, so you might as well save your energy for later. I let Bernice borrow my car, so I need a ride anyway. Do you mind picking me up?"

Bethany sighed. No way would she be able to get out of this, so she might as well stop trying. "Of course, I don't mind." Besides, after all the things Naomi had done for Bethany after Charlie passed away, there was no way she could turn her mother down, even if it meant going somewhere she wasn't in the mood to go.

"Good. Gertie said to be there at six thirty, so why don't you swing by around six, and I can show you the new vegetable garden at the Village? It took a half dozen of us a whole week to get the ground ready, but I have to admit it was all worth it."

After they hung up, Bethany rocked back on her heels. It was already past four, so she didn't have much time to finish putting all the photos in the albums she'd picked up. Her daughter Ashley had pulled down all of the boxes of pictures from the attic last time she was in town during semester break. If Bethany had known how many there were, she might have left them up there. Now she had dozens of boxes stacked almost as high as she was tall in the kitchen, with the photo albums covering the table. At least she didn't have to worry about clearing a place to eat now that she was going over to the Sprocketts' place for supper.

Bethany had known the Sprockett family all of her life, and she'd spent many hours at their house. Miss Gertie had made sure all of Pete's friends felt welcome by preparing platters of snacks and setting extra places at the table if the fun lasted until mealtime. No one cared that she stretched the meals with extra potatoes and rice because they loved Pete's mom. Between Miss Gertie and her mother, most of the kids in Bethany's crowd stayed well fed and entertained.

Her mother had tried to get Pete's mom more involved in the garden club, but Miss Gertie had always said someone needed to watch the kids while their mothers were off beautifying Bloomfield. Now that she was ready to commit the time, the garden club was making her jump through all kinds of hoops. Bethany knew the only reason they did so was because they could, and if Miss Gertie put her foot down, she'd be fine. The group needed more hands to accomplish their goal of making the town desirable enough to boost the population to ten thousand. They consistently hovered close to that number, but they'd never quite made it, because as soon as a baby was born, someone would move or pass away.

Bethany was tempted to go as she was, but she hadn't seen Miss Gertie and Mr. Frank in a while, so she decided to change into something a little nicer than her yard work jeans and bank-issued T-shirt. A quick glance in the bathroom mirror let her know she needed a little color on her face, or she'd risk having Naomi—or worse, Miss Gertie—ask if she wasn't feeling well. So she brushed a light dusting of powder blush over her cheeks and smeared on a bit of coral lipstick. Fortunately, she'd just gotten her hair cut, and her blonde waves fell in some semblance of order over her shoulders.

At a quarter to six, she headed out to pick up Naomi. As she drove through the downtown section of Bloomfield, she took long, deep breaths. The town hadn't changed much since her childhood, but Bethany had changed beyond anything she ever would have imagined. Once upon a time, she'd imagined she and Charlie would move back into his family's home after he retired, and she would jump into the Bloomfield Garden Club with gusto. He used to laugh at that notion, reminding her that as soon as they moved into their house, all the flowers died.

Rows of potted evergreens lined the sidewalks on either side of the faded red-brick road. Shop owners still posted signs in their windows announcing specials and HELP WANTED. Young Bloomfield residents rarely relied on the Internet for their first jobs, because they did things the old-fashioned way, just as their parents and grandparents had done before them. They would take off on foot downtown and ask managers and shop owners to hire them. In a town the size of Bloomfield, reputations were stronger than references, so no one had to wait for an answer.

Bethany had held a variety of part-time jobs when she was a teenager, including one summer at the Lake Bliss Retirement Center dining room, which eventually led to busing tables at the Pink Geranium Tea Room and then being a courier for City Hall. All her work lessons had been valuable, but the one lesson that stood out the most was that her mother was considered eccentric—even by quirky Bloomfield standards—something she'd learned when people forgot whose daughter she was.

Bethany drove around the town square toward the Lake Bliss Retirement Village where her mother lived. As she passed the Fontainbleu Apartments where quite a few of her unmarried friends and some of the younger adults from town lived, she noticed Pete pulling out of the parking lot. If she didn't own her former in-laws' house, she might have enjoyed some of the amenities of apartment life. But realistically, she probably wouldn't have taken advantage of most of them, and she doubted there would be enough room for all of her mementos.

Everything about the Lake Bliss Retirement Village, affectionately called the Village by its residents, was immaculate—from the freshly paved and marked visitor parking lot to the butterfly, vegetable, and herb gardens scattered throughout the property. The Village golf course was pristine and well managed. Naomi lived in the farthest building from the parking lot, but Bethany knew better than to ask if she should drive around to pick her up. Active in Zumba for Seniors, garden club activities, helping construct playgrounds with hopes of attracting more families with children, and her daily meddling wherever she saw the need, Naomi prided herself on staying in shape.

Just as Bethany pulled into a parking spot and got out of her car, she saw her mother running toward her.

"Get back in. I don't want to be late," Naomi said as she opened the car door and slid into the passenger seat. "Took you long enough to get here."

"You said to be here by six. I thought you wanted to show me some of the gardens."

Naomi frowned and then nodded as she got out of the car. "Okay, so you're on time. C'mon, and I'll show you the gardens." She pointed as they walked along the edge of the parking lot. "See the butterfly garden over there? We just finished planting some asters and zinnias along the northeast edge."

"Nice."

"Wanna go look at the vegetables?" Naomi fidgeted with the hem of her jacket.

"Isn't it a little early to be planting all these gardens? What if there's another frost?"

Naomi shrugged. "That's a chance we like to take. If we have a frost, we just have to replant. If we don't, we're ahead of the game."

"Such gamblers." Bethany chuckled.

"Yeah, that's how we roll around here. Throw caution to the wind and take a ride on the wild side—that's what we always say."

"So tell me what Miss Gertie is up to."

Naomi's head snapped around. "What're you talking about? What makes you think she's up to something?"

"Um . . . I didn't mean anything by that. I just—"

"Oh, never mind. Let's just go, okay?" Naomi turned and started toward the car.

"Sure." Bethany followed her mother.

The look of steely determination on Naomi's face as they buckled their seat belts sent an alarm buzzing through Bethany. She knew the signs of her mother's scheming, and the signs today were flashing neon.

Bethany backed the car out of the spot as soon as Naomi had her seat belt buckled. "What's going on?"

Naomi smoothed her shirt and then fidgeted with the gift bag in her lap. "I don't know what you're talking about." She cleared her throat. "Today was beautiful, wasn't it?"

"Yes." Bethany hoped it would remain that way.

As she drove toward the Sprockett house, Naomi chattered about all kinds of insignificant things—from the weather to fashion, which she hadn't cared about for as long as Bethany could remember. Something was definitely going on, but Bethany knew her mother wouldn't let on until she was good and ready.

Chapter 2

"Why are you pacing, Mom?" Pete grabbed a stick of celery and shoved it into his mouth. "Don't be silly. I'm not pacing."

Pete swallowed, leaned against the kitchen counter, and folded his arms. "Then what are you doing?"

"Getting dinner ready." She motioned her head toward the door. "Do me a favor and get a couple of the folding chairs from the garage."

All of Pete's life, his mother invited anyone to dinner who didn't have other plans, even when money was tight, so it was no surprise she was expecting more folks. What puzzled him was her nervousness. Normally, she was relaxed enough to hold a decent conversation, but now her nerves appeared to be strung tighter than a fiddle. He pondered the possibilities as he found the chairs and carried them into the kitchen. Maybe his parents had an announcement, and Mom was worried about how he'd take it.

He remembered when one of his buddies got the news that his parents had sold the house, bought an RV, and planned to travel around the country for the next year. Somehow, that didn't seem like something Mom and Dad would do.

"Dad said you were cooking a pot roast. What's all this other stuff?"

"Put that chair over there." She nodded. "I just want to make sure we have enough food, and the pot roast will only stretch so far."

Pete followed his mother's orders, placing chairs and moving them around again after she changed her mind. Her normally smooth gestures had turned into jerky motions, and when she stood still, she fidgeted.

The doorbell rang. Pete glanced over at his mother across the dining room table and saw the deer-in-the-headlights panic.

"Want me to get that?" He lifted an eyebrow, as her cheeks flamed pink.

"If you don't mind." She turned her back and scurried back into the kitchen. Whatever had her in this nervous tizzy sent her into hiding. Must be a doozy, and he suspected he'd get an answer as soon as he opened the door.

"Hey, Naomi." He glanced over at Bethany who appeared slightly confused. "Bethany." He took a step back. "Come on in. Mom said we had some people coming, but she didn't say who."

Naomi forged toward the kitchen, leaving him standing in the foyer with Bethany, who gestured toward the older woman. "I have no idea what's going on, but Mom was a nervous wreck all the way here."

"My mom's acting weird too. They're up to something." Pete had a good idea what it was, but he didn't want to scare Bethany. One night in a moment of weakness, he'd divulged his attraction to Bethany during a family dinner. At the time, he assumed his parents would accept it for what it was—a fantasy—but that obviously wasn't the case.

"Do you cook for yourself?"

He chuckled. "I cook a little, but it's mostly stuff from a box.

Mom likes to lure me back every once in a while with one of her home-cooked meals." He rubbed his tummy, and she laughed.

"Our moms are both such great cooks."

He nodded. "Yes, except Naomi started on a health kick, and my mom is stuck in the meat-potatoes-and-gravy mode."

"The best of both worlds." She smiled, lighting up the room.

"So what do you think? Any idea what they might be up to?"

"I think I know what it is." Bethany put her purse on the floor behind the foyer table, leaned over, and pulled out a figurine. "I have something for your mom."

"Isn't that from one of Charlie's mother's collections?"

She nodded. "I remember Belva saying she and your mom both liked these."

He shrugged. "I wouldn't know. So why do you think our mothers are acting so skittish?"

"I'm not sure, but I think they're both considering running for the garden club board, and they might have a plan to join forces." She shrugged. "But I don't see how that would make them act so . . . weird."

Pete laughed at the face she made, with one side of her nose crinkled, lifting her lip Lucille Ball style. She might be pushing fifty, but her shoulder-length blonde hair, silky smooth skin, sparkling blue eyes, and impish grin made her look much younger.

"Are you kids going to help me get the food on the table, or do you plan to stand out there yapping all night?" The sound of his mother's voice echoed through the house, and Bethany grinned up at him, making his heart pound double-time.

"We'll be right there," Pete said. He sighed. "I hope you're hungry. Mom fixed enough food to feed all of Bloomfield and then some."

"She's always done that." Bethany took a step toward the kitchen but stopped. "Remember when Charlie and I broke up right before our last Homecoming game?"

Pete did remember, and he'd tried to put it out of his mind ever since. His mother had gotten the notion that food would cure Bethany's pain. She'd invited Bethany over for dinner and presented her with a smorgasbord that provided his family with leftovers for an entire week.

"Did you hear me?" she asked.

He jerked back to the moment. "Uh, yeah, I heard you."

She shook her head and sighed. "Your mother plied me with country fried steak, barbecued pork chops, roasted chicken, mashed potatoes, and brownies to help me get over Charlie—stuff my mother would never fix. I must have put on a good five pounds that week."

Naomi appeared at the other end of the hall. "You two best start helping, or you'll be stuck cleaning up this mess by yourselves."

Pete shot a glance at Naomi before turning to wink at Bethany. "Then by all means, we'll help now."

As Pete took a step toward the kitchen, Bethany playfully nudged him out of the way and rushed past. "Last one there is a rotten egg."

He hesitated for a split second before taking off after her. "You're on."

♡ ♡

Bethany's heart hammered so hard against her chest, she thought Pete would surely see the effect he was having on her. He'd always managed to bring out her playful side. They used to kid around when they were younger, saying Charlie was the straight man to set up Pete's punch lines. At times during Bethany's marriage, she wished they lived closer so Pete could help lighten up Charlie. Her late husband's serious nature sometimes sucked all the joy from their lives.

Ashley brightened things up, though, and Bethany was

thankful their daughter had her disposition. She'd wanted more children, but Charlie said they needed to be cautious, because raising kids was so expensive. Over time, Bethany had become more reserved and serious. Pete brought out the lighter side of her she'd forgotten existed.

By the time she reached the kitchen, she was out of breath, with Pete right on her heels. She turned around and saw the gleam in his eye.

"Why are you looking at me like that?" she asked. "I won."

"I let you win." A hint of a smile twitched at the corners of his lips.

"Did not. I won fair and square."

Miss Gertie rolled her eyes and shoved a stack of dishes into Pete's arms. "Some people never grow up."

"Growing up is overrated." Naomi chuckled as she grabbed an olive from the relish tray and popped it into her mouth. "And don't ever accuse me of doing it, because I'll call you a liar if you do."

"Where's Dad?" Pete stood by the kitchen door still holding the plates.

"I think he smelled work and took off."

Bethany saw the look of annoyance flash across Pete's face, but he didn't respond. Instead, he turned and carried the dishes into the dining room.

"I'll get the silverware," she said. "Do you keep it in the same place?"

Miss Gertie nodded. "Naomi, why don't you make the iced tea? No one else can make it as good as you."

"You're just tryin' to get me out of the way," Naomi said, even though she did what Miss Gertie asked. "Got any lemons?"

Her friend pointed to the refrigerator. "I stuck them in the top vegetable crisper. See if we have enough to make lemonade."

As Bethany walked past the mirror over the buffet table in the dining room, she caught her reflection and almost gasped. Some of the color she'd lost in her cheeks had returned, and she actually looked younger than she had in a long time. And it wasn't just the blush she had applied before leaving home.

Pete put down the plates and turned to face her. "What's wrong? Are you okay?"

She couldn't tell Pete, so she just nodded. "Let's get the table set so we don't get in trouble."

He laughed as he turned back around. "This is just like old times, isn't it? Only . . ." His voice trailed off, but Bethany was pretty sure she knew what he was thinking. It was just like old times, only now, Charlie wasn't there.

As Pete carried the flatware into the dining room, Bethany remembered she needed some serving spoons. She'd reached the kitchen door when she overheard Miss Gertie say, "I think our plan to get the kids together just might work. Have you seen the way they look at each other?"

So she was right. They were scheming. Bethany cleared her throat to alert them before walking toward the utensil drawer. The guilty look on Miss Gertie's face was comical, but when she turned to look at her mother, all she saw was a stern expression.

"Better hurry up and get back in the dining room, or Pete will think you're shirking your responsibility."

Bethany nodded, grabbed some spoons, and left the two mothers staring after her as she headed back to the dining room. Pete glanced up and winked. Her heart thudded.

They set the table in silence until Naomi joined them. "Why's it so quiet in here? I thought you two had abandoned us."

Bethany looked Naomi in the eye and smiled. Pete lifted his hand and pointed toward the kitchen. "I'll grab the bread basket, so I can steal a roll. I'm starving."

Naomi shook her head. "You haven't changed a bit, I see." She clicked her tongue. "Go help him, Bethany, and while you're at it, make sure he doesn't eat all the bread before he gets to the table."

When Bethany went back into the kitchen, Pete stood there, his lips in a straight line, eyebrows comically arched, a bowl of lettuce and other assorted vegetables in his hand. "Mom won't let me near the bread."

"You got that right, son." Miss Gertie chuckled. "We all know there's not much chance of you snitching too much salad. Go on and put that on the table."

Bethany grabbed a bowl and followed Pete but went to the opposite side of the room. After they put their bowls on the trivets, Pete looked around the table and counted chairs. "I wonder who else is coming."

"No telling, knowing our moms." Bethany smiled and shook her head.

Miss Gertie entered the dining room carrying a casserole dish, with Naomi following right behind. Naomi scooted around her friend and placed another trivet on the table for the hot casserole. Their synchronized movements made it obvious they'd done this before.

"We heard you talking," Naomi said. "And you're right. We do have something up our sleeves. We want Pamela to know she's not the only one with good ideas." She looked directly at Bethany with a Cheshire-cat grin. "So we invited her and Andy."

Pete leaned back, still smiling, and folded his arms. "What kind of ideas are you talking about?"

Naomi turned to Miss Gertie. "Do you want to tell them, or should I?"

A stricken look flashed across Miss Gertie's face. "I don't know if that's such a good idea."

"Too late now, Mom. Spill." Pete's smile faded.

"Don't get all worked up, Gertie. These are smart kids. They'll know what's going on as soon as we open our mouths."

Miss Gertie made a harrumphing sound and stomped out of the dining room, leaving Bethany and Pete to stare at Naomi. "Okay, so what's going on?" Bethany asked.

Naomi lifted her hand and tapped her finger to her chin. "You know how Pamela is always trying to concoct a way to bring more people to Bloomfield, and once they're here, she does everything she can think of to make them stay?"

"She's always done that," Pete said.

"It's obviously not working all that well, because we still haven't reached our population goal of ten thousand." Naomi rolled her eyes. "Even though I think it's about the silliest thing I've ever heard of, I've decided to go along with her and help her out. You know how—"

Bethany planted her fist on her hip and glared at her mother. "Stop going off track. What's your latest plan?" She had a bad feeling about this, but she also knew there was nothing she could do once her mother set her mind to something—especially if she had a partner in crime.

"A reward program."

"Reward?" Pete unfolded his arms and looked at Naomi with suspicion. "As in paying people?"

"Something like that, yeah." Naomi glanced around, discomfort written all over her face. "We need to give people incentive to make Bloomfield their home."

"Isn't the reward of living here enough?" Bethany asked.

Naomi shook her head. "Obviously not, or we'd be overflowing with new house permits." She chuckled. "Actually, Gertie and I thought up the most ridiculous thing we could to get Pamela off our backs."

"If it's so ridiculous, what makes you think she'll buy into it?"

Naomi cackled. "Oh, trust me, she won't. Pamela's a smart woman."

"Then why bother?"

"She will either embrace it to keep us busy or she'll tell us how stupid our idea is and then back off and let things happen naturally." She cast a glance at Gertie who nodded. "I don't really care which way it goes 'cause I don't have anything better to do."

"But—" The doorbell rang before Bethany could finish. "I'll get that."

The second she opened the door, Pamela Jasper burst into chatter, waving her hands around, showing off her latest manicure—this one featuring pearlized snowflakes against an azure background. "Sorry we're late, but Andy didn't want to leave his precious bird alone." Even though Pamela rolled her eyes, Bethany could tell the woman didn't mind.

Andy hung back, a sheepish expression on his face and a birdcage dangling from his hand. "Is it okay . . . I mean, do you mind that I brought Murray?"

"I'm okay with it if everyone else is," Miss Gertie said, looking at Bethany.

Bethany glanced down at the gigantic parrot staring at her. "Of course, I don't mind. That is, he'll be in the cage the whole time, right?"

Andy chuckled. "As long as I don't turn my back on him, yeah, he'll stay in his cage."

Pamela made a face. "That bird is an escape artist. I don't get why you don't just put a lock on it."

"You know how it upsets him." Andy's frown let Bethany know this was a long source of contention.

"He'll get over it." Pamela forged ahead. "I don't want to just show up and eat. What can I do to help?"

Naomi let out an incredulous huff. "You're already late, Pamela. There's not much left to do."

"You don't have to get testy with me." Pamela's eyes bulged as she and Naomi did one of their stare-downs. "I'm being nice."

"Mom," Bethany said as she touched her mother's arm. "Please don't . . ."

Naomi yanked her arm away. "I just tell it like it is."

"C'mon, Ms. Jasper. You can give me a hand with the ice."

As Pamela followed Pete into the kitchen, Bethany heard Pamela chattering nonstop. "Ice is a one-person job, Pete. I don't have to give you a hand. One of us can get it, but not both."

Pete glanced over his shoulder at Bethany and grinned. "Okay, just let me know if you want to do it, so I can do something else."

"I don't *want* to do it, but I will."

The sound of Andy mumbling behind Bethany caught her attention. She spun around and saw that he was still standing there holding the cage. "Would you like to put Murray down?"

"That would be nice. Where will I be sitting? Murray likes to be close to me, or he might squawk us right out of the dining room."

Bethany had heard the volume of noise Murray could make, so she knew exactly what Andy was talking about. "I'm not sure. Let me go ask Miss Gertie."

Fifteen minutes later, everyone was seated, and Murray was perched in the cage directly between Andy and Pete. Pamela insisted on saying the blessing. She was halfway finished when Murray decided it was time to remind everyone of his presence. "Amen . . . *squawk* . . . Let's eat!"

Pete had to bite the insides of his cheeks to keep from laughing. He opened one eye and caught Andy scowling at his bird.

Pamela cleared her throat and continued. "Lord, bless this food we are about to eat, and remind us of how fortunate we are to be surrounded by such good friends—"

"Good food, good friends, let's eat . . . *squawk* . . . Amen!"

This time, Pete couldn't hold back the laughter. Pamela finally expelled a breath of exasperation and said, "Amen." When Pete opened his eyes, he noticed amusement on everyone's faces, except Pamela's.

Chapter 3

Throughout dinner, Murray made up for Andy's reticence by letting his voice be heard. He had opinions about everything from beautifying Bloomfield, "Beautiful flowers . . . *squawk* . . . win the trophy!" to increasing the population, "Ten thousand or bust . . . *squawk* . . . ten thousand or bust!"

"Cut it out, Murray!" Pamela snapped.

Andy leaned away and gave her one of his you're-kidding looks. "What're you talkin' about, Pamela? You taught him to say that."

Pamela lifted her chin. "He needs to learn there's a time and a place . . ."

"He's a bird." Andy shook his head and laughed. "What do you expect?"

"Nice birdie . . . *squawk!*"

Everyone laughed, until Pamela gave each person one of her no-nonsense scowls. Pete had to use his napkin to cover the smile he couldn't erase, and he saw Bethany struggled with the same thing.

"Oh, for Pete's sa—" Naomi grinned at Pete. "I mean, for heaven's sake, I think Murray is a cute bird. A little too much of a ham, but even you have to admit, Pamela, he's pretty funny."

The low growl that came from Pamela's throat showed just how amusing she thought he was. Pete glanced over at his mom and saw she'd started fidgeting again.

By dessert, Pamela's annoyance toward Murray grew to epic proportions; her fingernails fluttered double-time, and her voice grew shriller by the second. Pete continued to hide his amusement as Naomi took every opportunity to pop a retort back at Pamela's comments. Those two women were so much alike they appeared not to like each other, but he knew better. They'd been friends ever since Pamela took over presidency of the garden club, a job Naomi once held but didn't want any more, even though she wasn't willing to give up all control.

"Can't you make him be quiet?" Pamela finally said. "We're trying to hold a conversation here, and his squawking is making it nearly impossible."

"Bad birdie . . . *squawk*!" Murray buried his head beneath his wing. Pamela turned to Naomi. "Okay, so tell me what you and Gertie cooked up."

"We were thinking . . . at least I was thinking and Gertie agreed with me . . . that maybe we can have some sort of reward program to bring people to Bloomfield."

"Reward?" Pamela tilted her head. "I don't think—"

Naomi lifted her hand. "You want people to move here, right? We can give them some sort of incentive."

"Like what?"

Pete's mother spoke up this time. "For starters, we can give prizes to existing residents for bringing people to one of our events."

Naomi nodded. "And once people sign a lease or a contract to move, we can give them a welcome-to-Bloomfield gift."

"That sounds—"

"Ridiculous?" Andy offered.

Pamela scowled at Andy, pursed her lips, and gave the concept some thought. "When would you want to do this?"

"Soon." Naomi looked at Gertie who nodded her agreement. "In fact, the sooner the better."

Pamela's forehead crinkled. "We already have the Annual Bloomfield Rummage Sale coming up. Maybe afterward . . . or . . ." Her eyes lit up. "We can have a festival and do both!" She waved her hands around in excitement, almost smacking Andy in the face. "It'll be a regular party, and that'll certainly make people want to move here. Everyone loves a party!"

"Party hearty . . . *squawk!*"

"Stop that, you silly bird!" Pamela glared at Murray. "You need to learn when to keep your beak shut."

Pete noticed Naomi's lips twitching, and he didn't miss her exchanged glance with his mom. Fortunately, they didn't say what he suspected they were thinking—that Pamela's squawk was just as annoying as Murray's.

"Did you ever go through that junk Belva collected?" Naomi asked Bethany, clearly to change the subject and take the attention away from Pamela.

Pete cringed. This didn't seem like the time or place to bring up that topic, but Bethany stood up to her. "You know good and well I can't just get rid of her stuff. She wanted Ashley to have some of it."

"Then you might want to donate some of your knickknacks to our . . ." Naomi looked around at everyone and smiled. "Our cause. Your house isn't big enough for junk from the houses of two pack rats." Naomi leaned back, glanced at Pamela who nodded, and turned back to face Bethany. "You can do double good by letting us sell some of it at the rummage sale."

Bethany frowned. "Maybe I can go through it when Ashley comes home on break. I just don't want to give away anything she might want later. That wouldn't be right."

Naomi's eyebrows came together as her face puckered. "What's not right is the fire hazard you've created. When was the last time you dusted the baseboards? You can't even see 'em because there's so much clutter in that little house of yours—"

Pamela nodded her agreement. "You really need to listen to your mother, Bethany. It's not healthy to have such a mess in your house."

Pete had heard enough. "That's enough, ladies. I think she knows how you feel."

"We just wanted to make sure—"

He scooted his chair back and stood to further drive his point home. "Anyone want anything from the kitchen while I'm up?"

His mother jumped up. "I'll go with you and get more tea."

He started to tell her he'd get it, but she gave him a look that let him know she wanted to talk. Once they were out of hearing distance, she shook her head. "Those two women can be so overbearing on their own, but when they agree on something . . ." She sighed. "Poor Bethany."

"Yes, poor Bethany, but you knew how they could be before you invited them." He paused. "Now I'm concerned about how Naomi backed Bethany into a corner."

"Naomi has always done that." His mom's gaze slowly met his. "I suspect that's why all her kids moved away, and why I tried so hard to let you live your life as you saw fit. Maybe I went too far in the other direction."

"What are you talking about?" Pete closed the distance between them and placed his hand on his mother's shoulder. "You've always been the perfect mom."

"But you haven't given me any grandkids yet, and I'm afraid it's too late." She cleared her throat. "My only hope now is that you'll meet someone who already has children."

He removed his hand, took a step back, and leaned away. "Oh, so that's what this is all about."

"What what's all about?"

"This whole dinner tonight. It's a setup."

"You should know better than that. I think it's pretty obvious we were trying to give Pamela some ridiculous idea about how to bring more people to Bloomfield . . . not thinking she'd actually buy into it."

Pete held her gaze. "So you don't have any notion of getting Bethany and me together? Be honest with me."

She blinked and glanced down. "I can't honestly say I wasn't hoping something would happen . . . you know."

"Look, Mom, I've known Bethany all my life." He paused. "We're good friends, and I want it to stay that way."

"But—"

He lifted a finger to silence her. "Let's just hope Bethany hasn't caught on, or she might never want to see me again."

A stricken look crossed his mother's face. "That would be awful."

He didn't want her to feel too bad. "If that's the case, I'm sure she'll get over it. Bethany and I are good enough friends that I think we can get through this little setup without too many scars."

"Let's hope so." She took a step toward the dining room, stopped, and glanced around the kitchen. "I better not go out there empty-handed, or they'll think we were talking about them."

Pete laughed. "We wouldn't want them to know the truth, would we?"

The look she gave him made him laugh even harder. She opened the refrigerator and pulled out a pitcher of tea. "I'll see if anyone wants a refill."

The instant Pete and his mom returned to the dining room, Bethany sensed something different between them. Not only did Pete avoid her gaze, his mom's overly polite demeanor toward him seemed awkward.

Andy's gaze darted back and forth between her and Pete, so she suspected he was aware of something as well. Even Murray remained quiet—at least for a few minutes—until the conversation got back on a more natural track. Then he started squawking again.

Pamela finally pushed back and picked up her plate from the table. "Let's clean up now. I don't know how much more of Murray's interruptions I can take."

Bethany wondered how Pamela and Andy ever had time to themselves with Murray around. They'd been dating for at least a dozen years. Both of them were widowed—Andy as a young man when his wife was killed shortly after they were married and Pamela when her much older husband died of a heart attack. Bethany had heard the story many times about how Andy came to her rescue during her grief, and how he'd never left.

That reminded her of how Pete had been there for her after Charlie had passed, but her situation was a tad different. She and Pete had always been good friends, so any thought of romance would be awkward. That still didn't erase the tingle she felt whenever he looked at her a certain way. She glanced over at him and gasped before rubbing the goose bumps that prickled her arm. He was doing it again!

"Stop acting like a love-struck schoolgirl and help us clear the table," Naomi whispered as she continued moving toward the kitchen without giving Bethany a chance to argue.

Bethany picked up the butter dish and bread basket from the table and headed for the kitchen. Pete passed her and whispered, "Don't hold me responsible for anything happening here tonight."

"Trust me, I won't, as long as you promise the same."

It only took them fifteen minutes to clear the table, load the dishwasher, and settle in the living room. Pamela glared at the bird by Andy's side. Bethany suspected there might be some thoughts of birdie torture going through Pamela's mind, but she'd never act on it. Pamela might be bossy, but kindness ran through her veins, and she'd never physically hurt any of God's creatures.

"Okay, now let's talk about your plans." Pamela looked back and forth between Naomi and Miss Gertie with shoulders squared and body rigid.

Miss Gertie glanced at Naomi, who nodded, before turning back to Pamela. "We've already told you what we were thinking." She paused. "But I actually like your idea better."

"What do you think?" Pamela shot a quick glance at Naomi.

Naomi nodded. "I like it too. Folks in Bloomfield are mighty competitive, so we figured we should tap into their nature to get what we want. But like you said, everyone loves a party." She turned to Gertie and winked. "The bigger the party and the more we have going on the better."

Pamela grinned. "This is a very intriguing idea, giving prizes to folks for inviting people to Bloomfield. I think it'll work if you take the lead on this. We should probably come up with a theme and a name for the festival." She leaned forward. "So how will this contest work, and where will we get the prizes?"

Bethany listened in amazement as Naomi and Miss Gertie listed some of their preposterous ideas, each one building on the last. Caught up in the excitement, Naomi added, "As soon as you get one family to sign a lease or put a down payment on a house, you get a small prize and move on to the next level."

Pamela tilted her head and smiled. "So they won't be competing with each other as much as trying to move to the next level?"

"Sort of," Naomi explained. "Each level gets a small prize, like maybe dinner for two at The Fancy Schmantzy or breakfast at The Pink Geranium Tea Room. But we can still offer a grand prize for the person who brings in the most folks."

"Like what?"

Andy held up Murray's birdcage. "A weekend with Murray?"

Pamela shot him a silly look before rolling her eyes. "We're trying to attract people, not scare them away."

Naomi pointed to Bethany. "We'll decide on the grand prize later. We can offer a variety of smaller prizes, though, like my daughter's . . . antiques."

Bethany caught the tone of her mother's voice as she said the word *antiques*. Naomi had never understood Bethany's collections—from the shaped and scented erasers she collected when she was a little girl to the posters and T-shirts of her favorite bands when she became a teenager. She also had shoeboxes filled with memorabilia from dates with Charlie and fun times with friends.

"Why don't we have an official meeting about this so we don't leave anyone out?" Pamela said. "The garden club members get mighty testy if they think we're working behind the scenes."

The only people Bethany saw as testy were Pamela and Naomi, but she didn't say a word. Pete looked at her and smiled his understanding. At least she had one ally in the room.

Murray started squawking again, so Andy stood. "We best be getting on home. I think Murray has had just about all he can take for one night."

"Why did you even bother to bring him?" Naomi asked. "It's not like you were here all that long. Can't he stay home by himself for a couple of hours?"

"You know how lonely he gets. I've been gone most of the afternoon, so I figured it wouldn't be a good idea to leave him again."

Pamela glared at Murray. "That bird is worse than having a toddler around. At least you know the child will eventually grow up."

After Pamela, Andy, and Murray left, Naomi chatted with Miss Gertie for a few minutes. Bethany stayed in the living room, remembering the days when she couldn't see through some of her mother's schemes.

Once again, the overwhelming urge to pull Bethany away from the crowd for a kiss had to be squelched. Every time Pete looked into her blue eyes, he felt as though he'd lost another piece of himself. But right now, he could see she was doing everything she could to avoid looking back at him.

After Pamela and Andy left, Naomi and his mom went into the kitchen to do more planning, leaving him alone with Bethany. "So what do you think about our mothers' new scheme?"

She shrugged. "That's exactly what I think—it's a scheme. They always have something brewing. I suppose this is as good as any of the others."

He laughed. "Yes, that's true. Wouldn't it be hilarious if their plan backfired and more people came here to live?"

"I'll be shocked if that happens, but . . ."

"This is Bloomfield, after all, right?" He laughed as he finished her sentence. "And I bet some people will love getting some of your tchotchkes."

"Tchotchkes?" She tilted her head.

"Yeah. Your knickknacks."

"Is that what you think of my collectibles?" She pursed her lips and glanced down.

"Um . . . no. I'm just speaking in general." He needed to stop talking. Her nerves were already raw enough. "Look, Bethany, I don't want to upset you . . . ever."

Her shoulders rose and fell as she sighed. "I know, Pete, and I'm really sorry for being so sensitive. It's just that Mom's been after me to clear out the clutter, and then the way you looked at it last time you were over . . ." She lifted her hands and let them fall to her sides. "Plus all the comments tonight. Everything I own means something—memories and happier times. I know I need to get rid of some of that stuff, but . . ." She shrugged. "Well, it's just not that easy."

He wanted to tell her she needed to clear out the clutter to make way for more happy times, but he didn't. Instead, he pulled his bottom lip between his teeth as he gave her what he hoped was a reassuring nod.

Naomi's voice coming toward them snapped them to attention. Bethany stiffened, and Pete leaned back on the sofa.

"Ready to go?" Naomi stopped in her tracks. "I didn't interrupt anything here, did I?"

"No, of course not." Bethany tossed her shoulder-length blonde hair over her shoulder and smiled at Pete. "We were just talking about what a brilliant plan our mothers had. I mean, how can anyone resist trying for one of my figurines that has been in the Hanahan family for forty or more years? Who wouldn't uproot a family and leave a job just to get their hands on a complete collection of Hummel figurines? We'll wind up with more people in Bloomfield than we have room for."

Naomi tilted her head and frowned. "Are you being sarcastic?"

Bethany pointed a thumb to her chest. "Me? Sarcastic? Why would you ever think that?"

Pete kept quiet.

After a restless night of tossing and turning, Bethany schlepped to the kitchen, nearly tripping over the stool she'd moved from the foyer to the small eating area. If she ever did decide to declutter, the stool would be first on the list. But then, how could she let go of a precious memory decorated with creative, loving hands? She sighed. This was too much to think about before her first cup of coffee.

She'd barely sat down with her muffin and coffee when the phone rang. It was Pete.

"Have you gone anywhere today?" he asked.

She glanced at the clock. "It's only ten, and I slept in, so no, I'm just now eating breakfast."

"Then I guess I better warn you. Our mothers haven't wasted a second."

Bethany felt that old familiar tingle of alarm. "What have they done now?"

"Are you sitting down?"

The closest thing to sit on was the stool, so she lowered herself to it. Before she had a chance to say another word, it gave way, and she crashed to the floor. As she righted herself, she saw two of the four legs on the stool had broken off.

"Bethany! What happened? Are you okay?"

She rubbed her bottom and sighed. "I'm fine. I just broke the stool." She picked up the remnants and set them by the back door to take to the garbage. Then she crossed the kitchen, pulled out a chair, and sat. "So what did our mothers do?"

"Maybe I better wait to tell you. Sounds like you're not quite ready yet."

"No, tell me now." If the worst thing that happened to her all day was breaking the stool, she'd be fine. But she suspected that was only the beginning.

Pete cleared his throat. "They've already plastered posters and handbills all over town."

"I'm not surprised. Once my mother sets her mind to something, she doesn't waste a second."

"That's not all. Apparently, your mother considers all your collectibles fair game for the prize selection, and she's offering three complete sets of Hummels, heirloom quilts, and other stuff she's calling antique bric-a-brac."

"Maybe it's not my stuff she's offering."

"I just happened to wind up with one of the flyers, and here's what it says." As Pete read the list, she mentally ticked off the items throughout her house. Her mother hadn't come right out and put her name on the flyers, but there was no doubt it was Bethany's stuff. Anger welled in Bethany's chest as she remembered why she and Charlie had decided to move away in the first place.

Bethany forced her voice to sound calm, until she got off the phone with Pete. Then she let out a low growl. Naomi's interference had to be stalled. It was time for a confrontation, but she didn't feel like facing her mother, so she picked up the phone and punched in Naomi's number.

"Mom, we need to talk."

Naomi's breath whooshed through the phone line as she let out a deep sigh. "I was afraid of this."

"You really need to stop making decisions for me without at least discussing them with me first."

"If you're talking about the donations, I thought you were ready to let go of some of your things." She paused. "You are, aren't you?"

"Well . . . yes."

"Listen, sweetie, I was just trying to help. If it upsets you that much to do this, tell me now, and I'll find someone else who has stuff to get rid of. Do you need some time to think about it?"

Naomi had taken some of the sting away, and now that Bethany thought about it, she was ready to move forward. Donating some of her collectibles—and junk—might be painful at first, but after it was over, she didn't think she'd miss it. "No, I'm ready."

"Good. So did you need something else?"

"Yes," Bethany replied. "In the future, before you commit me to anything else, you need to discuss it with me first."

"I will." The sound of contrition in her mother's voice warmed her heart. "I'm sorry I didn't do that this time, but from now on, I'll try to behave."

Bethany laughed. No matter how overbearing her mother was, she couldn't stay mad at her long. "Thanks. I'll hold you to that."

Chapter 4

Even with her eyes tired from lack of sleep, Bethany wouldn't have been able to miss the hot pink signs on every lamp post and store window in town. Pete was right. Her mother didn't waste time.

She went into the card shop where Sherry Butler stood behind the counter. "Do you know about this new contest?"

Sherry grinned and nodded. "The garden club had an emergency breakfast meeting this morning."

"Were you there?"

"Yes, and I even had some reservations about their plan. I mean, it is rather strange, but . . ." She shrugged. "You know how Pamela and Naomi can be when they get their minds set on something."

Bethany chuckled. "And when they're on the same team, they're formidable."

"Fortunately, that's not usually the case." Sherry came around from behind the counter. "Can I help you find a card or new figurine? We just got some new ones in last week."

As tempting as it was to browse, Bethany shook her head. "Better not. I don't need to give my mother more prizes for her little contest."

"So it's true they're using your collectibles. That's really sweet and generous of you. I know how much you love Hummels."

Bethany offered a closed-mouth smile but didn't say a word. No point in showing what might appear to be a lack of generosity at the moment. Even after her talk with Naomi, she had a knot in the pit of her stomach about letting go of so many of her things.

"Do you think the contest will work?" Sherry asked. "It seems like a rather odd plan."

"I have no idea if it'll work, but this is Bloomfield we're talking about."

"True." Sherry grinned. "We're supposed to get as many donations as possible. Businesses all over town have offered items and gift cards. I'll call the owner of the card shop to ask if we can donate something to the cause, but I'm still not sure that's enough incentive for someone to pick up and move to Bloomfield."

"I know. I think this is just an excuse to have another festival."

"We've barely gotten past the Christmas and New Year's festivals and parades. I would think they'd want a break." Sherry frowned. "Being vice-president of the garden club, I'll have to do a lot of the work. This isn't such a good time for me, having to work full-time and plan my wedding."

"Let me know if you need help with the wedding," Bethany offered. "That's something that actually makes sense."

Sherry grinned. "I might take you up on that. Naomi offered to help, but I thought I'd ask her to act as mother-of-the-bride . . . that is, if you don't mind."

"Of course, I don't mind." Bethany smiled. "You were always like a sister to me. Naomi has always loved you."

Sherry cleared her throat as her eyes started to glisten. "I love Naomi too. And you." She dabbed at her eyes with a tissue. "So is there anything else I can help you with?"

"Do you have any extra flyers I can have?" Bethany asked.

Sherry pulled one out from beneath the counter. "Here you go."

Bethany left the card shop and went straight to Pamela's house to see if there was any way she could change the garden club's tactics. She knocked on the door, and Pamela answered within seconds.

"What do you need, Bethany?" Pamela blocked the doorway and didn't even bother to ask her in.

Bethany lifted the flyer. "I wondered about this. Where are you getting all the prizes . . . that is, besides the ones I'm donating?"

Pamela tilted her head, squinted her overly mascaraed eyes, and gave Bethany an incredulous look. "You were there last night, so you know pretty much everything." She took a step back as something apparently dawned on her. "Oh, I get it. You're upset that we didn't call you in for the breakfast meeting."

"No, that's not—"

"I understand, but time was of the essence, and since Naomi was there, we didn't see the need to bother you so early."

Bethany sighed. This wasn't going well. "It's not that. It's just—"

A slow smile spread across Pamela's lips. "I hope you know how much we appreciate your donations. It's such a wonderful cause. Once we reach a population of ten thousand, we shouldn't have any trouble getting into the *Best Small Towns in America* book, and that will do wonders for all our fine homegrown businesses. Then the town will grow without any help from us. I have to admit, your mother's idea for this festival was brilliant."

"She and Miss Gertie came up with the reward program. The festival idea was yours."

Pamela's grin widened. "Oh yeah, that's right. It was my idea, wasn't it?"

"But do you think—?"

Pamela's smile quickly faded to a look of concern. "It's such a shame our businesspeople have to struggle so much to keep their doors open. We simply don't have enough residents here in Bloomfield to support all of our many small businesses. People like you are such assets to the community." She stepped back and gestured for Bethany to come inside. "Why don't you come on in for some coffee?"

Pamela had just zapped Bethany's will. "No thank you. I just wanted to know if there was anything else I can do."

"Oh, I'm sure there'll be plenty for you to do once we start working on the Welcome to Bloomfield parade."

"Welcome to Bloomfield parade?"

"Yes, we decided since we're having a Welcome to Bloomfield festival, we'd do it up big and add a parade," Pamela explained. "We thought it might draw more attention from visitors if we had a big show."

"Does the mayor know about this?"

Pamela's hesitation was all the answer Bethany needed. "Well . . ."

"So what all are you doing besides a parade and rummage sale?"

"Everything." Pamela nodded and made huge, sweeping gestures with her hands, fluttering her fingernails. Today they were peach colored with small, opalescent crescent shapes painted on each one. "Pony rides and arcade games and talent shows—the works." She sighed. "We're planning a huge campaign with radio spots in all the big cities within five hundred miles." She tilted her head forward. "I think you should come inside so I can tell you all about it. I've been working on plans."

"What if it snows?"

Pamela forced a frown. "Yeah, that could be a problem. We

discussed the possibility of inclement weather at the breakfast meeting." Her eyebrows shot up. "But if that happens, we can bring indoors as much of the entertainment and games as we can fit in the community center. On the flip side, if the weather is nice, we can add more outdoor events like lawn bowling and horseshoes and sack races and—"

"I—"

Before Bethany could finish her sentence, Pamela grabbed her arm and yanked her inside, closing the door with her other hand. "I have a nice big basket filled with all sorts of delicious treats from the bakery. Would you like coffee or tea?"

Knowing Pamela's take-no-prisoners manners, Bethany went along with her. "Coffee."

"Good, because that's what I'm having. I hope you like cinnamon-pecan."

Fortunately, Bethany liked any type of coffee. "Yes, I like it very much."

"Come on back," Pamela said, as she let go of Bethany's arm. "And relax. You're way too uptight. I don't understand why so many people act all buttoned-up around me. It's almost like folks are afraid of me, or they think I'll judge them or something. And you know me . . ." She turned around and smiled at Bethany. "I'd never judge anyone. That's the Lord's job. My job is to keep things running smoothly in Bloomfield."

Actually, her job was to run the Bloomfield Garden Club as president, but Bethany never would have said that to Pamela. The aroma of fresh-brewed flavored coffee wafted from the kitchen and down the long hallway, melding with the fragrance of lemon-scented household cleaners. Bethany had been to Pamela's house a number of times, and it always smelled wonderful.

When they reached the kitchen, Pamela pointed one of her talons toward the table. "Sit. I'll bring some plates and the basket of pastries to the table."

Bethany had to scoot one of the chairs around to a clear spot on the table. "Are we holding this talent show, parade, and festival on the same weekend you were originally planning the sale?"

Pamela turned around with the basket and moved toward her. "Probably, but that's something we'll need to discuss with the garden club. Speaking of which, when do you plan to start attending meetings regularly? Naomi said you wanted to get more involved. What's stopping you?"

Bethany hated being put on the spot about anything related to the garden club. Naomi had always been so active, Bethany sometimes wondered if her mother knew the difference between family and her club. "I don't know that I'd be all that much help."

"Maybe not." Pamela went back to the cupboard, extracted a couple of plates, and returned to the table. She placed her hands palms down on a stack of papers and leaned toward Bethany. "But sometimes we just need warm bodies."

At least she was honest. "I can certainly be one of those."

Pamela returned to the table, her arms loaded with the plates, napkins, forks, and spoons. "You're Naomi's daughter, so I suspect you can be much more than a warm body. Don't tell her I said this, but she's one smart cookie."

Bethany chuckled. "That'll be our little secret."

"I just wish I'd gotten to know you better when you were younger, so I could see what kind of talents you have. As soon as you hit legal age and got married, all we saw was your backside when you made your way out of town."

Bethany laughed. "Charlie had a better opportunity elsewhere."

"From what I understand, he always wanted to move away." Pamela sat down and brushed some papers away to make room for her coffee. "His mother told us how he wanted more than what Bloomfield had to offer." She shook her head and sipped her coffee. "Lord only knows why anyone would ever want to leave this beautiful little town."

Bethany knew Pamela had tunnel vision about boosting the population, so she decided it was time to stop talking about herself and Charlie. "Do you really think having another festival will make more people want to move here?"

A brief flicker of doubt darted across Pamela's face, but it quickly faded. "Of course, it will. Everyone loves a good festival."

"So tell me more about the reward program to lure people here." Bethany figured she might as well know where her donations were going and how people would win them.

"I'm glad you asked." Pamela put down her cup and leaned over to pick up some papers across the table. "We're using this reward program to tie everything to our history. Like if they win one of the floral quilts your mother-in-law made, they'll get a note about how the garden club influenced her choices in color and design. The winner of a landscape makeover will get a free one-month trial membership to the Bloomfield Garden Club. The garden club will hand out flyers and calendars so folks can see what we have to offer, and we'll take names and e-mail addresses to let people know of upcoming events."

This plan sounded more like it was about recruiting new members for the Bloomfield Garden Club than bringing in more people to establish roots in the town of Bloomfield, but Bethany would never call out Pamela. "I suppose it's a good cause."

"Oh, it absolutely is a good cause. It'll benefit everyone in this town." Pamela sighed. "We've gone far too long without getting the kind of attention we deserve. This Welcome to Bloomfield festival will make everyone feel special—from the current citizens to the visitors."

Especially Pamela. Bethany had known Pamela all of her life, and she couldn't remember a time when Pamela wasn't the center of attention.

"One thing I've noticed, though," Pamela said slowly. "You haven't actually come out and volunteered any of your collectibles. It's always your mother who mentions them." She leaned back, eyebrows lifted, as she remained uncharacteristically silent. "So tell me, are you onboard with this?"

"Yes." Bethany was glad she'd had the conversation with her mother, or Pamela might have been able to see her reluctance.

"Are you sure? I mean, if you aren't ready . . ." The softness in Pamela's voice caused Bethany's throat to tighten. Pamela reached for Bethany's hand and closed around it. "If it's too hard to offer those things, just say so. I would never want to take something away from you if you're not willing to give it up. If you're that attached to all your things, well . . ." She lifted her hands and let them drop, slapping the table and making Bethany jump.

That did it. The tears that had caught in Bethany's throat now streamed down her cheeks. She rubbed her face with her sleeve, but there was no way she could hide them from Pamela whose gaze remained fixed on her.

"I honestly don't mind donating some of my things." She sniffled. "I have way too much in that small house anyway."

"Look what I've gone and done. I didn't mean to make you cry." Pamela leaned toward her as she closed her hand around Bethany's. "Are you absolutely sure?"

Bethany nodded. "Positive."

"Okay then, let's make an itemized list. It can't be just any old junk . . ." She smiled apologetically. "That didn't come out right, but I think you know what I mean. We have to show the value of the items so people will want to win them." She lifted a pencil and pulled a notepad toward her. "It would be nice if the items were either antique collectibles, limited editions, or handcrafted items made by a Bloomfield resident. Belva was the craftiest person I ever knew. She could sew, quilt, knit, crochet, paint, and do anything else she set her mind to. All that, and she managed to have the prettiest garden in town most years."

Bethany squeezed her eyes shut as she realized that was one area where she'd let folks down. The beautiful flower garden across the front of the house she'd inherited had withered and

died, so she'd let the grass creep into it, and now the lawn grew
flush with the house. The vegetable garden in the back had also
been sorely neglected.

"Bethany, are you okay, dear?"

Bethany nodded. "I'm fine." She leaned forward and glanced
at the paper where Pamela had listed numbers one through ten.
"Let's work on this."

By the time she left Pamela's house, she'd volunteered to
donate three handmade quilts, three complete collections of
Hummels, ten years' worth of Bloomfield Garden Club's cook-
books, and several of the many oil paintings her mother-in-law
had made of the town square.

"We won't use it all for prizes. In fact, I think putting most of
it in the garden club booth at the rummage sale will bring in some
much needed funds so we can keep up with all of our projects."
She paused. "What do you think?"

Bethany shrugged and then nodded. "Sounds good. I'll get
everything together as soon as I have time."

"It's not much, but it's a start," Pamela said.

"Do you really think all that stuff will make people want to
move here?"

"Well . . . I think these things will be attractive to Bloomfield
residents so they'll have incentive to bring out-of-towners to the
festival and show it off. Then visitors will see our pride, and it'll
make them want to move here." She stopped, crinkled her forehead, and smiled as her voice changed. "Oh, what am I saying?
Actually, no, I don't think any of this will make people want to
move here, but your mother and Gertie were so proud of themselves for coming up with the idea of the giveaway, I couldn't
very well say no, could I?" She shrugged. "I mean, who am I to
dampen anyone's enthusiasm? Everything can't be my idea, now
can it?"

Bethany had never seen this side of Pamela, and it cast a whole
different light on her feelings toward the woman. "No, but why

did you decide to turn the whole thing into a festival with the parade and all?"

"I got caught up in the moment. Their excitement was contagious." Pamela shrugged. "It sounded good at the time, and once I had Naomi and Gertie onboard, how could I back out?" She lowered her voice. "Actually, I think it's a rather silly idea, but please don't let on. I'm just glad someone besides me is excited about increasing the population here. I was beginning to think I was a one-woman army fighting an impossible battle. I'll do whatever it takes to keep folks happy and feeling like they're part of something bigger than themselves."

No wonder Pamela was president of the Bloomfield Garden Club.

Chapter 5

After Bethany left, Pamela strolled out the door to check the mail. As she turned back toward her house, a gray envelope taped to the front door caught her attention. She lifted it and checked the return address. Mayor Woody Hansen.

Pamela tossed the rest of the mail onto the side table and ripped into the mayor's envelope. She wondered when she'd hear from him. After all, she'd done everything in her power to let him know about the plans for the festival short of calling him herself. Last time she'd wanted something, she heard him groan the instant he saw her. And now, according to his short sentence, "Pamela, call me ASAP. Woody," he was beckoning her.

Not one to shirk responsibility for a single garden club activity—even one she thought was as silly as Naomi and Gertie's reward program plans—she'd taken the initiative to make things happen. She had a pretty good idea they were testing her with the cockamamie idea. So rather than show doubt, she latched on and showed her support to call their bluff.

Pamela chuckled as she reflected on how they'd hung tight to their scheme rather than back down. She had to hand it to them;

they followed through, and she knew they would until the very end.

She picked up the phone to dial the mayor's office, and then put it down. This was one of those times she'd have to exercise a little patience and make him wait. He'd certainly made her wait enough times. Maybe she'd give him a call in the morning.

Andy stopped by a little later to check on her. "I have to go to the fire hall early. One of the guys got sick, so I'm finishing the last couple hours of his shift."

"That's too bad." Pamela's mind wandered back to the mayor's note. "I hope he gets well soon."

Andy waved a hand in front of her face. "Earth to Pamela, are you in there?"

She blinked and looked him in the eye. "Of course. Why do you ask?"

"The question is, why are you acting this way? It's as though your mind is miles away." A look of consternation washed over his face. "You're not worried about that festival you've been talking about, are you?"

Andy knew her too well. "I might as well come out and tell you; I'm not so sure Naomi wasn't pulling my leg about it."

"She just might have been." He shook his head. "It would serve her right to have to go to all that trouble of actually having the festival."

Pamela rolled her eyes. "I'm the one going to all the trouble."

"I thought you put Naomi in charge."

"Are you kidding?" she asked. "I did, but you know how that goes. Oh, speaking of the festival, I got a note from Woody. He wants to see me right away."

He chuckled. "Isn't that what you were hoping for?"

"Why do you say that?"

"Because I've been around you quite a bit for the past twelve years, and I know how you operate. So do you have your speech planned out?"

"Speech?"

Andy nodded. "Yes, the speech you'll make before the city council, with all your buddies from the garden club standing behind you for support." He laughed again. "And to think you're doing all this for what might wind up being a joke."

"Hmm." Pamela sank down in the chair behind her.

"But . . ." He lifted a finger. "This festival actually isn't such a bad idea. Like you said at the Sprocketts' dinner table, this town loves a festival, and we can always use a good party."

"True. I suppose I should call some of the garden club members to go with me." She leaned back and frowned. "I bet that's what he expects."

"Of course, it is."

Resolve flowed through her. "Then that's not what I'm gonna do. I think this calls for an element of surprise."

Andy groaned. "Looks like I opened a can of worms."

"Nope. You're a genius." Pamela hopped up, gave Andy a quick kiss on the cheek, took him by the arm, and led him to the door. "I hate to do this, Andy, but you need to leave now so I can go to City Hall and see the mayor."

"By yourself? What about your friends?" He shot a concerned gaze her way. "I can go with you if you want."

She sighed. "Thanks, Andy. You're a sweetie, but I think I'll do better by myself."

Andy shook his head and laughed all the way to his car. Once he pulled away, Pamela ran to her room, freshened her makeup, thought about what to say, and rehearsed her spiel. This had to be an award winner, or she'd never get the rummage sale changed to a parade and festival. The city council had already started talking about scaling back on what they called costly events. This could serve more than one purpose—to show Naomi the error of pulling a fast one on Pamela and testing the mayor's loyalty to the garden club. He'd been blessed by their support during election season. Now he could show his willingness to back up his promises.

Fifteen minutes later, Pamela walked into City Hall. Mayor Hansen's assistant wasn't at her desk, so she walked right up to his closed office door, paused for only a second, and then knocked.

"Come on in, Ophelia."

Pamela opened the door and walked in with her shoulders squared, her head high. "Ophelia wasn't at her desk, so I took the liberty—"

"You always take liberties, Pamela," Woody said as he stood and gestured toward the chair on her side of his desk. "Have a seat." Once she was seated, he folded his hands in a manner that made him look more like a mayor and less like the boy Pamela once knew back in high school. "So what's this I hear about another festival?" He lifted one of the pink flyers and waved it.

She explained how they were close to reaching their population goal. "If we can have this one, teeny-tiny festival, I think we'll nail it."

He laughed. "This one teeny-tiny festival can set the city back quite a bit."

"How? It's not like I'm asking the city for money. You know everything the garden club does is self-funded."

He narrowed his eyes and held her gaze. She wasn't about to back down. "When I first caught wind of this, I thought it might be a joke and wondered what you were up to." He leaned forward, his eyes bulging. "But you're actually serious, aren't you?"

She only hesitated for a split second before giving him a clipped nod. "Yup. As Naomi would say, serious as a heart attack."

Tilting his head even farther forward, he cleared his throat. "This will be fully garden-club run and paid for?"

"Of course. All I'll need from you is a pronouncement of the Welcome to Bloomfield weekend, and we'll do the rest."

"How about shutting the street down for your proposed parade?" He looked at her with skepticism.

"Only for a day and a half." Pamela paused. "And it'll be during the weekend when there's never any city business anyway."

"From what I've heard on the streets, you plan to start it on Friday."

Pamela nodded. "Yes, but in the afternoon." She leaned forward to trump his gaze, raising her eyebrows. "How much work do you get done on Friday afternoons, Woody?"

"You've got a point." He raised himself slightly from his chair and looked around her. "Did you bring something to sweeten the deal?"

"What?"

"Like pastries from the Pink Geranium." He leaned back. "Not that I'm asking for a bribe or anything."

"Of course you aren't, which is why I didn't do it. I thought you wanted to see me right away, so I came straight here. I would never want the mayor to think I'm not a good citizen. You wanted to talk to me, so here I am." *Oh, that was good.* She made a mental note to use the citizen thing again in the future.

"I said to call."

She grinned. "So you did."

"Tell you what. You can have this festival, but I'll have to think about the Friday afternoon thing and run it by the city council." He smiled. "Let's not end it until Sunday after church."

"Whatever you say, Mayor. You're the boss."

"Are you being sarcastic?" he asked.

She forced a contrite look. "No, why would I do that? I'm just thankful you're onboard with us."

As she walked out of the mayor's office, she did a mental fist pump. One thing she'd learned was that it always paid to ask for more than she wanted. It didn't hurt to leave room for negotiation.

Chapter 6

On his way to a plumbing job, Pete spotted Bethany coming out of Pamela's house. He slowed down, lowered his window, and tapped his horn. She glanced up and waved.

"Need a ride?"

She shook her head and pointed to her car. "I drove, but thanks." Her gaze darted to the car that had pulled up behind Pete. "We're stopping traffic."

Pete pulled off to the side so the car could drive around him. "What're you doing tonight?"

He noticed the flash of trepidation on her face. "Call me later, okay?"

He lifted his hands, forced a grin, and nodded. "Fine, I'll do that."

As he pulled away, he realized something appeared different about Bethany—something more than her reluctance to talk to him. Ever since she'd returned to Bloomfield, she seemed distracted and in her own little bubble, but now, she looked as though she was aware of the rest of the world. She'd just left

Pamela's house, so he wondered if it was something Pamela might have said or done.

He turned onto the next street over, pulled into the driveway of his client, and got out of the truck. Jeremy Maples had asked him to come over and help replace some of the outdated kitchen plumbing. Ever since the Maples family had started renting Sherry Butler's house, they'd been updating it and fixing everything that didn't work.

At first, everyone was shocked that Sherry had gone through with renting the house out and moving into the Fontainbleu Luxury Apartments, but now she was having so much fun, he had to force himself to remember how things were before that. Before she'd been a quiet woman whose social life revolved around the garden club, but now she was a regular social butterfly who looked like she actually enjoyed life. Of course, the fact that she and Brad Henderson were now engaged made a huge difference.

Jeremy greeted him at the door. "C'mon in. Shouldn't take us too long. I managed to remove most of the old stuff, and I have all the new parts lined up, ready to install."

"I bet Gina will be glad to have her kitchen like she wants it."

"Yeah, but now she won't have an excuse to order carryout." Jeremy turned around, and Pete followed him through the house. "I miss her cooking something awful."

As he walked through the foyer and down the hallway, Pete noticed some of the changes the Maples family had made. The wallpaper in the living room had been stripped and the walls painted a pale yellow that brightened up the room. The dining room had a newer, more modern light fixture. Even the hallway felt more welcoming with the glossy coating on the hardwood floors and a carpet runner leading the way to the back of the house.

"You've done a great job with this place." Pete shrugged out of his jacket and leaned over to inspect the hole where the new sink would go.

"I'd like to take credit, but Gina's the decorator. When she said she wanted yellow walls in the living room, I thought she'd lost her mind." Jeremy grinned. "But now that it's done, that's my favorite room in the house. Let's get this job done, and she'll be really happy."

It took Pete and Jeremy until mid-afternoon to finish all the work in the kitchen. After they completed the job, they stood back to admire it.

Jeremy rubbed his chin as a self-satisfied grin crept across his lips. "Now all I have to do is put the finish on the cabinets, add the hardware, and the kitchen is done."

The sound of the front door opening made Pete smile. "I think we're about to have our first review."

"Daddy!" Jeremy's little girl bolted through the kitchen and straight into her daddy's arms. She wrapped her arms around his neck and gave him a big hug but pulled back when she noticed Pete. "What are you and Mr. Pete doing?"

"We finished the kitchen sink."

Her eyes widened. "Pretty. I like it, Daddy."

Jeremy picked her up, walked over to the sink, and showed her the new faucet. "Now we can use everything in the kitchen, see?" After that, he pulled a glass from the cabinet and showed her the water coming through the refrigerator door.

"That is so cool!" She clapped her hands. "Now Mommy can make yummy food again."

Gina laughed from the doorway. "Most kids beg for fast food, but not this one. She actually likes my home cooking."

Pete tweaked Lacy's nose. "I'm with you, kid. Home cooking is the best."

Jeremy put Lacy back down and turned to his wife who'd been standing there watching and smiling. "Where have you and Lacy been all day? I thought you were coming home after lunch."

"Working on the garden club festival committee." She walked around the kitchen, smiling as she inspected all the new equipment. "Naomi even gave Lacy some projects to do."

"Daddy, Miss Nomi said I can draw pretty pictures of flowers for the festival. I think I'll make 'em yellow and pink and red and orange." She tapped her finger on her chin. "And purple, but not blue."

Bloomfield had more festivals than any town Pete had ever seen, with half of them cooked up after Pamela took over as the Bloomfield Garden Club president. Her motto seemed to be "Festivals are fun, so let's have more." He'd heard some people on the city council grumble about the volume of them, but council members never failed to charm their constituents with smiles and plenty of handshakes during the events.

Bethany took a long look around her living room before squeezing her eyes shut. *Lord, show me true joy, and lead me to get rid of anything that bogs down my life. Help me move forward and remove the temptation to live in the past. Forgive me for hanging on to things, hoping they would give me the comfort I can only get from You.*

This would not be easy, but without the Lord's help, it would be impossible. She gathered as many items as she could bear to part with and carried them all to the living room, where she placed them in various stacks. She labeled one COLLECTIBLES and another HANDMADE QUILTS AND LINENS that might make good Welcome to Bloomfield prizes. Then there was the miscellaneous pile for the rummage sale.

The sound of knocking at the door made her groan. Pamela had said she'd be by to pick up some of Bethany's donations, but she was nowhere near ready.

When she opened the door, she noticed Pamela wore jeans

and a work shirt rather than one of her usual flamboyant, head-to-toe, color-coordinated outfits. "I'm here early to help you sort through your junk."

Bethany wasn't about to raise the woman's ire over a single annoying word. Junk. After the emotionally draining time of sorting through all of her belongings, she just smiled and took a step back so Pamela could enter.

"Here ya go." Bethany swallowed hard as she turned to Pamela. "And this isn't even all of it."

"Wow, that's more than I thought." Pamela stood at the living room door, eyes bulging, fingertips tapping the doorframe. "I need to call someone to help."

"You don't—"

Before Bethany had a chance to finish her sentence, Pamela had whipped out her cell phone and punched in the number. "Hey, Pete. Drop whatever you're doing and come on over to Bethany's place. We have a disaster, and we need your help."

Disaster? Bethany took a long look around and turned back to Pamela, who winked.

After Pamela hung up, she walked gingerly around the room, almost as though in fear of something leaping out and grabbing her. "Do you have any boxes?"

"Yes, I picked up a few on my way home from your house. They're in the garage."

"Go get them." Pamela found the pile of quilts and knelt down. "I'll look through these and see what we can use."

Bethany was glad to leave the room for a few minutes to collect her composure. She came back with the boxes and saw Pamela had surveyed everything and started making more orderly stacks. She lifted one of the paintings. "I remember this piece. It's part of a set. Do you have the rest of them?"

Bethany nodded. "They're upstairs."

By the time Bethany rounded up the other four paintings in the set, Pamela had put the figurine collections into groupings and lined up all the oil paintings according to types—from land-scapes to indoor settings. As annoying as Pamela could be, she sure knew how to organize things quickly.

"I think we can use everything here." Pamela took a step back and glanced over her shoulder. "Got anything else?"

Bethany opened her mouth, but nothing came out.

"Never mind." Pamela grabbed a box and started wrapping some of the collectibles in the newspaper that Bethany had put in the middle of the room. "After we get all of this out of here, you can make some more piles." She glanced at her watch. "I wonder what's taking Pete so long."

It had only been a half hour since she'd called, but Bethany knew patience wasn't one of Pamela's strong points. "I'm sure he'll be here when he can."

They had boxed up all of the fragile collectibles when Pete arrived. As he walked through the house, Bethany noticed his surprise. But at least he had the good manners not to voice his opinion, even though Bethany didn't doubt he had one. After all, when it came to her décor, there weren't many people who didn't.

Pete's willingness to stop whatever he was doing to help a friend wasn't lost on Bethany. From helping set the table without coercion to coming here now showed her the depth of his car-ing nature. She glanced up at him, and when their eyes met, her insides fluttered. She quickly glanced away.

When Pete entered the living room, Pamela glanced up, and without bothering with a greeting, pointed to the taped-up box. "Be a sweetheart and carry that out to my car so we have room to finish loading all these things."

Pete winked at Bethany and mock saluted Pamela. "Yes, ma'am."

"Good boy."

Any other man might bristle at Pamela's bossiness, but not Pete. He always took life in stride, something her mother once said showed his confidence in his own manhood. Charlie had been pretty good about that, too, but he wasn't a fan of Pamela's. When they visited his family or her mother in Bloomfield during any holiday season, Pamela was generally smack dab in the middle of things, barking orders and flashing her fingernails.

As soon as Pete left the room, Pamela spun around to face Bethany. "So what's keeping you and this sweet young man from getting together?"

The comment caught Bethany so off-guard, she coughed and sputtered. When she tried to talk, she wasn't sure how to answer Pamela.

"C'mon, Bethany. Is it that difficult for you to see?" Pamela lifted both hands out to her sides, palms up. "Everyone else knows there's a spark between you." She finally shrugged. "But sometimes people are so caught up in their own little worlds and how they think things should be they don't see the forest for the trees. Maybe one of these days, you'll come to your senses and let a little happiness into your life. Just because you're widowed doesn't mean you have to act dead. Look at me. I'm a prime example."

No point in arguing. "I'm trying my best."

"Good. Let me know if you need any advice because I have plenty to offer." Pamela glanced around the room. "In the meantime, we have our work cut out for us. After we get all this junk out of here, maybe there'll be some room for you to move around. Honestly, Bethany, I don't see how you can stand all this clutter."

Before Bethany had a chance to respond, Pete returned. "I'm ready for the next load."

"We're working on it." Pamela lifted a stack of quilts and lowered them into one of the bigger boxes. "Charlie's mama sure did like to do needlework, didn't she? I don't know where she found all that time, between raising her kids and doing so much with the garden club. And her gardens . . ." Pamela used the back of her wrist to push back the hair that had fallen over her eyes. "She had the prettiest English country gardens in town."

"She sure did." Pete took the box she'd just filled. "I remember her vegetable garden too." He turned to Bethany. "Remember how she got all the kids to eat vegetables by letting us pick our own? I think she even had so much she supplied your mom and mine with fresh veggies."

All this talk about Belva brought back the guilt she'd felt when she first started culling through Mom Hanahan's things. Pamela's chatter about the past reminded Bethany that she had no business even thinking romantic thoughts about Pete, but each time she was around him, she found it more and more difficult to push them aside. She shuddered and dared a glimpse at Pete who stood over her, watching Pamela pack.

When she met his gaze, he blinked as though something had struck him hard. Bethany's mouth went dry. But the sound of Pamela clearing her throat brought her back to the moment.

"Well, kids, I'm running out of steam. Help me get all this stuff packed so I can get out of here. I have a date with Andy." She snickered. "He even promised to leave Murray at home this time."

All three of them quickly packed the remaining items in boxes. Pete and Bethany carried all of it out to Pamela's SUV.

"Good thing you didn't bring out all your junk, or we'd never be able to close the car door." Pamela brushed her hands as though she'd done all the work herself.

Bethany held her breath, waiting for another snide remark. But Pamela only smiled at her.

"Do you need help unloading your car?" Pete asked. "I can follow you if you want."

"No, that's okay," Pamela said. "I'll get some of the nice boys who hang out at the community center to do that. You stay here and help Bethany gather the next load."

Bethany had never offered, or even mentioned, that there would be a next load, but she didn't say anything. Instead, she chewed her bottom lip until Pamela pulled away.

"That woman is a piece of work." Pete glanced down at her and frowned. "Are you okay?"

Bethany nodded. "Just a little annoyed, that's all."

"That was hard for you, wasn't it?"

She smiled. "You have no idea."

"Want me to stick around, or should I leave?"

Deep down, Bethany wanted nothing more than for Pete to come inside, but she knew she was vulnerable at the moment. "I'm really tired."

He smiled and placed his hand on her shoulder. "I can imagine. Why don't you go on inside and try to relax? I'll head over to the community center and let Pamela know you're not up to doing more today."

"I appreciate that."

"We can get together another time. I'd like to take you to dinner soon . . . that is, if you would like to go with me."

"Sure." She'd agree to anything that wasn't concrete. Well, practically anything.

After Pete drove away, she went inside and saw she had a voice mail from Aunt Mary, her mother's younger sister who'd moved away from Bloomfield. Bethany smiled. Aunt Mary was one of the few people who accepted Bethany at face value and didn't try to tell her what to do.

Chapter 7

I wish I'd known you were coming," Bethany said.

"Your mother finally talked me into coming home for a visit, but she made me promise to keep it a secret. She wanted to surprise you." Aunt Mary let out a deep sigh. "It took coming back to realize how much I missed this place."

"Where are you staying?"

Aunt Mary laughed. "Where do you think?"

"With Mom?"

"Yes, but I'm actively looking for a temporary place of my own." She paused. "Not sure if I'm staying permanently, but I might as well get out of your mother's hair before I drive her batty."

Bethany could hear her mother in the background touting the benefits of living at the Lake Bliss Retirement Village. But Aunt Mary was more the type to move to Fontainbleu because she loved being around younger people.

"So what are you doing tomorrow?" Aunt Mary asked. "I thought it would be fun to have a girls' day out, just like old times."

"I'd love that." Some of Bethany's fondest memories were of times spent with her favorite aunt—shopping, antiquing, and getting their hair done. "I have to do a little cleaning in the morning, though. Pamela just left with some of my collectibles, and now I can see all the dust they were hiding."

Aunt Mary's laughter still hadn't changed; it was exactly how Bethany imagined an angel's laugh would sound. "How about I pick you up around eleven, and we can have lunch—your choice of restaurant."

"Is my mother coming with us?"

"Heavens, no. She's too busy with her Zumba for Seniors class at the Village and a garden club committee meeting."

Relief laced with guilt flooded Bethany. "Maybe we can take her back some dessert."

"I'm sure she'll love that. I need to run now. Your mother wants to introduce me to someone." She lowered her voice. "And as I'm sure you know, that makes me want to gag, but I'm going along with her because she's so relentless. I just hope this guy doesn't drool."

Bethany laughed. "Maybe he'll have coupons for an early-bird special."

"Oh, I'm sure. They even have a coupon bulletin board for people to swap." Aunt Mary laughed. Her sense of humor hadn't changed a bit, so there was no doubt they'd have a blast tomorrow.

If there was one thing Pete knew after living in Bloomfield all of his life, it was to follow up on everything he was involved in, or he'd have a garden club member to answer to. So first thing the next morning, he drove over to the community center to check on all the items Bethany had donated. The second he walked into the multipurpose room, he was glad he did.

Along one wall sat a display with a sign stating LOVINGLY

Handcrafted by the Late Belva Hanahan. That was fine. But the other sign, the one that read More Beautiful Crafts to Come, gave him pause. He wasn't sure Bethany had it in her to scour her house for more donations.

One of the regular checker players motioned for him to come on over to the game corner. "Looks like Pamela's been mighty busy. That woman sure does work hard making this town a great place to live."

Pete bristled as he thought about all the hard, soul-wrenching work Bethany had put into gathering all those things on the tables. "Yes, Pamela does work hard, but so do a lot of people."

"Ah, that goes without saying. But Pamela's somethin' else." The man laughed. "I have to say she's quite the looker. You don't see too many women who look like her still willing to get their hands dirty." The older man pointed to a nearby chair. "Have a seat and get in line to play the winner. I'm about to cream Howard here."

Howard rubbed the back of his neck. "I don't know how you do it." He glanced up at Pete. "Claude's been the checkers champion for the past year."

"Then I better not challenge you," Pete said with a chuckle. "I'd hate to mess up your winning streak."

Howard leaned back and howled with laughter. "That sure sounds like a challenge to me."

"Trust me, it's not." Pete took a step back. "Besides, I just stopped by to see if I needed to do anything to help with the festival."

"Them garden club folks seem to have everything under control," Claude said. A twinkle formed in his eye. "I agree with Howard. That Pamela sure is a pretty girl. Andy better keep a close eye on her, or I just might take a notion to ask her out on a date."

"You're too old for someone like Pamela," Howard said. "She's not interested in a guy with one foot on a banana peel right outside the Pearly Gates."

That started a debate between the two older men, so Pete took the opportunity to slip out the side door. As he walked on the sidewalk flanked by tulip shoots, he took a deep breath to fill his lungs with clean, small-town air. No dirty factories in Bloomfield. One of the reasons the town screeched to a halt in population growth is they discouraged business that they deemed dirty. Mayor Woody Hansen said that kind of industry was best left to big cities that could handle smog and air pollution, and the city council agreed. Actually, a more accurate conclusion was that the Bloomfield Garden Club agreed, and when they set their minds to something, there was never any doubt they'd get their way.

Bethany had dusted the empty shelves and tabletops that once held her mother-in-law's collectibles. As she moved things around, she had to admit the house looked much better with less clutter. She knew it would look even better if she could bring herself to cull more stuff. But it was hard . . . and draining.

By the time Aunt Mary arrived, she'd finished dusting, and all she had to do was powder her nose and apply lipstick. "Come on in." She stood back to let Aunt Mary in.

"Wow. This place hasn't changed a bit, except maybe it's a little more . . ." She smiled at Bethany and cleared her throat. "So are you ready?"

Bethany knew what her aunt had decided not to say, and she was thankful Aunt Mary stopped when she did. "I have to powder my nose and get my handbag."

Aunt Mary nodded and turned around to look at the shelf behind her that held some of Belva's first-edition signed books, flanked by porcelain bookends that had never been moved since Bethany lived in the house. Bethany had read those books many years ago, and she doubted she'd ever read them again. But she still couldn't bring herself to get rid of something with such value—both monetary and sentimental.

After putting on her favorite color of coral lipstick, she appeared at the door and saw Aunt Mary standing there, holding a book open, and scanning the pages. Bethany gasped as she saw the gigantic dust ball rolling across the shelf.

"What's wrong?" Aunt Mary closed the book and stuck it back in its place on the shelf. "Are you okay?" Her eyes focused on the dust ball. "Oh, looks like the cleaning lady hasn't been here in a while."

Bethany laughed. "You're looking at the cleaning lady."

"You need to hire someone to help."

"I'm afraid I can't afford what this house needs."

Aunt Mary grinned. "I'm cheap. All you have to pay me is an afternoon of good company and maybe a nice cup of herbal tea." Her smile faded. "What's wrong? Did I stick my foot in my mouth again?"

"I-I haven't . . ." She smiled. "No, you didn't do anything wrong." As soon as she returned, she decided she would clean a little bit more.

Aunt Mary closed the distance between them. "Naomi told me what's going on. You're having a hard time getting rid of all the old stuff, aren't you?"

No point in denying the obvious, so Bethany nodded. She looked around at the remaining things she'd never use.

"You don't have to get rid of everything just because my sister and Pamela think you should." She tilted her head toward Bethany and offered a sympathetic grin. "You do realize what this whole festival thing is about, right?"

"To get more people interested in Bloomfield."

"Bethany sweetie, that's just a side benefit. My sister wants you to get rid of the clutter so you have room for love again, and this is what she came up with."

"I—"

"Don't be upset with her, though. She only wants what's best for you."

"I know." Bethany shrugged. "As much as I hate to admit this, I'm afraid I agree with her. I'm practically tripping over all the mess."

"Have you ever thought about putting everything in boxes and rotating some of it to the attic so it doesn't look so cluttered?"

That thought had never occurred to Bethany. "That's a good idea." But it would still mean moving her things, and the thought of it exhausted her.

"My offer to help is still open. I can at least do that since I'll be here a while. I can only take so much Zumba, polka, and garden club frenzy."

Bethany laughed. Her mom had enlisted her to join the garden club, but she did it in name only. As much as she'd wanted to participate for the sake of showing support, the garden club had never been her thing and apparently not Aunt Mary's either.

"Let's decide on a place to eat, and we can talk about it over lunch." Aunt Mary took her by the arm and led her outside. "I can help you plant some pretty flowers along the front of the house . . . that is, if you don't mind. I miss having my own garden."

"Do you think there's any chance you might be moving back to Bloomfield for good?"

Aunt Mary smiled but didn't answer. "So what are you in the mood for?"

"How about the Pink Geranium? I haven't been there in a while."

"Sounds great. I've missed Caroline's fabulous quiche." She closed her eyes and sighed. When she opened them, Bethany saw the look of pure bliss on her face. "Let's go. I don't want to have to wait in line."

By the time they arrived at the Old Towne Inn, half the dining area of the Pink Geranium was full. Bethany took a long look around. "I don't know most of the people here."

"Same here. These folks must be staying at the bed and breakfast." Aunt Mary nodded toward the woman coming toward them. "There's Caroline."

Both Bethany and Aunt Mary smiled at the petite woman with a salt-and-pepper braid who came toward them smiling, blue eyes twinkling, arms open wide. "It's so good to see you, Mary. I heard you were in town."

Bethany listened as the two old friends chatted, until Mary finally pulled away. "I don't mean to be rude, but I can't be held responsible for my actions if I don't get some of your delicious quiche and soon."

Caroline laughed and gestured toward a table in the back. "Then by all means, let's get you seated and served."

After they placed their order, Caroline came back to catch up some more. "I wish you'd gotten here earlier. We had a nice Bible study this morning."

Aunt Mary tapped her chin, frowning, and then nodded. "Maybe next week?"

"You know you're always welcome to join us. So how's Naomi? She used to come, but lately she's been so wrapped up in new projects for the garden club, she hasn't had time."

"She needs to make time." Bethany couldn't miss the hint of annoyance in Aunt Mary's voice. "My sister has always bitten off more than she could chew, and then she complains about it. If she'd put first things first and stop worrying so much about insignificant stuff, she wouldn't always be so rushed."

Bethany tensed. Even though Aunt Mary was her mother's sister, and she actually agreed with her, Bethany didn't like having to pick a side.

Caroline's soft, warm smile had a calming effect. "That's something Naomi has to see, and I'm sure she will. She always does."

One of the workers motioned for Caroline, so she stood. "I have to run. Let me know if you need anything." She placed her hand on Aunt Mary's shoulder but looked at Bethany. "Oh, and Bethany, I want to thank you for your generosity with all those collectibles. I have to admit I'm somewhat surprised you were willing to part with so much." Caroline offered a sympathetic smile. "I know how difficult that can be since I had to go through my parents' things after they passed, but once you're finished, you'll be glad you did it."

Before Bethany had a chance to respond, Caroline had floated away. Bethany knew how hard Caroline worked with her bed and breakfast and small dining room, but she never seemed rattled. In fact, Bethany couldn't remember ever seeing Caroline without a welcoming smile and gracious attitude. And she was one of the few people who didn't get upset with Pamela.

A basket of pastries arrived, and Aunt Mary didn't hesitate before selecting one off the top and sinking her teeth into it. Her eyes rolled back, and she let out a long sigh.

Bethany laughed. "Is it that good?"

With her mouth still full, Aunt Mary tilted her head toward Bethany and gave her a you've-got-to-be-kidding look. She chewed and swallowed. "What do you think?"

"In that case, I'll just have to try one—" As she spoke, she started to reach into the basket, until she spotted Naomi standing at the door looking around. "Mom's here."

"So she is." Aunt Mary's mouth twisted into a half-frown. "We could pretend not to see her, but that wouldn't be very nice, would it? I suppose we should ask her to join us."

Naomi spotted them and didn't waste a moment walking to their table. "You didn't tell me you were coming here," she said to Aunt Mary. "But that's okay. Enough people saw you, so it wasn't too hard to find you." She turned to Bethany. "Pamela is really pleased about all of the things you donated. She thinks that'll get everyone excited about bringing out-of-towners to the festival."

Aunt Mary snickered. "I think it's ridiculous to believe

people will move to Bloomfield for some trinkets and baubles. I'm
sure Pamela sees right through your plan to bring Bethany and—"

Naomi gave her sister a warning look that stopped her mid-
sentence. "You have no idea what's going on, Mary, and until you
do, I would appreciate it if you'd keep your thoughts to yourself."

Bethany held her breath, hoping this wasn't the beginning of
another one of their arguments. All of her life, she remembered
how her mom and aunt would get into verbal sparring matches.

"Oh, I can see what's going on. And there's no doubt in my
mind you'll have plenty of people coming to the festival, but as I
was about to say, that's definitely not enough to get them—"

"That's the difference between you and me, Mary." Naomi
glanced up and motioned for Caroline. "You don't understand
how all this works. People will visit for the festival, and they'll
take home some mementos to remind them how wonderful
Bloomfield is, and that'll get them thinking about making it
home."

Caroline arrived at the table and gave Bethany a sympathetic
smile before turning to her mother. "What can I get for you,
Naomi?"

"I'll have what they're having." She turned to Bethany. "By
the way, what are you having?"

"Quiche."

Naomi grinned and snapped her head in a nod. "Good. I love
quiche. Oh, and I'd like one of your delicious teas, and I don't
care what kind. Surprise me."

Caroline walked away, laughing.

"So here's the scoop." Naomi's eyes flashed with excitement
as she turned all her attention to Bethany. "We've copied a thousand flyers already, and Pamela is making some more. I came
up with the idea to get the men involved, and surprise, surprise,
Pamela agreed with me."

Aunt Mary smiled at Bethany before turning back to Naomi.
"That is unusual. Are you sure another festival is necessary,

though? It's going to be difficult throwing this together since it's only a couple months away."

"We're just trying to get the word out that this is the best place in the world. Even if it only brings us one or two new families, we'll consider it a success."

"How far away from your goal are you now?" Aunt Mary asked.

"All depends on what day you ask and who you talk to. Last week, I think we were up to 9,982, but then we lost a couple newly graduated kids who decided they wanted to try living in the big city for a while."

"It's always been that way, hovering close to the goal but not quite making it, hasn't it?" Aunt Mary cleared her throat. "Maybe if you . . ." Her voice trailed off, and then she laughed. "Look at me, will you? This is so contagious I'm getting caught up in the fever."

"That's easy to do." Bethany turned to Naomi. "What else has been donated besides all the stuff I sent?"

"There's the weekend here at the bed and breakfast . . ." Naomi lifted her hand and ticked off the items as she listed them. "The golf range is offering a bottomless bucket of balls for an afternoon."

"All good stuff." A thoughtful look came over Mary. "You're having a parade, right?"

Naomi nodded. "We're planning to."

"For a prize, why don't you let someone ride on a float as a special VIP guest? That wouldn't cost a dime, but it would give someone a powerful sense of belonging here."

Naomi's eyebrows shot up. "That's a brilliant idea!"

"Yes, I know." Aunt Mary teased.

Naomi gave her a sly grin. "I knew you were just funnin' me with all that talk about how you don't get how this festival will bring folks here. That's probably one of the best ideas yet."

"I'm sure I'll come up with a few more if I put my mind to it."

"Then you have to go to the garden club meeting," Naomi said.

An instant look of pain shot across Aunt Mary's face. "No, I don't think so."

"You really need to get over it, Mary," Naomi said. "Harboring guilt that's best put to rest will only make you sick."

"What are you talking about?" Bethany had never heard anything about guilt and Aunt Mary, and the look on her aunt's face let her know it was something serious.

"Never mind." Aunt Mary shot Naomi a look that made Naomi lean back and shake her head.

"Are you two going to keep this a secret from me?" Bethany looked directly at Naomi.

Her mother shot Aunt Mary a glance and then turned back to Bethany and looked her in the eye. "It's not my secret to tell, so if you want to know what it's all about, Mary will have to be the one to tell you."

"Don't do this, Naomi." Mary's voice came out in a low growl, totally unlike anything Bethany had ever heard from her aunt.

Bethany watched the dynamics change between her mother and aunt and knew this was an issue that ran deep. She wasn't normally the nosy type, but now she wanted more than ever to know what had gone on between Aunt Mary and the garden club.

When their quiches arrived, Naomi ate hers slowly, but Aunt Mary barely touched hers. Bethany looked forward to finding out Aunt Mary's secret so she could help wipe the look of guilt and hurt from the normally loving face. But she couldn't without knowing what had happened.

The next half hour was one of the longest Bethany could remember as they ate in an uncomfortable silence. Finally, Naomi stood. "I have to go meet with the garden club. I'll cover everyone's lunch."

"You don't have to," Bethany argued.

"I don't have to do anything." Naomi glanced back and forth between Bethany and her sister. "Except this. It's the least I can do after upsetting the apple cart."

After Naomi left, Aunt Mary stood and pushed her chair under the table. "Why don't we do a little shopping? I remember that was something you always enjoyed."

Aunt Mary clearly wanted to evade the topic, so Bethany nodded. She could bring it up later when they were alone.

Chapter 8

The first place they stopped was the card shop. Sherry greeted them as she pushed a cart toward the racks of cards.

"Hey, Bethany." She grinned. "Mary, I'm so glad you're in town. I heard you were thinking about moving back."

Aunt Mary shrugged. "Maybe. I still haven't decided."

Sherry laughed. "I'm surprised Pamela hasn't twisted your arm. She can taste victory when we get this close to the ten thousand target."

"If I move back, it won't have anything to do with the population goal."

"I understand." Sherry continued smiling. "But I would love to see you move back, as I'm sure everyone in the garden club would. You have such a way with flowers."

Bethany noticed Aunt Mary stiffen. "My decision has nothing to do with anyone else, and certainly anything Pamela can possibly say to me will absolutely not affect what I do."

"Okay then." Sherry's eyes bulged with confusion as she glanced at Bethany. "I unpacked more of the shipment we got in last week, and I discovered some of the brand new Hummels. They're over there on the display against the wall." She nodded toward the back of the store. "Oh, and I have some of last year's pieces on sale. I know how you like a bargain. Let me know if you have any questions."

Bethany's heart raced as she made her way to the display. Since she'd just gotten rid of some of her other collections, she had some room. The sale sign practically called her name.

"Oh, no, ya don't," Aunt Mary said as she yanked on Bethany's arm and steered her toward the cards. "It's tempting to tell you to go for it, but Naomi would never forgive me if I let you do that."

"What do you mean, *let* me do that?" Bethany planted a fist on her hip. "I'm a grown woman, and I can buy anything I can afford." She lifted the sale sign. "Besides, look at this. They're on sale. A *bargain*."

Aunt Mary held up her hands in surrender. "I realize that, but humor me, okay? If you want to buy Hummels, come back in here and do it when I'm not with you. I seriously don't want my sister ganging up on us, and you know she will."

Yes, Bethany did know that, so she forced herself to back down. "Okay, that's fair." She quietly wondered how she could get Sherry to hold onto some of the sale items until she could return.

"Whew. I was afraid you'd do it anyway. I don't want to upset you, but to be honest, making my sister angry is much worse." Aunt Mary lifted a card and pretended to read it before placing it back in the slot. "She's very protective of you, ya know."

"Yes, I do know that."

"She's always been a good mother from what I can tell."

Bethany had a feeling her aunt was skirting an issue, so she decided to come right out and ask, "Why are you stating the obvious?"

Aunt Mary smiled. "I still think it's rather weird that sometimes you call her by her first name."

"I've done it since I was in elementary school," Bethany reminded her.

"I remember, but I still don't know why. When I asked her, she said she didn't know either, but she thought it was cute . . . at least when you were a child."

Bethany did remember. "If you ask me really nicely, I'll tell you why."

"Okay, so tell me."

"That's not asking me nicely."

"Do I have to tell you it's okay to look at Hummels to get this out of you?"

"No, of course not," Bethany said. "Just say please."

"I can do even better than that." Aunt Mary stood straight, folded her hands in front of her, and tilted her head slightly. "Pretty please with whipped cream and chocolate sauce?"

"Add some almonds and a cherry, and I'll tell you."

"Consider it done."

Bethany gave her a clipped nod. "Remember how she used to want all the kids to call her Miss Naomi instead of Mrs. McCord?"

"Yes."

"That's when it started. All my friends called her Miss Naomi, so I started doing it. And because she was my mother, I left off the Miss. When I saw how much she enjoyed it, I kept calling her Naomi." She lifted her hands palms up. "I would have done anything to make my mother laugh."

"That's it?" Aunt Mary looked disappointed.

"Afraid so."

"And I thought I was going to get some deep, dark confession from you."

Bethany laughed. "There is one thing I can confess. When I think about her, I alternate between calling her Mom and Naomi."

Aunt Mary rolled her eyes. "Now that's a confession for the records."

"I know, I know, but it's the best I can do. I'm so boring."

"Bethany, honey, you are not boring. Just a little vanilla, that's all." She gave Bethany a squeeze. "And vanilla just happens to be one of my favorite flavors."

Sherry appeared from around the corner, her cart now empty. "You ladies finding everything you need?"

"Yes," Bethany replied. "So how is everything with you and Brad?"

Sherry inspected the diamond ring on her finger and sighed before looking back up at Bethany. "He's amazing."

Aunt Mary laughed. "Something about love makes people amazing, doesn't it?" Before Sherry had a chance to reply, Mary continued. "I bet he feels the same way about you. When's the wedding?"

"I was thinking next summer, but he wants to get married sooner."

Bethany nodded. "I understand. It's not as though you two just met."

"That's what he says. He thinks waiting might prolong the stress."

"Yes," Aunt Mary agreed. "Planning a wedding can be mighty stressful, as I remember with Naomi's. Might as well just do it and get it over with . . . sort of like ripping off a Band-Aid."

Both Bethany and Sherry laughed before Sherry spoke up. "There are so many arrangements; I don't know how we'll get it all done."

Aunt Mary shrugged. "Like what? All you need to do is get your marriage license, pick a day the church isn't booked, and have the ceremony."

"But what about—?"

"The rest of it will get done," Aunt Mary assured her. "Trust me."

"I'll think about it. In the meantime, we've got this festival coming up. Pamela wants me to run the parade committee." She contorted her mouth and rolled her eyes. "I've never done anything like that before. I'm always on the committees, but I've never led one this public."

"Oh, I'm sure Bethany wouldn't mind helping you." Aunt Mary grinned at Bethany. "Would you, dear?"

Bethany did mind, but now that she was put on the spot, she couldn't very well argue. "Sure, if you need help, give me a call."

"I just might take you up on that." Sherry glanced up at the clock. "I need to put this cart in the back. My part-timer is coming in a few minutes, so Brad and I can look at new trucks."

"We need to run anyway." Aunt Mary waved as she ushered Bethany out of the door. "Talk to you later."

On the sidewalk outside, Aunt Mary turned to her and said, "See what you're missing out on by not getting romantically involved again?"

"What? Looking at trucks?"

"No, silly. You know what I mean."

Bethany did know what she meant, but she wasn't falling for it. She'd been married once, and it was wonderful, but that didn't mean she needed to jump right back into another romantic relationship—even if Pete did give her the tingles. Besides, he'd already declared himself a confirmed bachelor, adding that a lifetime commitment scared him silly. If he'd only said that back in high school, she wouldn't have thought anything of it, but when she and Charlie saw him during their Bloomfield visits, he'd commented that he wasn't the marrying kind.

"Right?" A half smile formed on Aunt Mary's lips.

"Yes, I know what you mean." Bethany sighed. "And I appreciate your concern about me, but I'm doing just fine on my own."

"Are you sure?"

"Why would you think otherwise?"

"For starters, you don't get out much. And the only thing that keeps you company is your houseful of stuff you don't need . . . and that you're getting rid of." She lifted an eyebrow. "You are getting rid of it, right?"

There it was again, the clutter issue. "Of course. I think we've already established that."

Aunt Mary placed a hand on Bethany's shoulder. "Okay, sweetie. I didn't mean to upset you again. But you know how much I care about you, right?"

"Yes, of course."

"Would you like to see if Elsie has something new at the bookstore? I know how much you enjoy reading."

Bethany paused and then nodded. "Sure, let's do that."

She would much rather have gone home, closed the door behind her, and wandered around in her house, looking at all the mementos she had left that brought back happier times. She wasn't terribly unhappy now, but times like this made her reflect on the immense joy of having her husband and daughter at home, laughing and teasing each other about everything under the sun.

As they approached the one-story brick building that housed Bloomfield Books, Aunt Mary slowed down. "Let me know if you see something you want. I'd love to treat you to a new book."

"You don't have to do that."

"I never have to do anything I don't want, but I want to get you a book." Aunt Mary smiled.

"Okay, if that makes you happy."

As they opened the front door, high ceilings and a blend of the smell of old and new books greeted them. Elsie stood in front of her massive counter with the antique cash register Bethany remembered from her childhood.

"Good afternoon, ladies." Elsie walked around one of the cats that had taken up residence in the bookstore. "What can I help you with today?"

"Got anything new?" Aunt Mary asked.

Elsie pointed to a wall of books. "The best sellers are on the shelf in front, and I just stocked some new fiction in the inspirational section."

"Let's look there." Aunt Mary took Bethany by the arm and led her to the aisle of Christian fiction. "Whoa, you have quite a selection here."

"I like to stock what my customers want." Elsie pointed to a new release by a Christian mystery author. "This book has been quite popular, and I've had to reorder it several times. We just got it back in today."

Aunt Mary shot Bethany a questioning look. "Do you have this one yet?"

"She's my favorite author, but no, I haven't bought that book yet."

"We'll take two." Aunt Mary pulled the books off the shelf, handed one to Bethany and tucked the other close to her side.

Bethany chuckled. "I hope you know you'll be up all night once you start reading. All of her stories are spine-tingling."

"That's what I'm counting on. I'm ready for an all-nighter read-a-thon." She made a face. "At least now it'll be a book keeping me up late and not weighing the decision I have to make about moving back."

Bethany wondered if there was more to it than that. Perhaps immersing herself in a good book would help her avoid whatever bothered her about Bloomfield. "If I can help, let me know." Bethany held her aunt's gaze. "I would love having you here permanently."

"Let's not talk about that now." Aunt Mary cleared her throat. "Let me pay for these books and we'll get out of here."

After Elsie rang up the sale, they left the store. They'd barely stepped outside, when commotion from down the street captured their attention. A couple of elderly men scurried around the building, both of them shouting at each other. "It's all your fault!" was all Bethany could decipher.

"What in the world is going on at the community center?" Aunt Mary frowned.

"I have no idea," Bethany said, shaking her head. "That's the most excitement I've seen since I've been here. Let's check it out."

They quickened their steps and headed toward the uproar. The first person they spotted was Pamela, running around in kitten-heeled mules, her bright purple fingernails flashing through the air as she ordered people around.

"Claude, I want you to cover the side entrance. Howard, come with me."

"What happened?" Aunt Mary asked.

"Murray's loose. We think he's still inside, but we can't find him, so we're covering all the exits just in case." The sharp tone of Pamela's voice commanded attention.

"How did he—?"

"Never mind how," Pamela snapped. "Why don't you make yourself useful and give us a hand?"

Bethany nodded. She understood that Pamela didn't intend to be rude. She was worried about what Murray might do. "Where do you want me?"

"Inside. Someone needs to guard the prizes. Murray likes bright, shiny things, and I don't want to take a chance on having him mess up what we've been working on."

Bethany suspected Pamela wasn't terribly concerned about Andy's parrot. The Bloomfield rumor mill buzzed about Murray being the only thing that came between Pamela and Andy making their relationship more permanent. The couple was on the verge of breaking up on any given day because of something Murray squawked. If Andy's sister hadn't left the bird to him in her will, he would have been gone long ago. But Andy's sense of responsibility and love for his sister kept him from following his own heart. Bethany knew Andy's older sister had been a big influence in his life after their parents passed away when he was young, and he didn't want to let her down—even after her death.

Bethany and Aunt Mary slipped inside and saw a dozen people already looking for Murray. One of the city council members crawled around on his hands and knees, looking beneath tables, while another opened and closed cupboards, calling, "Here birdie, birdie."

Aunt Mary nudged her. "Why don't you take that side of the room, and I'll head over there?" She pointed to the kitchen area. "I have a feeling Murray won't be found until he's good and ready."

"I'm sure you're right."

As Bethany approached the corner where all her donations sat among hundreds more, she tried to imagine where a parrot would hide. She scanned the tables until a colorful head popped up from behind a collection of Hummels. Her heart thudded.

"Murray, what are you doing?" She slowly approached the bird.

He sidestepped, bobbing his head, not meeting her gaze. She didn't want to upset him for fear he'd start flapping his wings, sending the fragile porcelain figurine flying to the floor.

"Are you looking for something?" Bethany asked as she took another tentative step closer.

He bobbed his head again but didn't say a word. Fear of what he'd do if she shouted overrode the temptation to let everyone knew she'd found him. She glanced over her shoulder and saw no one had noticed her discovery.

"Do you want something to eat?" she asked.

"Murray wants candy . . . *squawk* . . . Murray wants candy!"

In a matter of seconds, everyone in the community center had dropped their own search and scrambled over to the collectibles table. Bethany held up her hands. "Please don't upset him, or he might break everything around him."

"We've been looking everywhere for that bird," Mayor Hansen said. "I'm not going to let some birdbrain get the best of me." He lunged for Murray.

Before anyone had a chance to stop him, Murray expanded his wings and started flapping, sending precious figurines crashing to the floor. A collective gasp filled the room.

"That bird is a public menace." The mayor stomped around the floor, pointing at Murray, his face red with fury. "Get him out of here."

Bethany glanced down at the fragments of figurines that had once belonged to Charlie's mother. Her heart sank. She had to protect the rest of the collectibles. "Please, Mr. Mayor. Let's give him some space."

"I don't—"

Andy came up from behind. "Bethany's right. Please, everyone, move away and let me deal with this."

Bethany took a step back as she whispered, "He says he wants candy."

"Yes, I'm sure he does." Andy pulled a plastic bag of carrot sticks from his pocket. "And that's exactly what I brought him." He lifted one of the carrots and showed it to his bird. "This is Murray-style candy."

The mayor let out a sound of disgust, but Pamela shook her finger at him. "I'm not trying to be critical, but if you'd start eating Murray-style candy, you might get in shape, Mayor."

"Are you telling me I'm—?"

She shrugged. "I'm just sayin' . . ."

He narrowed his eyes and gave her a long look, but he finally glanced away. Even the mayor knew better than to challenge the woman who pretty much got everything she wanted.

"Good boy, Murray," Andy said as his bird accepted the carrot and allowed his master to pick him up with both hands. "Now let's get you back in your cage where you belong."

Bethany let out a sigh of relief. "Glad that's over." Then she realized she hadn't seen Aunt Mary since Andy arrived. "Where's my aunt?"

Pamela pointed to the door. "She left ten minutes ago."

Bethany glanced back at Andy to make sure he had a good grip on his bird before bolting toward the door. She ran outside and halted in her tracks when she spotted Aunt Mary standing next to a lamppost, shielding her eyes from the sun. Aunt Mary turned to face her and waved.

As Bethany approached her aunt, she saw the tight lines around her lips and the way her eyebrows drew together. "What's wrong? Did something happen . . . I mean, besides Murray?"

"Nothing's wrong."

"That's not true, Aunt Mary." Bethany tentatively touched her aunt's back and tried to rub away some of the tension. "Please tell me what's wrong."

"I don't want to."

"But why? Don't you trust me?"

Aunt Mary's shoulders rose and fell as she inhaled deeply before letting out a deep sigh. "You might not understand." She sniffled and dabbed at her nose with a tissue. "I don't want you to hate me."

Bethany pulled her into a hug. "That is simply not possible. I'll love you no matter what."

Aunt Mary's tight jaw relaxed as she sighed and nodded. "Then I suppose I might as well tell you, or you'll never give me any peace." She pointed in the direction of Bethany's house. "I'll take you home and tell you the whole sad story."

Chapter 9

'll fix some tea," Bethany said once they reached the house. "Why don't you sit down and relax, and I'll bring it to you."

"Relax?" Aunt Mary forced a smile. "I hardly think that's possible, considering . . ."

"Okay, then sit down and fret. No point in trying to force yourself into relaxing if it's not possible." She offered a sympathetic smile as she pointed to the sofa. "At least get comfortable. I won't be long."

Bethany left her aunt in the living room, while she strolled to the kitchen. She had a feeling some huge revelation was about to rock her world, and for some reason, even though she was curious, she wasn't in a hurry to hear about it. One thing she did know was that it would take something really terrible to change her opinion of Aunt Mary.

The woman had always been there for her, even jumping into the ring when she and her mother had skirmishes. When she wanted to wear the clothes her friends were wearing and Naomi said no, Aunt Mary asked, "Why not? You have to buy her new clothes anyway." And when she wanted to stay out a little later, she even offered to be the one to pick up her and her friends.

Even though Aunt Mary never had children of her own, she seemed to understand them better than her parents did. Or perhaps that was why she understood them. Now that Bethany had raised her own daughter, she realized Aunt Mary never had to deal with the emotional aspect of watching teen angst from a parent's point of view.

As the water heated, Bethany loaded a tray with cups, saucers, small plates, crackers, cheese, and grapes. Then she filled a teapot with boiling water and placed a couple of tea bags in to steep. After a deep breath, she lifted the tray and carried it to the front of the house, where Aunt Mary sat on the edge of the sofa playing with the fringe on the blanket Charlie's mother had made for her own fifth wedding anniversary.

"You didn't have to go to all that trouble, Bethany."

"It wasn't a bit of trouble. I want you to relax."

"That looks so nice." Aunt Mary lifted a cup and poured herself some tea. "It's not easy talking about what happened, but I suppose it's time you knew."

Bethany prepared her own cup of tea and then chose a chair adjacent to the sofa so she could face her aunt. "I have to admit, there have been times I've wondered if something happened to make you . . . um . . . I don't know . . . not want to come back to Bloomfield." She gave her aunt what she hoped came across as a loving smile. "I've been worried about you."

Aunt Mary flipped her hand from the wrist as Naomi often did, and Bethany glanced down at her own hand, wondering how often she might have done that herself. "You never have to worry about me." She took a sip of her tea and grimaced. "I just have these inner demons I need to deal with periodically."

"We all have our demons."

Aunt Mary set her cup and saucer on the end table and nodded. She folded her hands in her lap. "Ready to hear about mine?"

Bethany nodded. "I guess."

"Okay, here goes." Her aunt sighed and sank lower into her seat. She closed her eyes, moved her lips as though in prayer, and finally looked Bethany in the eye. "It happened a long time ago. One of your mother's younger friends held a belated wedding shower for Andy's wife Cheryl. They'd been planning a wedding but decided to elope because the guest list and the arrangements had gotten so out of hand." She cleared her throat as tears formed in her eyes. Her chin quivered as she looked at Bethany.

Alarms went off in Bethany's head. "Aunt Mary, you don't have to talk about this if it's so distressing."

"No, that's okay. You probably need to know. I wish my sister had told you, but I think she might have been afraid it would change your opinion of me, and she knows how well we get along."

Now Bethany wasn't sure if she wanted to hear another word, but she didn't want to upset Aunt Mary more than she already was. She nodded and lowered her head for a few seconds before looking back at her aunt.

Aunt Mary continued. "Since Cheryl and Andy lived fairly close to me, we agreed she would ride with me. When I got to their house, she said she wanted to drive because their car was bigger and could hold the gifts. I agreed." She sniffled, so Bethany handed her a tissue from the box on the table. "Everyone was having such a good time, and the shower ran later than expected. I needed to leave early, because I had to go to work the next morning. Cheryl got her keys to leave with me because my car was at her house. Since the shower was in her honor, that didn't seem right. Your mother offered to drive me to her house to pick up my car, so I told Cheryl to stay."

Bethany could see where this was going. "You don't have to say any more."

Aunt Mary held up a hand. "No, I need to get this out. It's been bottled up inside me for so long, I feel like I might explode."

"Okay, I understand." Bethany took a deep breath and slowly let it out, hoping her aunt couldn't hear how shaky it was.

"Anyway, Cheryl actually argued with me and said she really didn't mind leaving. I finally put my foot down and insisted she stay." Her lips quivered as she tried to smile. "I even played the guilt card, saying she had to stay since she was the guest of honor, and it would be rude to leave before the rest of the guests."

Now Bethany understood why Aunt Mary had such a difficult time dealing with this. It wasn't rational, but guilt generally wasn't.

"Your mother drove me to my car, and then I went home and went straight to bed. The next morning . . ." Her body shook as tears streamed down her cheeks. "The next morning, I was awakened by the phone call . . . the one informing me that Cheryl had been in a fatal car wreck on her way home from the shower." Her body shook as she lowered her head into her hands.

Bethany got up from her chair and sat down next to her aunt. As she placed her arm around the woman who'd been living with guilt for nearly forty years, she understood so much more about situations that had happened over the years—the main one being why Aunt Mary had avoided Andy. There were other situations Aunt Mary had avoided as well—like participating in garden club social events and bridal showers for other friends. Knowing Andy, he never would have placed the blame on her aunt, but that didn't make things any better for her.

Aunt Mary pulled back and turned to face Bethany. "If I hadn't insisted on her staying and your mother driving me to my car, Cheryl never would have been in the path of that drunk driver who crossed the median and killed her." Her chin quivered as she continued. "She'd still be here, living in Bloomfield, probably a happy mother of a houseful of Andy's kids."

"Maybe not."

"She and Andy couldn't wait to have children."

Naomi's advice rang in Bethany's head, so she repeated it.

"There are so many what-ifs in life that if we dwell on them, we can make ourselves crazy."

"I know all that. Your mother and I heard it all our young lives from our mother. But don't you understand why this is different? It's not like things just happened. I argued with her. My last words were intended to make her feel guilty if she left the shower." Her body shook as she buried her face in her hands. "It was supposed to be a celebration. I played on her guilt, and look how things wound up."

Bethany took Aunt Mary's hands in hers and squeezed them. "But don't you see? Your last words to her are making you feel guilty, which is ludicrous because your intentions were so honorable."

She half shrugged and then nodded. "I thought I was doing the right thing."

"You were," Bethany said. "You can't look back and worry about things you can't change."

"But look at what happened. A beautiful, smart young woman was killed because I thought things should be a certain way. My bossiness caused her to die in a flash, her sweet young husband to be widowed before their lives together had a chance to gain traction, and—"

"Sweet? Are you talking about Andy?" Andy had quite a few positive traits, and she had seen the occasional softer side, but she wouldn't use the word *sweet* to describe him. He was honorable and kind, but he also had a gruff demeanor that was much saltier than sweet. "He's a grouch."

"I think I caused his grouchiness. After Cheryl died, he went into a shell and didn't bother with anyone, that is, until Pamela's husband passed away. Some of the folks from church encouraged him . . ." She made a face. "Or rather pushed him to be there to comfort her, and next thing we all knew, they were an item. I'd already left town by then, but your mother tried to use that to bring me back saying Andy was over his grief."

"But you weren't over *your* grief . . . or guilt."

Aunt Mary instantly stilled, blinked, and finally nodded. "You're right. And I'm still not over it."

"Obviously."

"So that's why I may not be able to stay in Bloomfield. Being here brings back too many bad memories. You understand."

"Yes, I do, but being here should bring back good memories too. Remember when you and I used to hang out at the soda shop in back of the drugstore?"

Aunt Mary grinned. "Of course I do. Your mother used to fuss at me when you wouldn't eat your supper, because I couldn't say no when you wanted French fries and sodas."

"And the times when we went to festivals together? Mom was always working hard with the garden club and didn't take time to have fun with me. But even though you had stuff to do, you didn't seem to mind kicking back and laughing with your needy niece."

"Yes, but remember I didn't have a family to tend to like your mother did. Between her family and garden club commitments, there was little time left for fun."

"True, and I understand that after having my own daughter." Bethany sighed. "But that doesn't take anything away from our relationship. I would love for you to move back here so we can recapture some of those happier days."

"I don't have to move back for that."

True. Bethany reached for her aunt's hand. "Why don't we say a prayer? We're both obviously dealing with things that are bigger than we can handle on our own."

"Good idea."

They bowed their heads and prayed in silence for a moment before Bethany spoke. "Lord, I pray that You work on our hearts, help us to forgive, and allow others to forgive us. Show us the way You want us to go."

When she paused, Aunt Mary took over. "And Lord, thank

You for this time I'm able to spend with my sweet niece Bethany who has always given to others without regard to what she wants." After they both said, "Amen," they opened their eyes and smiled.

Aunt Mary placed her hand on Bethany's shoulder. "Now it's my turn to give you advice. Stop trying to recapture happier days from the past and start enjoying the present."

Bethany held her aunt's gaze for several seconds. "That sounds good, but it's not so easy, you know?"

"Yes, I do know. When the past is painful, it's difficult to see the beauty and joy of the present and future." She waved her hands around the room. "I suspect that's why you're having such a hard time getting rid of some of this clutter." Her lips quivered as she smiled. "We're quite the pair, aren't we?"

Before Bethany could comment, a knock sounded at the door. "I better go see who that is."

Aunt Mary's playfulness returned as she picked up a pillow and pretended to hide behind it. "If they're looking for me, I'm not here."

Bethany laughed at the common line she and Aunt Mary used to share back when times were happier and simpler. She got up and went to answer the door.

"Hey, Bethany." Pete grinned at her. "Mind if I come in?"

She took a step back and made a sweeping gesture toward the foyer. "Come on in and join the party."

He gave her a curious look as he hesitated. "Party? I didn't mean to interrupt anything."

Aunt Mary stood. "You're not interrupting a thing, Pete. Come on in. I was just leaving." She avoided letting Pete see her reddened eyes as she leaned over and gave Bethany a hug and kiss on the cheek. "Thanks for everything, sweetie. Give me a call later, and I'll come back to help you sort through some more of your stuff."

♡ ♡

Pete sensed something he couldn't describe as he followed Bethany through her house. Her aunt had smiled and tried to act normal, but whatever happened before he arrived created tension in the air. Once again his timing was off, but how could he have possibly known?

"It's been quite a day, hasn't it?" he said once they reached the kitchen.

She set down the refreshment tray on the counter beside the sink and started unloading it without looking at him. "It sure has. I don't understand why Andy can't just leave his bird at home."

Pete lifted his hands, palms up. "You saw what the bird did in the community center. I can only imagine what he's done to Andy's house."

"True. But I would think that if he wants to take him out in public, he could train him to behave . . . or put a lock on the cage."

"Not that I know this first hand, but according to rumor, Murray gets so mad when he's alone for any amount of time, he can be heard squawking and kicking up a fuss a block away." Pete chuckled. "I suspect that's why Andy carries the bird around. He even takes him to the fire hall when he's on duty."

"Too bad his sister didn't leave him a Dalmatian." Bethany wiped off the tray and stuck it in a cabinet before turning around. "What does the bird do when there's a fire?"

"I'm sure he hangs around the firehouse waiting for the crew to return."

As they chatted about Andy's parrot, Pete realized this conversation was more about keeping the subject safe. He sensed Bethany's discomfort whenever he mentioned anything related to feelings or the past. Immediately after Charlie's passing, he understood, but enough time had elapsed, and he felt she should be willing to move on with her life. The problem was, he didn't know how to change the subject without being obvious.

"Do you want something to drink?" Bethany folded her arms as she looked at him.

"No, as a matter of fact, I can't stay long. I just wanted to stop by after I heard what happened. I thought you might need consoling after all your stuff was broken."

Her body tensed, but she shook her head. "It wasn't my stuff anymore."

"I know, but still . . ."

She forced a chuckle. "I'm okay, but it's too bad we have fewer *prizes* and *rummage sale items* to lure people to Bloomfield."

He noted the sarcasm and nodded. "Yeah, we might lose a few people who had their hearts set on a bunch of ceramics. We'll just have to think of something else to lure them with."

"I agree with all the garden club members. I think Bloomfield has a lot to offer, and maybe if Pamela would relax a little and enjoy some of our amenities without worrying about the population, it would happen on its own."

"You know that's not going to happen. Pamela will never leave anything to chance." Pete took a step back. "I best be leaving, but before I do, would you like to do something later?"

"I don't know." She gave him a contrite glance before looking away. "I mean, I'm really busy, and I've never been much of a night person, and it's getting late . . ."

Pete let out a sigh of exasperation. He wished he knew what it would take to get through to her—to bring back the fun-loving Bethany he once knew. Charlie was a fortunate man, and he knew it. Pete often wished he'd been the one who had asked her out first, but once Charlie laid claim to her, no way would Pete do anything to interfere.

He opened his mouth to persuade her to go out when another knock came at the door. "Want me to get that?"

"That would be nice," Bethany said as she made one of her funny faces. "Honestly! It's like Grand Central Station around here lately." She nodded toward the door. "I need to put the rest of these things away."

Pete opened the door to Andy, who clung to the birdcage with one hand, a bouquet of flowers in the other, and wore a sheepish expression. "Hey, Andy, what brings you here?"

Andy shot him one of his grumpiest looks. "Are you Bethany's bodyguard?"

"Does she need one?"

"I don't know, does she?"

"Maybe." Pete nodded toward the bird. "As long as he's around."

"Touché." Andy tilted his head forward. "Mind if we come in?"

"I guess that would be all right." He took a step back and closed the door behind Andy. "Why don't you and your bird have a seat, and I'll go get her?"

As Pete took off toward the kitchen, he overheard Andy mumbling something about gatekeepers to Murray. He sure hoped he didn't resort to talking to birds when he reached Andy's age in about twenty years.

"Who was at the door?" Bethany asked.

"Andy, and he's waiting for you in the living room." He paused. "With his bird."

Bethany groaned as she wiped her hands on the dishtowel. "What do they want?"

"I think they have a peace offering."

She gave him a shaky smile as she tossed the towel to the counter. "Okay, I guess that's probably a good thing. Stick with me, okay?"

"I'll be right there."

As they approached the living room, Andy stood and thrust the bouquet toward Bethany. Once she accepted it, he lifted Murray's cage to put the bird at eye level with her. "What did I tell you to say?"

"Bad birdie . . . *squawk* . . . bad birdie!"

"True," Andy replied with a pretend scowl. "But what did I say to tell her?"

"Tell the girl you're sorry . . . *squawk!*"

Andy glared at his bird. "Say I'm sorry, Murray."

Murray fluttered his wings, shook his head, and stepped side-to-side on his perch. "Say I'm sorry, Murray . . . *squawk* . . . Say I'm sorry, Murray."

Andy put the cage on the floor and cast an apologetic look at Bethany. "I did the best I could in the short time I had. It generally takes hours and hours of repeating the same words over and over before it becomes part of his vocabulary."

"That's okay, Andy." Bethany leaned down and looked at the bird. "As for you, I accept your apology. Just don't ever do that again."

Murray hung his head. "Bad birdie . . . *squawk* . . . bad birdie."

"Yes, bad birdie." Bethany straightened to look at Andy. "I appreciate all this, but you really didn't have to—"

Andy lifted a hand. "There's something else . . . a favor. I really hate to do this, considering what happened this afternoon, but I've exhausted all of my other options."

A bad feeling washed over Pete. Whatever Andy was about to say had to be a zinger for him to preface it with so much drivel.

"A favor?" Bethany tilted her head.

"Would you mind keeping an eye on Murray for a couple of hours? The bird-sitter I had lined up got sick, and—"

Pete held his breath as Bethany opened her mouth. He hated the fact that Andy had put her on the spot, but he was helpless to do a thing.

"I'm so sorry, Andy, but Pete and I have plans to go out in a little while." She smiled. "Maybe some other time?"

Chapter 10

Once they were settled in Pete's truck two hours later, he stuck the key in the ignition, but then paused and turned to her. "I'm glad you decided to go out with me. I have to admit, though, I was surprised." He grinned. "Still am, but I'm not complaining. You look pretty."

He'd told her to wear something nice, so she took a little extra time getting ready. She smoothed the sides of her satin blouse but didn't look directly at him. "Surprised?"

"Yes. I thought you said you were too busy, and it was too late."

She darted her gaze toward him but quickly looked away. "But I never said I wouldn't go."

He suspected she might have been on the fence about the date and eventually agreed to go out with him, but Andy had saved him from sweating it out. "True. But I do have one question."

"What's that?" Now she turned her attention fully in his direction.

"If Andy hadn't shown up and asked you to bird-sit, what would you have done? Would you have said yes?"

"Maybe . . . probably." She sighed. "Okay, so Andy showing up with his bird helped me decide. I appreciate that he apologized, but when asked the favor, I . . . I just sort of went into one of the zones Charlie used to tease me about. I knew I had to make a decision, and going out with you was my choice."

"So you're saying the reason you're with me is because you don't want to bird-sit?"

A distressed look washed over her face as she shook her head. "No, that's not what I'm saying. I—"

He knew better than to press her. If he didn't let up, she might wish she'd chosen to take care of Murray instead. "Okay, I'll stop."

She let out a breath. "Thanks."

Pete chuckled. "That bird is something else, isn't he?"

"Oh, he's something else all right." She smiled. "But I'm not sure what that something else is."

"I wonder if he knows what he's saying."

She nodded. "I think he does most of the time. I've heard parrots are pretty smart."

"All I know is, they talk a lot . . . or at least Murray does."

"According to my mother, they can have thousand-word vocabularies." She tucked one side of her hair behind her ear and looked over at him. "I'm pretty sure Murray is close to that already."

"That's crazy. Some people I know don't have thousand-word vocabularies."

"Be nice, Pete. Those people probably can't help it."

"Or maybe they can but don't want to."

"Speaking from experience?"

He laughed. It sure was fun bantering with Bethany again like this.

Guilt flooded Bethany as she focused on the road ahead. Pete deserved heartfelt acceptance, not the consolation prize of being the lesser of two evils. She enjoyed being with Pete, but the conflicting emotions welling up inside her lately had overflowed and rendered her craving more alone time. Aunt Mary's confession had drained her, and her heart ached knowing about the guilt her aunt had endured over the years. Ever since the confession, Bethany had prayed for her aunt's ability to let go of the suffering.

Bethany saw Pete glance in her direction every now and then as he drove toward The Fancy Schmantzy, the nickname of the finest restaurant in Bloomfield. People in town had called it that for so long the owners Fred and Rita had changed the sign, and she couldn't remember the original name.

"You really don't have to take me to such an elegant place," she said. "I would have settled for a sandwich or salad someplace more casual."

"I don't want you *settling* for anything tonight," Pete said. "You shouldn't feel like you have to settle. Ever."

Pete's words rang through her head. All of Bethany's life, she'd felt as though she'd settled for whatever others thought she should have. Growing up, Naomi had called the shots, and after realizing that trying hard to get her way was pointless, Bethany had settled for her mother's wishes. She'd married Charlie out of love, but even his desires took precedence over hers, so she often found that to keep peace in the marriage, she had to settle for doing things his way.

Then along came Ashley, and anyone who has ever had children knew their needs came first. Even now, with Ashley in college, she had to make do with the meager leftovers from the small income Charlie had set up for her to live on. Before Ashley started college, Bethany promised a long vacation for the two of them, so she'd been tucking away a few dollars from her monthly income Charlie to pay for that trip.

Pete reached for her hand, squeezed it, and let go, returning his hand to the steering wheel. "This is your special evening. Order anything you want and don't even bother looking at the prices."

The more time she spent with Pete, the more she remembered how giving he'd always been. She let out a nervous chuckle. "Aren't you worried I'll take advantage of your generosity?"

"That's what I'm counting on." His half-smile faded as a more serious look came over him. "No one else seems to mind taking advantage of you and making you feel guilty, so now it's your turn to have what you really want."

Bethany leaned her head back and closed her eyes for the last few minutes of the short trip to the restaurant. Nothing in Bloomfield was far, so they were likely to run into someone they knew—the main reason she stayed home most nights. The thought of running into an acquaintance and having them assume anything about her relationship with Pete bugged her, but she knew it would probably happen. The bump leading into the parking lot jostled her from her thoughts.

"I meant what I said about ordering what you want," he said, as he opened her door and gave her a hand.

"Okay, you asked for it." She sent him a teasing glance. "I hope you have deep pockets."

He shoved his free hand in his pocket. "Yep. It's deep enough."

Pete was surprised that Bethany didn't let go of his hand, and he wasn't about to pull away, even if it meant an awkward moment when they reached the restaurant door. He was about to maneuver around when the massive oak door swung open.

"Good evening," the young woman said as they entered. "Reservations?"

Pete nodded. "Yes, for two. Pete Sprockett."

The hostess glanced at the book behind the counter, grabbed a couple of menus from the nook, and motioned for them to follow her. "I have the table you requested ready."

"You requested a specific table?" Bethany asked.

"Absolutely. I wanted the best in the house."

A giggle bubbled up from her throat. "Is that a line you give all the ladies, or do you mean it?"

He gave her a horrified look, but when he saw the teasing grin, he rolled his eyes. "I'll leave that for you to figure out."

"Hey, Bethany. Fancy seeing you here."

The sound of Pamela's voice scraped Bethany's last nerve. She held her breath as she turned toward the person she least wanted to see tonight.

"Hey, Pamela." She glanced at the man across the table from Pamela. "Hi, Andy. I see you got someone to watch your bird."

"No, I left him home alone. No telling what he'll get into with my being gone so much lately." His humorless voice cracked. "But some people—" Pamela's sharp glare cut him off.

"Aw, that's too bad." Bethany tried her best to sound sorry, but she wasn't sure she'd pulled it off when she saw a hint of a smirk on Pete's lips.

Andy shot her a look of defiance. "No one was willing to help me out, so I had no choice."

Pamela pointed one of her long, snowflake-painted fingernails at Andy. "That bird rules your life, Andy, and no one feels sorry for you."

Andy shrugged. "He's spoiled. What can I say?"

"And whose fault is that?" Pamela bobbed her head.

Pete gestured toward the hostess who patiently waited for them by a table in the corner of the dining room. "Sorry, folks, but we need to get on over to our table."

Andy waved them off as he turned back around and picked up his fork. "That's fine. Don't you worry for a moment about Murray. He might get out of his cage and get into something he shouldn't, or worse, eat something poisonous, but that's not your concern."

"Oh, for crying out loud," Pamela growled.

It took every ounce of self-restraint to keep Bethany from responding. When she sat down, she looked Pete in the eye, and they both laughed softly.

Pete held up a hand and covered one side of his face for privacy. "Don't look now, but I think they're still squabbling."

"I know, and it's all about the bird."

"Remind me not to get on the bird-sitting list," Pete said. "Looks like once you're on it, there's no getting off."

After the server took their order and left, Bethany leaned back in her chair. "Thank you for getting me out of the house tonight. I've sort of gotten into a miserable routine of staying home and wondering what everyone else is doing."

"Sort of?" He gave her a teasing look. "But seriously, I don't know about being in a miserable routine. I think it's more like you've forgotten to look for the sunshine."

"Am I really that bad?" She scrunched up her face as she watched the pained expression wash over Pete's.

"I don't—"

"Never mind." Bethany forced a smile. "I have to admit, getting rid of some of the clutter makes me feel much better. Lighter even."

"Yes, and that's wonderful."

"My aunt wants me to tackle the rest of it in small amounts." She laughed. "She probably thinks if I take baby steps, I'll eventually wind up where I should be."

Pete nodded his understanding, but he didn't interject any comments. Bethany suspected he had plenty to say.

"Look, I get it. I know everyone is worried about me, and I understand why." She paused. "I just need the comfort of the familiar sometimes."

"Comfort doesn't come from things," Pete said softly. "The Lord doesn't want you to be bogged down with possessions that can be taken away in a flash. You saw what happened when Murray got loose."

"Yes, you're right." She knew deep down that was true, but when she wrapped up in one of the blankets her mother-in-law had crafted or admired some of the Hummel collections Charlie had given her for her birthday shortly after they'd gotten married, she remembered the happier times. If she closed her eyes, she could return to that moment. "Maybe I'll pick out a few things that mean the most and then have someone come in and box up the rest."

"Would you like my help?"

She shook her head. "I appreciate the offer, but I think it would be better if someone else did it. Maybe Aunt Mary will."

"And don't forget Naomi." He smiled and winked. "I bet she'd like nothing better than to get her hands on your collectibles."

"Oh, I'm sure that's right. But no, I think Aunt Mary can do it without Naomi's help."

Pete laughed.

"What's so funny?"

"You're doing it again. I always thought it was strange that you called your mother by her first name."

"I know, but it's an old habit that's hard to break. Would you believe I sometimes have to stop and think to call her Mom?"

"Everything about you is so different and interesting," he said as he propped his elbows on the table and leaned forward. "I would like to—"

The server arrived with their dinners, so he pulled his arms off the table and leaned back. As she placed the plates filled with steak, baked potatoes, and green beans in front of them, the aroma wafted to her nostrils. Bethany's mouth watered.

"This looks and smells delicious," she said.

"Then let's eat."

"But first, the blessing."

"Of course." Pete bowed his head and said the blessing. Then he didn't waste a moment before lifting his fork and knife. "Oh, and by the way, save room for dessert. I want to treat you to the works."

Bethany couldn't help but grin throughout the meal as she watched the obvious delight on Pete's face as she enjoyed her food. The Fancy Schmantzy was expensive, but everything about it—from the fabulous food and first-class service to the white tablecloths and ambient lighting—made it worth the price. But all that paled in comparison to how good she felt sitting across the table from Pete. Even the moments of silence were pleasant. She knew she needed to guard her heart, but being with Pete gave her a sense that all was right in the world.

Pete awoke the next morning with a smile on his face. When he first picked her up last night, Bethany had been tense and quiet, but once the evening wore on, she'd come out of her shell and actually laughed at some of his silly jokes. He filled a travel mug with coffee and grabbed a blueberry muffin on his way out the door. His mother still fussed at him for not eating a hearty breakfast, but he didn't have time to do that every single morning. Once in a while, he'd scramble a couple of eggs, but that was rare.

He arrived at work, still smiling. Charlotte, the office manager, greeted him right away.

"You look like you've been bitten by the bluebird of happiness." She put down a paper and took his travel mug to refill it. "I heard you were out with Bethany last night."

"That's right." He followed her to the small break room in the back of the shop. "Where did you hear?"

She laughed. "You're kidding, right? This is Bloomfield. You do something in public, and word gets around. So you're smiling because you and Bethany had a date last night?"

"Yep."

"I'm glad you had a good time." She handed him some papers. "After you come back down to earth, you need to take a look at these orders before I fax them."

"Will do." He'd almost made it to his office when Charlotte cleared her throat, catching his attention. "Did you need something else?"

"I have some advice if you want to hear it."

"Sure." He knew this would come eventually, so he leaned against the doorjamb.

"Don't try to resurrect the past. You're not a teenager anymore, and people change after life happens." She remained standing at the beverage counter after she topped off his coffee.

"Are you trying to tell me something?" he asked.

She hesitated before nodding. "I've seen Bethany around town and at church, and she doesn't look like she's having much fun anymore."

"When Bethany lets down her hair, she's a lot of fun."

Charlotte handed him his freshly poured coffee, filled her own mug, and tilted her head forward. "The key phrase being 'when Bethany lets down her hair,' right?"

He took a sip of coffee. "Afraid so, and it doesn't happen nearly often enough anymore since Charlie died."

"It's not easy losing a spouse," Charlotte said. "It takes some people more time than others to resume a sense of normalcy."

"I understand that, and I'm working on—" He stopped himself before adding he felt a personal responsibility for getting her back to living.

Charlotte gave him an understanding nod. "I'm sure if anyone can pull her out of her sadness, you can." She lifted a slip of paper. "Oh, by the way, Jeremy Maples called in this morning and asked if you were available sometime today to help with some bathroom plumbing."

Pete crinkled his nose. "Any idea of the specifics?"

"He's having some trouble replacing the wax ring on the toilet."

"I can do that in my sleep."

Charlotte chuckled. "You can do more plumbing in your sleep than most plumbers can do after five cups of coffee."

Pete knew his dad was one of those people, and he suspected Charlotte was aware of that too. But neither of them was disrespectful enough to come right out and say it. Pete's loyalty to his family ran deep, and Pete's dad took a chance on hiring Charlotte, a friend of the family, when she couldn't find work anywhere else.

Pete's grandfather had started a business that his dad never had any desire to run, so it had been a source of contention for the rest of Grandpop's life. Once he passed, Pete's dad tried to pour himself into the work, but his heart had never been in it, no matter how much he labored. At the end of every single day his dad worked at the family business, he looked as though he'd been in a street brawl. Pete, on the other hand, loved his work and thrived on helping customers with their plumbing problems.

The only thing Pete missed since he'd taken over running the company was being out and about among the customers. That was when Charlotte reminded him he was in charge, and if he wanted to help customers personally, he could. So he'd set that as a policy, and so far, it worked well.

After a morning filled with paperwork and payroll, Pete left for lunch. He'd barely made it out the door when Charlotte ran after him. "Jeremy's on the phone. He wants to know if you can go to his house right away." She made a face. "He says it's extremely important that you get there right away."

Pete thought for a moment and nodded. "Tell him I'm on my way." He could grab a bite to eat after they finished.

The instant he pulled onto the street where the Maples family rented their house, he spotted Bethany's car parked at the curb. He chuckled as he realized this was another setup, and now Gina was most likely in on the act.

As he walked into the Maples' house, he saw Bethany was as surprised as he was. She smiled as she reached up and twirled the end of her shoulder-length blonde hair.

Gina Maples popped in, wiping her hands on a towel. "Glad you could make it for lunch."

"Lunch?"

She nodded as she cast a curious look in her husband's direction. "You did invite him to lunch, right?"

Jeremy's face reddened as he shrugged. "I didn't actually speak to him. I just told his receptionist I needed him to come early . . . and it was important."

Gina laughed. "Oh, well, you're here. I hope you haven't eaten yet."

"As a matter of fact, I haven't." He looked at Bethany and saw that her smile had faded a tad.

"Then you'll stay for lunch, right?"

Before Pete could reply, Jeremy spoke up. "He has no choice since we're not starting on the bathroom until after we eat." The look on Jeremy's face left no doubt in Pete's mind that Gina had gotten him involved in the matchmaking.

Chapter 11

Once again, Bethany had been blindsided by the fix-up, but after the initial shock of seeing Pete, she was flattered these people would go to so much trouble for her. The look on Pete's face was priceless. He'd obviously been as surprised as she was, and somehow that made her happy. Of course, it didn't hurt that he seemed pleased about it.

"Let me help you in the kitchen," Bethany said as she followed Gina toward the back of the house.

Gina glanced over her shoulder. "You don't have to. Why don't you stay out there and chat with the guys?"

Bethany cleared her throat and decided honesty would be best in this situation. "Because I need a few minutes to regroup, or I just might make a bumbling idiot of myself."

The smile on Gina's face let her know she'd made the right decision. "In that case, would you mind ladling some of that salad dressing into the bowl?" She crinkled her nose. "I think even a bumbling idiot can do that."

Bethany laughed. "Then by all means, let me at it."

They chatted as they assembled the rest of lunch, until Jeremy wandered into the kitchen. "Will we be eating any time soon?"

"Yes." Gina cut him a playful eye roll, and she swatted at him when he reached for the bread. "We'll be out there in just a few minutes. Why don't you and Pete wash up while you're waiting?"

"Aw, do I hafta?" He winked at Gina as he left the kitchen.

Still grinning, she shook her head. "Sometimes I wonder whether I have one kid or two."

"He's very sweet," Bethany said. "But I thought he had a job. What's he doing home in the middle of the day?"

"They don't like the workers putting in too much overtime, and he had to work last weekend, so . . ." She opened her arms wide and shrugged. "I'm stuck with him."

"At least he's able to do stuff around here. My husband Charlie wasn't real handy."

"Jeremy is a little too handy sometimes. We always have a mess around here with one project or another." Gina handed Bethany a platter filled with cold cuts. "I've heard Charlie was a sweet guy. Your mother really liked him."

Bethany nodded. "Sometimes I thought they might even be in cahoots. It was uncanny how they could practically finish each other's sentences."

"That happens."

"Yes, especially with Naomi." Bethany noticed Gina's look of confusion when she called her mother by name, so she explained once again.

Gina grinned. "I've been wondering about that. Let's go eat before the guys scarf down all the bread."

Pete led them in the blessing. Jeremy was the first to add his "Amen," and he instantly reached for the cold cuts before Gina swatted at him again.

"Guests first. Where are your manners, Jeremy?"

"Sorry." Jeremy sheepishly handed a bowl of salad to Bethany

and waited for it to come all the way back around the table before
he dug in.

Pete winked at Bethany before turning to Jeremy. "You don't
have to worry about Bethany. She can hold her own at the table."

Bethany darted a playful frown back at him. "You should
talk."

"This is good," Pete said. "Kudos to the cooks."

Gina rolled her eyes. "We didn't actually cook anything."

"Hey," Bethany said. "I'll take any compliments he's willing
to give."

"Are you saying he doesn't compliment you enough?" Gina
lifted an eyebrow as she glanced at Pete.

He held up his hands. "Hey, I think Bethany's great."

Gina smiled at him before turning toward Bethany. "We all
know that."

Bethany enjoyed the banter with friends and thought about
how they should get together more often. Jeremy and Pete acted
as though they'd been friends all of their lives. Lunch was over
much too quickly.

Pete pushed back from the table and stood. "I hate to eat and
run, but we need to get on that project." He gave a comical bow
toward Gina and then turned and bowed to Bethany. "Thank
you, ladies, for a scrumptious lunch."

Jeremy nodded and headed for the bathroom, while Pete followed. Bethany could hear them discussing the best way to fix
the drain in the tub.

Bethany stood and started gathering plates. "Let's get this
stuff cleaned up."

"You don't have to."

"But I want to." Bethany turned to face Gina. "So did you
really need my advice on something festival related, or was that
just a ruse to get me over here?"

Gina smiled. "Busted. But you have to admit, it was fun."

"It was."

"Then let's do it again sometime soon, and maybe next time we can include Sherry and Brad. We've gone out with them several times, and it's always a blast. I used to think Sherry was quiet, but Brad really brings out the fun side of her."

Bethany started to say getting together as couples sounded like a good idea, but then she thought about the signal that might send to Pete. She knew he enjoyed hanging out with her, but she also remembered how he used to say he had no intention of being tied down. "I don't know."

"Do you have a problem with Pete?"

"No, of course not. Why would you ask that?"

Gina leaned against the counter and folded her arms. "Because you seem to have a good time with him, until you remember where you are. Then you clam up."

Bethany shrugged. She didn't want to put any of the blame on Pete. "I guess that's because I had such a good marriage."

"And that's the very reason you should enjoy yourself now. I didn't know Charlie, but I'm sure he would have wanted you to go on living. Loneliness is such a terrible thing."

Bethany lifted an eyebrow. "Something you know firsthand?"

"Yes, but not anymore. In fact, even if I wanted to be lonely, I don't think that's possible in Bloomfield."

"True."

The sound of commotion coming from the front of the house caught their attention. "Did someone have a party and forget to invite me?" Naomi popped into the kitchen, grinning and glancing over her shoulder every couple of seconds. "Where did that sister of mine go? She was supposed to be right behind me."

"Mom, what are you doing here?"

"That's not a nice way to speak to your mother." Naomi turned and grinned at Gina. "Where is that precious little angel child of yours? I brought her something."

"She's still at school." Gina closed the distance between

herself and Naomi as she went in for a hug. "What did you bring her?"

Naomi fished around in the oversized hobo bag and pulled out a figurine that looked exactly like one Bethany had donated to the festival committee. "This sweet, adorable little girl knickknack looks just like Lacy when she chased butterflies in the garden a few months ago." Naomi cut a glance toward Bethany and nodded. "Yes, that used to be one of yours, but you donated it, and I bought it from the garden club, so it's not yours anymore."

Gina looked at the ceramic face. "She does look just like her. Lacy will like that." Then she turned to Bethany. "Is it okay with you?"

"Yes, of course. Like Mom said, I donated it, and she bought it, so it's perfectly fine with me."

Bethany didn't want to be rude, so she stopped, bit her tongue, and decided to save the questions for later. Naomi cast a cautious glance her way but quickly redirected her attention.

Silence filled the kitchen for a few seconds, but Bethany knew that wouldn't last long with her mother in the room. "In case you're wondering, no, I didn't let myself in. Jeremy opened the door before I even had a chance to knock."

That did answer one question for Bethany. "Are you here just to bring that?" Bethany pointed to the figurine Naomi had placed on the counter.

"Nope. I wanted to see if you and Gina had some time this afternoon to attend a meeting." She glanced over her shoulder. "Where is Mary? Sometimes that girl wanders off like a toddler in a toy store."

"What meeting?" Gina asked, bringing her back to the reason for Naomi's visit.

"The Welcome to Bloomfield Festival committee meeting." Naomi glanced back and forth between Bethany and Gina.

Jeremy entered the kitchen, walked up to Gina, and placed his arm around her shoulders. "I'll be here when Lacy gets home from school if you want to go."

Gina nodded. "Sure, I'll go, but I don't know what good I'll do."

Naomi looked at Bethany. "Can I count on you to be there too?"

How could Bethany say no with three pairs of eyes looking at her? "Sure, I'll be there. What time?"

Naomi glanced at her watch. "In about fifteen minutes. We're meeting at the community center."

Jeremy stepped away from Gina and motioned for her to go. "You better start getting ready then." He turned to Naomi. "I don't know why, but she never leaves the house without doing something to her face." He winked and gave his wife a flirty smile. "I think she looks great now."

Bethany grinned. "I suppose I could use a little lipstick."

Naomi started toward the door and stopped. "There you are, Mary. Why didn't you come inside?"

"I was looking at the flower garden." Mary straightened up and grinned at Gina. "You've done a wonderful job with these plantings."

Naomi looked at the flowers as if for the first time. "Your yard does look pretty. Maybe we can have you present a new member workshop and talk about how to start a flower garden. The rest of us are repeating ourselves, and I'm sure Pamela would like some new blood on the speakers' bureau."

Gina obviously enjoyed the flattery. "I'd love to . . . I mean, that is, if you really think I'd have something worthwhile to say."

Naomi flipped her hand. "Of course, you have something worthwhile to say. C'mon, Mary, let's go on ahead and start setting everything up."

As soon as the door slammed behind her, Jeremy chuckled.

"She's a sweet lady." He paused. "Interesting, but nice. I bet it was fun growing up with her for your mother."

"Yeah, a laugh a minute," Bethany agreed. "She is very interesting."

He gave her a curious look but didn't hold it long. "We'll be done in the bathroom in a few minutes. I'll let Pete know you're leaving soon to go to your meeting."

Pete came out and thanked Gina for lunch. Bethany watched him shift his weight from one foot to the other, clearly uncomfortable as he finally turned toward her. "Mind if I call you later?"

"Sure." Bethany smiled, knowing Jeremy and Gina were trying hard not to interfere.

Bethany and Gina decided to walk to the community center, since they were only a couple of blocks away, and it would be easier than finding a parking spot downtown in the middle of a weekday. Bethany was happy to hear Gina in such a good mood as she chattered away about how much Lacy loved school and how she had quite a few more friends than she'd had back home. And now she was excited at the prospect of getting more involved in garden club activities.

"If it weren't for your mother, I don't know where we would be right now," she said. "Naomi has been one of the most influential people in my life, and I've only known her a short time."

"Mom has always had that effect on people."

Gina frowned. "I'm puzzled about something."

Bethany stiffened. "What's that?"

"You and Naomi seem rather uncomfortable around each other. Is there something I'm missing? Did something happen that upset you?"

"No, not at all. I love my mother dearly, but I never know what she's going to do next, so I'm always a little on guard around her. She's been that way all my life. That was fine when I was a little girl, but once I became a teenager, I didn't like it so much."

"Do you like it now?"

Bethany shrugged. "I can't say I like it, but I don't dislike it either. It's just that sometimes I think she needs to back off."

Gina laughed. "That's not her nature—to back off, I mean. Jeremy noticed right away that she treats everyone younger than her like we're all her children."

"Even though we're not children anymore. I've always hated that."

Gina held up a finger. "Aha! So that's why you always seem so annoyed around her. You feel as though she treats you like a child."

"Pretty much."

"There's something else, isn't there?" Gina waved her hand around. "Oh, never mind. It's really none of my business. So what do you think we're going to do at this committee meeting?"

Bethany laughed. "There's no telling, knowing my mother."

"Or Pamela." Gina let out a hearty laugh. "This should be a lot of fun."

"Like I told Jeremy, a laugh a minute."

Gina grinned at Bethany. "You have a rather wry sense of humor. No wonder Pete likes you so much." She paused. "He's such a nice, good-looking guy, I've wondered why he's still single."

"That's one question I know the answer to."

One of Gina's eyebrows arched as she looked at Bethany. "And the answer is?"

"He's a confirmed bachelor. He likes to date different people and doesn't want to be tied down to one woman."

To Bethany's surprise, Gina erupted into a fit of laughter. "Is that what you think?"

"I'm pretty sure that's the case. He used to tell us all the time that he was happy for other couples, but no one would ever catch him getting married."

"Was that when you were with Charlie?" Gina asked.

"Yes. In fact, there wasn't a time I wasn't with Charlie."

"So you never dated Pete when you were a teenager?"

"No," Bethany replied. "But I'll tell you a secret if you promise not to let anyone else know."

Gina pretended to zip her lip. "Not a word to anyone."

"Before I started dating Charlie, I had the biggest crush on Pete."

"Aha! I knew it must have started a long time ago."

"Oh, nothing actually started back then. It was unrequited puppy love."

Gina chuckled. "Something is simmering below that strong, silent surface Pete wants you to see. He really likes you. I can totally see why. You are one special lady."

"Thank you." Bethany wished she had the confidence Gina exuded. She couldn't help but compare herself to the woman who'd traveled to Bloomfield with her daughter when her husband was out of town, gone back home, and convinced him they should pick up and move everything to a place they'd only visited for a short while. It took strength and guts to do what she'd done. And now they were so happy and connected, Bethany forgot they'd only been in Bloomfield for a little more than a year.

"Here we are," Gina said as they reached the sidewalk leading up to the front door of the community center. "I hope I can help, at least in some small way."

"Oh, I'm sure you can help more than you realize."

Gina shook her head. "I've never felt like anyone really valued my opinion all that much. Growing up, I was always just the pretty girl in town. No one ever expected me to have brains." She paused, looked Bethany in the eye, and tapped her head with her index finger. "But I do."

That admission surprised Bethany. She'd never thought of Gina as anything less than smart, and her obvious beauty never overshadowed that.

Bethany grinned back at her friend who clearly trusted her to share her own hang-ups. "I know you do. If it makes you feel any better, my mother thinks you're really smart, and even more importantly, you're a wonderful mother."

Gina positively beamed. "Thank you so much for telling me that. By the way, you're more like Naomi than you might think."

"How so?"

"You're an encourager just like her."

Bethany blinked. She'd never thought about herself being anything like her mother, and she took it as a compliment. "Thank you, Gina. What a sweet thing for you to say."

"It's the truth." Gina pushed the door open with one hand and grabbed Bethany by the arm with the other. "Now let's go inside and do some committee work." She giggled. "Even saying that is so cool! I've always wanted to say I was on an important committee."

Her enthusiasm made Bethany laugh. "I don't know how important a festival committee is, but sure, let's go."

"Oh, it's important. It shows off what a fun place Bloomfield can be."

Once they entered the community center meeting room, it took a few seconds for Bethany's eyes to adjust to the dim lighting. Before she even saw Murray, she knew he was there from all the squawking.

"Took you two long enough," Andy said.

"What took you so long . . . *squawk* . . . What took you so long?"

"You're late." Naomi glanced at the clock. "You two should have been here at least ten minutes ago."

"Late for an important date . . . *squawk!*"

"Such a silly bird," Pamela said with affection-laced annoyance.

"Silly bird . . . *squawk* . . . Silly bird." Murray stilled as Pamela glared at him, and then he slowly turned his back to the people sitting at the table. "Quiet on the set . . . *squawk!*"

Andy planted his face flush with the cage. "Stop it right now,

Murray. If you can keep your beak shut for the next half hour, I'll give you some candy."

As Murray jumped around squawking about getting a treat, Gina headed straight for Andy and Pamela, wedged herself between the two of them as she placed her arms around their shoulders, leaned down, and gave both of them a hug. "I'm so excited to be on a committee with this group."

Bethany had to hold back her amusement at the discomfort she saw on Pamela's face. She glanced at Naomi, who'd also noticed. Naomi winked at Bethany and lifted the stack of papers in front of her to hide her own smile.

Aunt Mary grinned and patted the seat next to her. Bethany took it and leaned in for a hug. "How are you doing, girl?"

Bethany shrugged. "Okay, I guess."

"You'll be fine." She placed her hand over Bethany's and turned to look at Naomi.

Once Bethany got settled, she looked around and saw Aunt Mary had positioned herself so she wasn't facing Andy. Bethany decided right then to have a chat with Aunt Mary about asking for forgiveness, even though Andy didn't appear to hold her responsible for his wife's death.

"Let's get this show on the road, now that we're all here."

"Get this show on the road . . . *squawk* . . . What are you waiting for?"

Andy frowned at his bird. "Hush, Murray."

"Hush little baby . . . *squawk!*"

"Did you hear what I said earlier?" Andy growled at Murray, who pulled his head down deep into his shoulders. "Try to behave and stop being such a bad bird."

"Bad birdie . . . *squawk* . . . bad birdie."

Naomi narrowed her eyes, scanned the room with her gaze, and then picked up another stack of papers and handed them to Gina. "Take one off the top and pass it around. I'll wait until everyone has a chance to look it over."

The first page was the agenda for upcoming committee meetings, and the second had an outline with blank spaces beneath categories. After Pamela looked at the information, she lifted her glasses and propped them on top of her head. "All I see are a bunch of blank spaces. What are we supposed to do with this, Naomi, and why are we here?"

"We're here to fill in the blanks. We can't just go through the motions without some direction."

Pamela glared at Naomi but softened her look as she turned toward Gina and then Bethany. "It's not like we haven't had a festival before. I think everyone knows what to do."

Naomi tapped her pen on the table. "This one's different. It's new and untried. If we want it to be a success, we have to make it different from everything else going on here in town. We're expecting a lot more out-of-towners, as well as prizes from folks in Bloomfield. We need to put out the word that people should go ahead and rent booths so we can pay for the extra security to keep the city council from putting the skids on future events."

Gina timidly raised her hand. Naomi turned to her and gestured for her to speak.

"Do we have one person in charge of a group of chairmen, or chairwomen, who lead each thing on here? Like someone who oversees the others who gather all the prizes and keep track of security?" She offered an apologetic shrug. "I know I'm new and all, so I should probably just sit and listen, but it seems like an awful lot for one person to be responsible for."

Pamela shook her head. "No, we always just have one person doing all of it. It's best—"

Naomi tapped her pen again. "Since that one person is usually me, I like Gina's idea. I've had a frightful time getting everything done by myself."

"I don't know what you're saying, Naomi. I've done quite a bit as well. Besides, you never complained about being in charge before," Pamela said.

"And I'm not complaining now. All I'm saying is Gina has a good idea, and I think we should consider it."

Pamela rolled her eyes, fluttered her bright purple fingernails with silver tips in the air, and nodded. "Then Gina, what do you want to be in charge of?"

Gina's eyes filled with fear as she turned to Naomi. "I didn't mean to—"

"Like I said, Gina," Naomi tilted her head toward her, "your idea is excellent. I think you'd be good at organizing, promoting, and keeping track of the booth rentals."

Bethany felt like a lump on a log. Finally, she decided she might as well offer her services. "I'd like to do something."

"How about collecting the donations?" Pamela asked.

"Step right up and win a prize . . . *squawk* . . . step right up."

Everyone laughed until Bethany cleared her throat. She opened her mouth to speak, but Naomi spoke up before she had a chance. "Anything but that. She already has way too much stuff in that little house of hers. I think she'd be good at publicity."

Bethany felt her eyes bulging as she looked at Naomi. Was she kidding? Publicity? How could her mother even suggest something so out of character for her?

Gina grinned at her. "I agree. Everyone likes Bethany, and I think she'll be able to get folks to help get word out."

"I—" Bethany began.

Pamela pointed to Bethany, shushing her before she could finish. "Then you're responsible for publicity and promotion."

Bethany opened her mouth to say something, but she didn't want to do it in front of so many people. Instead, she slid down in her chair. "I'll do my best."

She really needed to have a private chat with her mother—or move out of town again to get away from her. Sometimes that seemed like the best option. Moving away from Bloomfield had given her an opportunity to stand up for herself without her mother's shadow constantly looming over her. People assumed that since she was a cheerleader in high school she was an extrovert, but she had to force herself to appear outgoing. Deep down, she was shy.

She'd managed to form a few friendships at the church she and Charlie attended, but she never felt connected. Charlie had such a big personality that she'd shrunk back to being quiet and withdrawn after being married to him for a while. She made a mental note to work on that. She'd done it as a teenager, and she could do it again.

Aunt Mary leaned over and whispered, "I'll help as much as I can."

Andy spoke up next. "I'll see about security and fire safety."

"Yes, of course, you will," Pamela said. "That goes without saying." She paused, glanced at Naomi, exchanged nods, and smiled at Gina. "Now that I've seen you in action, I think you'd make an excellent coordinator of the whole festival. Naomi and I have already discussed it, and she says it's time to bring in some fresh, new people who can take over after we step down. You can oversee all of the other chairpersons. I'll find someone else to take over the booth rental. How about it?"

Gina's eyes practically bulged out of her head. Bethany started to speak up and ask folks to give her a chance to get her feet wet when Gina spoke up for herself.

"Seriously? You'd actually let me be the coordinator?" Her chin quivered as she swallowed hard, placed her hand over her heart, and grinned. "Absolutely!"

Chapter 12

After the meeting, Naomi asked Gina to stick around to get more information about how to prepare for a festival. Aunt Mary hovered by the door, so Bethany approached.

"How's your visit going?"

"So far, so good. Are you going straight home?" Aunt Mary asked.

"I left my car at the Maples' house, and Gina and I walked here."

"Fine." Aunt Mary turned toward the street. "I'll walk with you, then."

Bethany glanced over and spotted Andy and Pamela at the door. "First, I want you to talk to Andy."

"Not now."

"When?" Bethany planted a fist on her hip. "Now is just as good a time as any. If you don't go ahead and talk to him, it will just keep getting more difficult."

Aunt Mary closed her eyes and took a deep breath. "Okay, I'll do it."

"Would you like for me to go with you?"

"No, this is something I need to do on my own."

Bethany smiled and gave her aunt a gentle nudge. "I'll be right here waiting."

She watched as Aunt Mary approached Andy and Pamela. After she said a few words, Pamela hugged her and left. Bethany glanced away, but every now and then she snuck a glance toward them to see how things were going. Relief flooded her as she saw that Andy wasn't angry. He actually put down Murray's cage and gave Aunt Mary a hug.

When Aunt Mary walked back to Bethany, a slight smile played on her lips. "I gather it went well?" Bethany said.

"Yes, very well. He said he never held me responsible for what happened and told me I should move on. This conversation was long overdue."

"I agree." Bethany gestured toward the door. "Ready to go?"

They'd barely gotten twenty feet when Aunt Mary started in on her mission. "I hate to do this to you, but I promised Naomi. Have you had a chance to go through more of your stuff yet?"

Bethany sucked in a breath and pondered what to say next. All the events and surprises over the past few days had worn her out. She needed some time to regroup. She wanted to tell her aunt—and everyone else who nagged about her clutter—to leave her alone and let her deal with it in her own time. But that would hurt the feelings of the people she loved most.

"No, but I will." She maintained a steady pace and kept her focus straight ahead.

"You didn't really plan to, did you?" Bethany met her aunt's gaze and slowly shook her head. "I didn't think so." Aunt Mary draped her arm over Bethany's shoulder. "But that's okay. I've decided that you need me to help and cheer you on." She grimaced. "Actually, that's not true. My arm has been twisted by you-know-who, and I sort of agreed to do it."

Bethany hated that her mother left the dirty work to her aunt. "If I tell you no that lets you off the hook. I still haven't pulled everything down from the attic."

"Please don't tell me no." Aunt Mary's quivering chin surprised Bethany. "Not only do I want to be part of your life while I'm here, I want to do it with your mother's blessing." She held her arms out to her sides. "She's given it."

"That's only because you offered to help, right?" Once Aunt Mary nodded, Bethany sighed. "Okay, fine. I'll take care of the attic next."

"Want me to start there, then? Since your things are still stored in the attic, you obviously don't need any of it. I can get the boxes down and take them straight to the—"

"No." The harshness of her own words stopped Mary. "I mean, thank you, but I'd like to go through it myself."

"If the boxes are as full as I think they are, that could take you all day, every day, for months."

Bethany shrugged. "What else do I have to do with my time? I'm home all day."

"That's another thing we need to work on. Even though you've been out with Pete a few times, you're still home alone way too much. You need to socialize more."

"I enjoy being alone," Bethany argued. "As long as my mother is still living, I'll have plenty of human contact. She's pretty good at seeing to that."

"Your mother doesn't count."

"Tell her that," Bethany said.

Aunt Mary's lips twitched. "I wouldn't dare, and I don't recommend you telling her either."

Bethany changed the subject to something she knew would interest Aunt Mary. "I've heard there's a folk music tour going through the area."

Aunt Mary's eyebrows shot up. "Do you think they would play at the festival?"

"I hadn't thought of that, but it wouldn't hurt to see if they have room in their schedule."

"We need to contact their management company and get them here." Aunt Mary's face scrunched up, and her pace quickened. "I wonder if Peter, Paul, and Mary are in this tour. They've done the folk tour before."

"I don't know, but that's something else you can ask."

Bethany had to hold back her amusement as Aunt Mary chattered with excitement. She'd clearly scored a surefire way to get the focus off of herself and on to one of Aunt Mary's other passions.

When they reached Bethany's car, Aunt Mary got in and continued talking about all the ways Bethany could promote the festival. "You can make flyers, send press releases to all the neighboring towns, and maybe we can even talk Pamela into letting go of some of the money from the garden club treasury to pay for ads in the nearby big cities." Aunt Mary paused to take a breath. "I'll work on getting free signed albums from the artists and maybe even some T-shirts and other souvenirs. This will be the best festival Bloomfield ever had. We might even get on *Good Morning America* if we can talk the folk tour into playing." She smiled at Bethany and sighed. "This is the kind of thing that really revs my engines."

"I can tell."

"I have a bunch of old clothes I've been dying to wear again. Naomi always said they looked silly on me, so I put them away."

Bethany feigned shock. "You saved them? I would have thought you'd get rid of anything you didn't use anymore. I mean, after all the nagging about my junk."

"Touché. They're at the Storage Locker past the Village." Aunt Mary leveled her with a head-tilted gaze. "But don't think that lets you off the hook. I still plan to sort through all your stuff with you and donate or toss out whatever you don't use." She folded her arms and jutted out her chin. "You can call me a hypocrite all you want, because quite frankly, I don't care if I am."

"I never said you were a hypocrite." Bethany smiled as she rounded the corner to her house. "Tell you what. We can go through my stuff as soon as we get to the house. I'll carry the boxes down from the attic and stack them in the spare bedroom. If you want to separate things into piles, I'll work on sorting and discarding some more of the decorations in the rest of the house."

"Fair enough." Aunt Mary got out of the car and waited for Bethany. "I might even overlook some junk in exchange for your tip on the folk tour."

"We make a great team, don't we?"

Three hours later, Bethany and Aunt Mary stood back and admired their progress. "Whoa, girl. I had no idea you'd be willing to purge so many things all at one time."

Bethany was surprised too. "It's strange, but I have to admit, it's also invigorating."

"Good. When do you want me to come back?"

"You're not ready to stop now, are you? Because I'm just getting started."

Aunt Mary smiled. "Are you serious?"

"As my mother would say, serious as a heart attack."

"I've heard that more times than I can count." Aunt Mary pointed to the stack of still-sealed boxes. "Okay, then. Grab the one off the top and set it over here."

Pete had just walked in the door of his apartment when the phone rang. "Come quick. I need your help."

"Naomi?"

"Yeah. I need you to come over to my place right away."

"What's wrong? Are you hurt?"

After a pause, she said, "No, I'm not hurt. I need a plumber and fast."

That made no sense. Naomi lived at the Lake Bliss Retirement Village, and he knew all the guys on the maintenance crew. Occasionally, they needed his family's plumbing company to come out with their large equipment for big problems, but they were all perfectly capable of taking care of most of the residents' emergencies.

"Are you coming or not?" The impatience in her voice amused him.

"I will if you come clean and tell me what this is really about." He rocked back on his heels and waited to hear what kind of story she'd cook up now.

"What are you talkin' about?"

"Naomi, you have maintenance men right there at the Village. Now tell me why it's so important I drop everything right this minute."

She made some coughing sounds, and he heard her mumbling something to herself, but he couldn't make out what it was. Finally, she chuckled. "Okay, you've caught me. We're having a variety show in the recreation room here at the Village, and I thought it might be fun for you and Bethany to come as my guests."

"Have you asked Bethany yet?"

"Well, no, but what would be the point if you couldn't make it?"

"You'd have some quality time with your daughter," he replied.

"I have plenty of quality time with my daughter. Now it's your turn."

He couldn't deny that Naomi's persistence could wear down a brick wall. "Tell you what. You call Bethany and tell her what you just told me—that you want both of us to join you for the show—and if she agrees, I'll be there."

"I like to surprise—"

"I know you do, but this time, no surprises. Tell her the truth, and then call me back." He paused. "Or better yet, ask Bethany to call me."

"Aw, c'mon, Pete. You know she'd never do that."

Pete thought about it for a moment and realized Naomi was right. "Okay, you call me then."

"Hang tight, and I'll call you right back. Don't go anywhere." The sound of her hanging up made him chuckle. Naomi not only made sure things went her way, but she had a sense of urgency that matched Pamela Jasper's.

He waited for about ten minutes before he came to the conclusion that Bethany had turned Naomi down. No matter how much he tried to tell himself it didn't matter, the fact remained, it did. He cared about Bethany, and he wanted the feelings to be mutual. Sure, he knew she liked him, but from what he'd seen, only at arm's length.

Pete wanted what Charlie once had—a loving relationship with a woman whose glance could make his insides go all funny. He'd just about given up on hearing back from Naomi when his phone rang. It wasn't Naomi.

"Mom asked if I'd like to go to the variety show," Bethany said. "And she told me she asked you first."

He rubbed the back of his neck as he tried to decipher her tone and figure out if she was upset. "Are you going?"

"That's why I called you. She wants us both there."

"Yes," he said. "I know. Do you want to go?" He still wasn't sure how she took Naomi's invitation, and he certainly didn't want to mess anything up—for himself or for Naomi. "I think it would be fun."

"Yeah, me too." She chuckled. "They have some pretty crazy talent over at the Village."

"So, do you want me to pick you up?"

"I'd like that."

Then Pete remembered Naomi hadn't given him a time. All she'd said was she needed him right away. "Do you know what time it starts?"

"In about an hour. Mom said we can meet at her place, and she'll fix us something to eat."

"I haven't eaten yet, so let's do that. Let me take a quick shower and change clothes. I can be at your place in fifteen minutes."

She laughed. "When you said quick shower, you weren't kidding."

Pete hung up and let out a deep breath. Naomi could be the most annoying woman he knew, but at times like this, he wanted to give her a big fat hug.

♡ ♡

The full visitor parking lot surprised Bethany. "I can't believe it's so hard to find a parking spot. Normally, I can find one on the first row."

Pete turned down the last row. "Maybe everyone is here for the variety show."

"Could be," Bethany said. "I wouldn't be surprised if my mother invited every single person in town."

They found a spot at the far end of the lot, got out, and walked straight to Naomi's condo. She opened the door before they knocked. "You're late." She stepped back so they could enter. "Come on in and grab a bite to eat. I put some plates on the counter, and all the food is still on top of the stove."

Pete took a deep breath and smiled. "Smells delicious."

"It is. Both of you like barbecue sandwiches, so that's what you're having." She took a step toward the credenza. "I have to run on down to the multipurpose room and help out. I'll save you two seats as close to the front as possible, but don't take forever."

She grabbed her handbag, hustled toward the door, and then stopped. "We'll have dessert after the show." Then she left.

Pete chuckled. "Hurricane Naomi."

"That's an excellent description." Bethany pointed to the kitchen. "We better eat and run, or we'll have to deal with the storm's wrath later."

The barbecue was delicious, but not as yummy as the man sitting across the table from her. Bethany found it increasingly difficult not to notice the way a small lock of his hair occasionally fell across his forehead or how the corners of his eyes crinkled when he smiled. The man's masculinity oozed from his pores, yet he had sensitivity unlike anyone she'd ever known.

Charlie had been a sweet guy, but he was sometimes clueless about what she wanted. If she didn't come right out and ask for something, he assumed she didn't want whatever it was. Pete, on the other hand, seemed to have much stronger intuition, and he acted on it. Plus he made her laugh.

She needed to stop comparing the two men. It wasn't fair. Charlie loved her and provided an excellent home for her and Ashley. He worked hard during the week and spent time with his family on weekends. They rarely missed church, and he loved the Lord as much as anyone. She had absolutely no complaints about her life with Charlie.

Comparing anyone to Pete wasn't fair to him either. He'd never been married, so the biggest thing in his life was his family business. She'd noticed when she returned to Bloomfield that the Sprockett Family Plumbing Company had thrived under Pete's management. Before she and Charlie moved away, she vaguely remembered the Sprocketts struggling to stay in business. Pete had even confided in Charlie that he didn't always receive a paycheck because his dad barely had enough to pay the other plumbers. Charlie asked Pete what was keeping him in Bloomfield, and Pete said he could never leave his family when they needed him.

Now Bethany saw exactly why. If it weren't for Pete, the business might have gone belly-up.

"Bethany?" Pete had finished his sandwich and sat watching her. "I don't want to rush you, but you heard Naomi. If we don't get on down to the recreation room, we'll hear about it later." He made a face. "Or worse, she'll come looking for us."

She nodded as she chewed what she had in her mouth. "I'm full anyway." She stood up from the table, carried her plate into the kitchen, put the uneaten part of her sandwich in a baggie, and tossed it in the refrigerator. "I'll eat the rest of this later."

Pete rubbed his tummy. "Not me. I'm having some of that delicious looking cherry cobbler I saw in the oven."

Bethany laughed. "Snoop."

He playfully shrugged. "Guilty as charged." He extended his elbow. "Ready to be amused, m'dear?"

She stuck her hand in the crook of his arm and nodded. "Most certainly. Let's go watch a variety show."

Being with Pete felt natural and lightened her heart. His playful manner brought out the joy she'd long since tucked away.

When they reached the hallway leading to the multipurpose room, a screeching sound (followed by shouts and gasps) halted them in their tracks. "Uh, oh." Pete glanced down at her. "Sounds like a Murray moment to me."

"Too bad Andy has to bring him practically everywhere he goes." Bethany shook her head. "I can't imagine being that tied down to a bird he never asked for."

"How do you know he didn't ask for him?" Pete grinned. "For all we know, he could have begged his sister to leave Murray to him." He laughed.

Bethany tilted her head. "That doesn't sound likely to me. If it weren't for Murray, he and Pamela might get married."

"Maybe Andy likes it that way."

Bethany instantly went numb. Was there some hidden meaning in his words?

A shrill scream echoed through the entire area. Pete shook his head as he pulled away from Bethany. "I better go see if I can help."

"I'm right behind you."

They took off running toward the multipurpose room, where pandemonium had hit hard. Murray fluttered slightly above the reach of the tallest adult. Some folks had jumped up onto their chairs, flailing their arms, and the emcee stood at the front of the room, eyes wide, appearing more shocked than anyone else.

"Where's Andy?" Pete hollered above the din. "He's still here, isn't he?"

"I'm right over here." Andy shot his hand up. "You don't think I'd take off at a time like this, do you?"

Naomi walked toward Pete and Bethany, looking over her shoulder at Andy. "I wouldn't put it past you. You knew better than to bring that bird to this show. What were you thinking?"

"I had a talk with him before we left the house, and he promised to behave." Andy's sheepish look belied his belief in the bird.

"Mommy, that birdie's gonna bite me." Lacy burst into full-blown sobs as Murray flew in circles above the little girl, still out of reach of everyone around. "Make him stop."

Gina cast a helpless glance at Jeremy, who sprang into action. "Please calm down, folks. We have to get this bird under control, and all this commotion isn't helping." The pleading sound in Jeremy's voice seemed to work as people lowered their pitch.

Jeremy jumped up and tried to grab Murray, but the bird flew away toward Andy. Instead of lighting on his master, though, he swooped down and grabbed one of Pamela's earrings. She lifted her silvery fingernails in a claw-like motion and made a hissing sound.

Murray dropped the earring as he perched on the indoor flagpole. "He's on the flagpole," Pamela said as she put her earring back on. "Someone go up there and get him down."

"Flagpole . . . *squawk* . . . I pledge allegiance to the flag!"

Jeremy quietly slipped up behind Murray and whispered something. Murray glanced over his shoulder and said, "Murray wants candy . . . *squawk* . . . Murray wants candy."

Andy approached Jeremy and handed him a bag of sliced carrots. Then Andy gestured for everyone to slowly back away.

"Everyone can relax," Jeremy finally hollered. "I've got him."

Within a minute, the audience had settled down, and a low murmur filled the room. Blood dripped from one of Jeremy's hands as he held Murray, but he didn't flinch. Finally, he handed the screeching parrot back to its owner.

"Why don't you take him on home now, Andy?" Naomi said.

Pamela walked right up to Naomi, her fist on her hip. "After all we went through, are you kicking us out?"

"Nope." Naomi planted her own fist on a hip and got right in Pamela's face. "I'm kicking Murray out. We have a policy."

"Ladies," Andy said as he placed a hand on Pamela's shoulder. "I think it's best to get Murray out of here so everyone can enjoy the show. Pamela, why don't you stick around? Murray and I can stop back by later and take you home."

"We'll take her home after the program," Pete said.

Bethany stifled a groan, but she knew Pete had done the right thing by coming to Pamela's rescue. Naomi looked at her with concern, so Bethany turned away to prevent showing how she really felt about sharing her date with Pamela.

Chapter 13

The emcee had lost some of his *savoir faire*, and he stumbled over every single introduction of the evening. Before the Maroon Clowns came on stage, he gestured toward them and said, "We'd like to welcome the moron . . . er, buffoon . . . um . . . the . . ."

He glanced over at the lead clown who slapped his forehead and went straight up to the microphone, grabbed it from the emcee, and gently pushed the befuddled man to the side.

"We don't normally talk when in costume, unless we have extenuating circumstances." He gestured toward the emcee. "And this is obviously one of those times. We are the Maroon Clowns, and our goal is to entertain and delight each and every one of you." He popped a suspender over his maroon-colored billowy shirt. "We are named after the glorious color maroon." He lifted a tiny horn and blasted it over his head. This was clearly the signal for all his clown friends to join him on stage.

As the grown men in clown suits bounced around on stage, their painted faces smiling at the audience, a cacophony of sounds erupted throughout the room. Horns blaring, carnival music playing, and clunky thuds reverberated with every movement.

Bethany sank back in her chair, surveyed the crowd, and studied how mesmerized everyone was by the antics on the stage. Even Lacy, who'd been shrieking earlier from fear of Murray, sat in her chair transfixed by the horns, bounces, fumbled juggling, and silliness of the Maroon Clowns. When they finished their act, the audience applauded. Bethany wondered how many people were clapping out of joy that the clowns were finished.

Next up was Johnny Johnson's polka band. Johnny walked up to the microphone and announced that due to the large crowd in the room, there would be no dancing. A few people groaned, and he held up his hand. "I know, I know, but there's simply not enough space for everyone to dance. So we'll keep it short for those who have happy feet." A few people snickered, and he waved to his band to start playing. After they finished, he and his buddies took a bow and left the stage.

There were still a few acts standing to the side of the stage when Pamela left her seat and walked straight up to Pete and Bethany. "I'm ready to go home now."

"But—" Bethany pointed to the stage where a new act was about to begin.

"Now." Pamela raised her eyebrows, and her voice grew louder. "Do I need to find another ride?" She glanced over her shoulder and had a stare-down with the man who couldn't see around her.

Pete leaned over and whispered, "Do you want to stay here while I take her home?"

Bethany shook her head and got up. "No, that's okay. I'll go with you."

Naomi stood guard by the door at the back of the room. "Where do you think you're going? The best act hasn't even performed yet."

Pamela walked right past Naomi without saying a word,

leaving Pete and Bethany to explain. Pete looked at Bethany, and she gestured for him to go ahead. "I'll be right with you." After he left, she told Naomi what had happened.

"That's ridiculous. All that woman ever thinks about is herself." She scowled. "I reckon it's for the best, though. If she's miserable, she'll take everyone else down with her. You and Pete can come back and have dessert with me."

Bethany nodded. "If Pete wants to come all the way back."

"All the way?" Naomi made a silly face. "It's not like the Village is in the outback. It'll take you ten . . . fifteen minutes tops to take Pamela home and drive back."

When Bethany walked up to the truck, Pamela was already buckled in the front seat next to Pete, so she slid into the tiny backseat. Pete gave her an apologetic look in the rearview mirror. All the way to Pamela's house, the older woman delivered commentary on the variety show.

"I can't believe I'm saying this, but the best part of the show happened before it even started." She chuckled. "Can you believe that little bird had everyone in such an uproar?"

"Little bird?" Pete laughed. "He's a monster."

"Tell me about it." Pamela shook her head. "But seriously? Why did everyone freak out just because he got out of his cage? If folks had just stayed calm, he would have eventually gotten back in without all that hullaballoo."

"We don't know that," Bethany interjected.

"Oh, but I do. He gets out of his cage all the time. All Andy has to do is pull out that bag of carrots, and Murray will do anything."

"Maybe next year Andy can sign up for the show. Murray can do tricks for carrots."

Pamela wiggled her fingers and flapped her hand, practically blinding Bethany with the sun reflecting off her shiny fingernails. "Not a bad idea, but I'm afraid that would be too undignified for Andy to even consider. Maybe we can get someone else to do it."

She glanced over her shoulder at Bethany. "I hear you have more items for the festival. When do you plan on taking them to the community center?"

"After what Murray did to some of the collectibles, I think I'll hang onto them until the festival."

Pamela scowled. "Andy's right. People in Bloomfield really do have it out for his bird."

Pete cut a glance in her direction. "It sounds to me like you're a Murray fan."

"I didn't say that." Pamela grew quiet as she turned toward the window. "But I do sort of relate to the little guy."

Bethany locked gazes with Pete in the rearview mirror as he pulled up to a traffic light. The corners of his eyes crinkled.

Pamela angled her body sideways to face Pete. "Murray and I don't see eye-to-eye on a lot of things, but we both stand out in a crowd, and people don't understand us."

Bethany thought Pamela had a point as she stared at the woman's profile, with the extra-long eyelashes, brightly blushed cheeks, and deep red lips. Both Pamela and Murray commanded attention everywhere they went. As Pamela fluttered her fingers around in the air to make her point, Bethany had to bite the insides of her cheeks to keep from laughing about how much she reminded her of Murray flapping his wings.

"Do me a favor, you two," Pamela said, tossing a glance over her shoulder at Bethany and then back to Pete. "Don't tell Andy I said any of that. I don't want him thinking I actually like Murray . . . or that I can relate to him."

This time, Bethany couldn't help herself. She belted out a loud chuckle that started Pete laughing. Before either of them could stop, Pamela joined in to Bethany's relief.

Pete pulled the car up in front of Pamela's house. "We'll keep your little secret."

"Thanks." She got out of the car and leaned over. "What do you think you're doing, girl?" She yanked the back door open and gestured. "Don't stay in the backseat. Come up to the front and ride with your guy."

Pete lifted an eyebrow and gave Bethany a humorous look. "You heard her."

As Bethany got out of the truck to join Pete in the front, Pamela leaned toward her, cupped her hand, and whispered, "And stop letting Naomi tell you what to do all the time. She might be your mother, but that doesn't give her the right to be so bossy. Do what you want to do and don't give any mind to what other people say or think."

"I'll try." Bethany smiled back. "It was nice seeing you, Pamela."

"Oh, and don't forget to replace all those things Murray broke. I know you have more stuff, because Naomi said Mary was spending time at your place going through your junk."

"Bye, Pamela." Bethany lowered herself into the car, buckled herself in, and waved.

Pete waited until Pamela went inside before pulling away. "Talk about bossy. The pot calling the kettle black."

"Yup. And it's so Pamela." Bethany cut a glance over to Pete. "I'd be disappointed if she acted any differently."

"You have to admit, she's hilarious."

They rode in silence for a while, until Bethany noticed Pete's expression had turned a little sullen. "What's wrong?"

"I just remembered something I said to you not long ago." He looked in her direction and turned his attention back to the road. "I made a negative comment about all your knickknacks. I hope you don't think I was being disrespectful or bossy."

Bethany remembered that day he'd fixed her faucet. "I wouldn't exactly call you bossy."

"Whatever you call it, I had no right to make such a rude remark. I'm sorry."

"No worries." Actually, Bethany was getting numb to all the comments about her décor. "It is what it is."

He flinched. "Ouch. That's what I'm talking about."

"Huh?"

"That was a rude comment, so I suppose that makes me a rude person. I'm really sorry."

"Stop it, Pete." She swallowed hard and squirmed in discomfort.

"Let's change the subject. Do you think the variety show will still be going on when we get back to the Village?"

Bethany glanced at her watch. "I doubt it. They only had a few acts left."

"Good." He licked his lips. "Why don't you call your mom and ask if we need to bring back some ice cream to go with the cobbler?"

She was happy to have something else to do, so she whipped out her phone and punched in her mother's number, thinking Naomi wasn't likely to be back at her apartment yet. But she was.

"What's taking you two so long?" Naomi cleared her throat. "Sorry about that. I'm annoyed that Pamela hoodwinked you into being her chauffeur and made you miss the show. The last act was the best. So are you on your way?"

"Yes, and Pete wants to know if we should stop off and pick up some ice cream."

"I thought he knew me better than that. I have four different flavors in my freezer, but if he doesn't like vanilla, chocolate, strawberry, or butter pecan, he can pick up whatever flavor he likes."

"Okay, I'll tell him." Bethany pushed the off button on her phone. "She said—"

"I heard." He stopped for a red light, turned to her, and smiled.

A warm feeling flooded Bethany as their gazes remained locked. "I should have known my mother would have plenty of ice cream in her freezer. I can't remember a time when she didn't."

Pete nodded and turned his attention back to the road.

"Yeah, I don't think Naomi will ever suffer from an ice-cream deficiency."

By the time they arrived at Naomi's apartment, Bethany's mom had set the table with bowls, spoons, and water glasses. "Would you like some coffee?"

Pete shook his head. "No thanks. You've already gone to way too much trouble."

"You think this is trouble?" Naomi laughed. "Trouble is when people you love get sick. Trouble is when you don't have enough money to pay the bills. Trouble is when—"

Bethany held up her hands. "I think we get the message, Mom."

Naomi smiled and put her arm around Bethany's waist. "I like when you do that."

"Do what? Interrupt you?"

"No, not that. I like when you call me Mom."

Pete's gaze darted back and forth between Bethany and Naomi. At first, he looked stunned, and then he took a step back, appearing uncomfortable.

"Well, you are my mom, so that makes sense."

"Yes, it does, doesn't it?" Naomi pulled away and gestured for them to sit down at the dining room table. "Have a seat, and I'll bring the cobbler out."

"No, *Mom*, you sit down. I'll get it." Bethany tipped her head forward and gave her mother what she hoped came across as a stern look.

Naomi's lips twitched as she nodded. "Okay, bossy lady."

"I come by it honestly." Bethany placed one hand on her hip and flipped her other hand, mimicking her mother. "So what kind of ice cream do you want, Mom?"

"Butter pecan."

Pete wiggled his eyebrows. "I'll have the same."

"Why don't you just bring the whole carton back?" Naomi said. "I think I'll have seconds."

Pete appeared amused. "Good thing you're active."

"I have to stay that way to keep my girlish figure. I've always eaten like a horse, and I don't plan to stop now."

As Bethany ferried ice cream from the kitchen to the dining room, she heard the low murmur of conversation between her mother and Pete. Based on the small snippets she caught, they weren't discussing anything of significance, which was a good thing. She heard the words "clowns," "accordion," and "trio."

Once she sat down, the tone and subject changed. "The festival will be here before we know it, and we still have a bunch of stuff to finish up," Naomi said as she plopped the second scoop of butter pecan ice cream on top of her cherry cobbler. "I'm afraid we didn't give ourselves enough time."

Bethany looked at Pete and saw the amused smile on his face. She turned to her mother. "What all do I need to do to make this run more smoothly?"

"You have plenty to do with the prizes and publicity." Naomi shoved a big bite of cobbler and ice cream into her mouth, winced, chewed, and swallowed. "Brain freeze." Then she took another bite, this one almost as big.

"Mom, you really need to slow down."

Naomi contorted her mouth and looked at Pete. "Do you talk to your mother this way?" She folded her hands in her lap. "It's like I'm now the child and she's the mother."

Pete chuckled. "My parents tell me I've gotten too smart for my own good. So yes, I must talk to them that way."

Naomi playfully pointed a finger at Pete and shook it. "Don't forget who raised you and took care of you the first eighteen or so years of your life."

"Have you and my mother discussed this already? She keeps saying that exact same thing."

Naomi grinned. "I've always thought your mother was a smart woman."

As Pete and her mother bantered, Bethany thought about

how similar her upbringing was to Pete's. They both had in-your-face moms who wanted to be involved in every aspect of their children's lives. However, there were some significant differences too. Pete's parents allowed him to take over the family business, but if Charlie hadn't wanted to move away, Bethany was certain Naomi would have tried to control their lives. She never doubted her mother's love, but it could be suffocating. Moving away had been good and forced her to develop in areas where she'd relied on her mom. The only problem was she'd centered her entire life on Charlie and what he wanted. This should be her time to do what she wanted. She lifted her chin and looked her mother in the eye.

"What're you thinking about, Bethany?" Naomi had propped her elbows on the table and leaned toward her. "You've been mighty quiet for the past few minutes."

The door opened, and in walked Aunt Mary, saving Bethany from having to answer. "Hey there." Aunt Mary's focus settled on the cobbler. "Why didn't you wait for me?"

"Because we didn't know where you were," Naomi said. "There's plenty left, so grab a bowl and spoon and join us."

Aunt Mary nodded as she gripped the back of a chair with both hands and grinned. "I will in just a minute. But first, I wanted to tell you about the big prize Caroline Short just gave us for the festival."

Naomi's forehead crinkled. "She already donated some meals at the Pink Geranium. Did you get her to donate something else?"

"Another weekend for two at the bed and breakfast, with all meals included." Aunt Mary beamed with pride. "She's releasing that one room she normally reserves for close friends and family. I managed to convince her that whoever stays in that room will become close friends if they move here. And that's not all. I got a year's worth of oil changes at the lube place."

Naomi leaned back in her chair. "Good job, Mary. Now how are you going to break the news to Pamela?"

Aunt Mary frowned. "What do you mean *break* the news? It's a good thing, right?"

"Yes, I agree, but you know how Pamela can be. She likes taking credit for stuff."

"Okay, so I'll give her the credit. I really don't care." Her shoulders sagged slightly.

Naomi sighed. "Oh, you care all right, but at least you're gracious enough to step aside and let the boss think she did something special."

"I'm just glad to help." Aunt Mary slowly turned to face Bethany. "How's everything coming along at your place? I can come over later if you want."

"Give my daughter a break, Mary. You're pushing her mighty hard."

Both Bethany and Pete burst into laughter. Naomi glared at Bethany.

"Sorry, Mom. It's just that—" She cut herself off. No point in antagonizing her mother when she was trying to help. "I appreciate your offer, Aunt Mary, but not today. Maybe later next week?"

"Call me when you're ready." She backed away toward the kitchen. "I'm ready for my cobbler now. Did you put beets in it like Mother did?"

"Of course." Naomi made a face. "And that was supposed to be a secret."

"I don't think it's any big secret that you sneak all kinds of things into food," Bethany said as she lifted her fingers and touched them, one at a time, as she ticked off the different ways Naomi snuck veggies into prepared dishes. "Cauliflower in mashed potatoes, zucchini in lasagna, carrots in muffins and cookies . . ."

Pete leaned back in his chair. "I'm impressed. Does my mom do this too?"

Naomi shrugged, obviously annoyed. "I don't know, and

even if I did know, it's not my place to blab all her secrets. Why don't you ask her?"

Aunt Mary came out of the kitchen with a bowl and spoon. "I can't wait to dig in. One of these days I might even take up cooking."

"You're a good cook," Bethany said. "You used to make the best macaroni and cheese, and I always enjoyed your pies."

"Boxed mac 'n cheese and pies from the Pink Geranium." Aunt Mary grinned and shoved a bite of cobbler into her mouth.

Naomi nodded. "The rest of us had to learn to cook, but by the time you came along, Mother was tired of teaching. We made things way too easy on you, but I suppose that's the way it is with the youngest kid in a big family."

Bethany's insides tightened. Both she and Aunt Mary were the youngest children in their families. She wondered if Mom was implying something about her own life being too easy. After all, she did leave home and move right in with Charlie immediately after they married. She'd learned to cook and do things around the house, but until Charlie passed away, she'd always had someone else to rely on.

Pete wasn't sure what happened, but Bethany instantly tensed, and she clammed up. It was right after her mother commented on Mary's cooking.

Mary got up, carried her bowl to the kitchen sink, said her good-byes, told Naomi not to wait up, and left. Naomi went into the kitchen, mumbling about how Mary had left her bowl in the sink without rinsing it. Bethany was in an odd frame of mind and didn't act like she wanted to talk.

"I'll do the dishes," Pete said. "And then I'll take Bethany home. It's been a long day."

Naomi shook her head. "Nah, you two run along, and I'll clean up. I don't have anything better to do with my time."

Bethany gestured toward the door. "Okay, let's go, Pete."

All the way to her house, she stared straight ahead. He wanted to ask what happened—if it was something he'd said or done—and find a way to make her feel better, but he didn't know where to start. She didn't seem mad at him, but she clearly wasn't happy. He knew she adored her aunt, and a simple jab from her mother shouldn't have put her in this state.

Pete pulled up in front of her house and put the truck in park. "Bethany, if you want to talk—"

"No, I'm fine. I'll talk to you later, okay?"

"Um . . . sure." He started to turn off the ignition, but she held up her hand.

"You don't have to walk me to the door. I'm perfectly capable of going by myself."

"Yes, I know, but . . ." His voice trailed off as she got out, slammed the door shut, and scampered up the sidewalk, pulling her keys from her bag as she went. After unlocking the door, she turned and gave him a half-smile, waving before she went inside and closed the door behind her.

Whatever had happened obviously had a huge impact on Bethany. As he drove home, he replayed the situation in his mind, but he still had no idea what had gotten her in such a mood.

Chapter 14

Bethany leaned against the door, closed her eyes, and thought about how similar she was to Aunt Mary. All of her life, she'd been compared to her favorite relative, and until now, she'd considered it a compliment. After her mother's comment, though, she realized the comparison wasn't always good.

Being the youngest of four, Bethany had to admit her parents didn't have the same expectations of her they'd had for her siblings. Her two older brothers were overachievers in their fields—one a doctor and the other an engineer. Her sister had married a corporate climber, and now that her children were older, she'd gone back to work as the head of a large nonprofit agency, using her volunteer résumé to get the job. She doubted any of her siblings was truly happy, but on the surface, they were all accomplished.

The only comments her siblings had about Bethany were that she married young, and she was a clutter-hound. As she looked around her house, she couldn't deny they were right. Even after ridding the house of a dozen boxes of knickknacks, she still had so much stuff she couldn't see the tops of some of her furniture.

She squeezed her eyes shut and took a deep breath before plunging into another prayer for guidance. *Lord, once again, I ask for mercy and the strength to get through this.*

When she opened her eyes, she took a long, hard look around and sighed. The volume of knickknacks and other memorabilia was still staggering. Even though she'd cleared so much away, she knew it was superficial. Now she needed to figure out where to put a serious dent in what was left.

Her mother's words from many years ago played in her head. "Take one bite at a time until it's all gone." Naomi had always said that whenever Bethany was overwhelmed, whether by a messy room or a massive homework project.

Bethany decided to tackle one corner of the living room, where she'd already removed a few collectibles. At least it wasn't quite as cluttered as her bedroom.

She went into the garage and grabbed a couple of the boxes she still hadn't gotten rid of when she'd moved in. As she walked inside with the huge boxes, she changed her mind. This required more of a tiptoe into the shallow end than diving into the deep end, so she went back out to the garage and exchanged the large boxes for a couple of medium-sized ones.

She placed one in the middle of the floor and the other beside the ornate antique side table, and then she picked up a ceramic piece her mother-in-law had created. She turned it over in her hands and inspected some of the fine workmanship before putting it back down. This was so hard.

Maybe she should move on to purchased collectibles rather than handmade items that meant more than money. Her favorite Hummel collection had a place of honor on the built-in bookshelves behind the table. She'd painstakingly collected each piece, one at a time, until she had the complete collection. Although she enjoyed her collection, she had no idea who'd made the pieces.

A knot formed in her stomach at the very thought of letting go of this set. After all, many of them had come as gifts from Ashley and Charlie, who knew how much she loved Hummels. Others she'd purchased after saving for them. Exhaustion overwhelmed her as she thought about the task ahead, and it seemed to grow by the minute.

The phone rang, so at least she had a brief reprieve from making decisions. It was Naomi.

"Hi, sweetie. I just wanted to call and check on you. Are you okay?"

"Yes, Mom, I'm fine."

"I didn't mean to upset you."

Bethany cleared her throat. "I know you didn't. It's just that—"

"Your mean old mother said some pretty rough things and scared you away. I know, I know. I should be more careful about what I say to you. After all, you've always been the sensitive one in the family."

"That's just it. I hate being labeled. I was always the messy kid, or the sensitive one, or the child who made the family late for everything." The instant she blurted out those words, her breath caught in her throat.

Naomi chuckled but quickly stopped. "In my family, I was always the bossy one."

Bethany let out her breath and relaxed. Obviously, nothing had changed.

"And the one who liked to cook, although to be honest, there are times I'd much rather eat out. Oh, and I'm the one who hates shrimp, but that's not true either."

"You like shrimp?"

Naomi laughed. "Yes, I like shrimp just fine. Granted, they're not my favorite food, but I like them once in a while."

"I wonder how you got that label."

"I'll tell you how," Naomi said. "One night when we were at my aunt's house, I was too tired to eat. So when they passed around the platter of shrimp, I turned it down. Someone asked if I'd like some shrimp, I said no, and from that moment on, no one ever offered it to me again." She let out a snort. "Just because I turned it down one time, folks figured it was because I didn't like it."

"Why didn't you ever say anything?" Bethany asked.

"No point in it. There were more important things to talk about."

"So where are you going with this?"

"I'm thinking that we might need to start fresh . . . now that you know I like shrimp." Naomi laughed at her own comment. "Instead of continuing to nag you about your clutter, I'll accept you as you are and your belongings at face value. I like shrimp, and you like your stuff." She paused. "How's that sound?"

"Sounds great."

"Good. I need to go now."

"Mom, before we hang up, I have something to say. When I came home, I took another look around and actually saw what everyone else sees. I have to admit it's not a pretty sight. You've always said I needed to do something about my clutter, even when I was a kid. I think it's time."

Naomi chuckled. "But I don't want you to think I don't love you just the way you are. Everything you have means so much to you."

"Yes and no. I've decided to clean everything out—and I mean really clean and not take a token action of getting rid of a few things under the guise of helping the garden club. My problem is, I don't know where to start."

"Want me to help?" Naomi made a clicking sound with her tongue. "Oh, never mind. That would never do, especially after I just told you I don't want to try to change you." She paused. "How about if I send Mary over again?"

"No. I have to do this myself." Bethany glanced around the living room and then walked back into the hallway. "I just have to figure out where to start."

"Remember what I always said—"

"Yes, one bite at a time."

"I'm happy to know you actually listened to me." Naomi chuckled. "Why don't you take everything off the shelves and put it into three piles—a keeper pile, a donation pile, and a maybe pile. Put the maybe pile in a box that you can store for a year. After that, if you don't need or want any of it, you can get rid of it."

That sounded like an excellent plan. "Mom, you're a genius."

"Of course I am. And the apple doesn't fall far from the tree." She laughed again.

"I love you."

Naomi stopped laughing and sighed. "Back atcha, kiddo."

After hanging up, Bethany felt a surge of energy and a fresh desire to get to work. She walked straight back into the living room, took a sweeping look around, and plowed forward. She took her mother's advice and created three piles without too much thought about any single item. Within a couple of hours, she had three impressive stacks, and she was pleased to see that the donation pile was the largest.

She stood back and brushed her hands together as she admired her work. Nothing remained on any visible surface, so now she could dust without worrying about breaking anything. She dug out a dust rag from a kitchen drawer and the furniture polish from under the sink and went to work cleaning, admiring the wood grain as she polished the antique furniture, and wondering why it had taken her so long.

Then she turned around and looked at the piles. The medium-sized box wasn't big enough for any of them, so she went back out to the garage and got more boxes—this time without that sick feeling that had formed in her stomach earlier.

By the time she finished packing all the items she wanted to give away or put in the attic, it was past suppertime, and her stomach had started rumbling. Leaving the things she planned on keeping in the middle of the living room floor, she padded into the kitchen to fix herself a sandwich.

As she ate, she pondered the feelings that surged in her chest. Surprised by how liberating it felt to have the most difficult part behind her, she decided she might as well tackle her bedroom tomorrow and the guest room the next day. But after supper, she knew she needed to finish the job in the living room so she could be free to move on.

On Thursday, with all her hard work behind her, Bethany loaded up her SUV to take more things to the community center. It didn't all fit in one load, so she left what she couldn't get into the car stacked in the foyer of her house.

After driving to the community center, she pulled up in front at the loading area and got out of her car. Before she had a chance to open the hatch, she heard Pamela's voice.

"Bethany, where on earth have you been? No one has seen you in days. We wondered if you might have decided to pack up and move back to the big city." She snickered. "No one would blame you after what folks have put you through lately." She glanced down sheepishly, kicked the pointy toe of her animal print shoe on the curb, and slowly looked up. "I have to admit I was one of the worst. I am so sorry. I hope I haven't scared you off."

"Apology accepted." Bethany smiled. "And no, I'm not going anywhere. You're stuck with me." Bethany gestured toward her SUV. "I've been gathering up more things for the festival."

Pamela's eyebrows shot up as she looked at the massive number of boxes. "That's a lot of stuff. Are you sure about this?" She cleared her throat. "Oh, never mind. There's too much to give away as prizes. I'll go through it later and decide. We'll put most of it in the garden club rummage sale booth . . . that is, unless you want to rent a booth yourself and keep the money."

"The garden club booth is perfect. I like the idea of donating to the cause."

Pamela smiled and touched the top box with one pastel fingernail and quickly drew back. "You can't unload all this stuff by yourself. Let me get some of the boys to give you a hand."

Before Bethany had a chance to remind her that she was the one who loaded the SUV, Pamela had darted inside. Bethany carried one box to the door and was met by three men who were old enough to be her father. These "boys" didn't seem to mind helping, and she wasn't about to argue. It was rather amusing watching them try to outdo each other, proving they were still virile. Pamela egged them on, letting them know how strong they were.

"Ooh, look at that muscle, Howard," Pamela said. "I remember when you won the Fourth of July arm wrestling contest."

He flexed his muscle. "And I still got it."

Pamela grinned. "Yes, you sure have." As soon as he turned to make sure the other guys heard her, she made her way back to Bethany's side. "It was nice of them to give us a hand, wasn't it?"

Bethany blinked. "Um . . . extremely nice."

One of the seniors returned for another load. "Is this all ya got?"

"Yes . . . at least for now. Thank you so much for doing all this."

"Aw, that's what we're here for," Howard said.

Claude snorted. "No way. You're here because you still haven't beaten me at checkers."

"Now that's not true, and you know it."

"Is *too* true." Claude leaned toward Howard. "Admit it. I'm a better checker player than you."

Pamela wedged herself between the men. "Boys, boys, I'm sure you're both excellent at checkers, but what does that really matter? You have both been such gentleman . . . until now."

Howard hung his head. "Yeah, you're right."

Claude jutted his chin. "Say you're sorry."

"Me say I'm sorry? Now that's a bunch of . . ." He glanced over at Pamela who glared at him with raised eyebrows. "Okay, if it makes you happy, sorry."

Pamela turned to Claude. "Now it's your turn."

Claude frowned and mumbled, "Sorry."

"Okay, then it's settled. You're both gentlemen who were chivalrous when we needed you, so run along and finish your checkers game. We'll let you know when we need you again."

Howard grinned at Bethany and winked. "You sure do have some nice things here. I just might pick up a few of them and take them home with me." He stuck his hand in his pocket and pulled out a weathered wallet. "How much do you want for this stuff?"

Pamela shook her finger at him. "You'll just have to wait until the festival and shop along with everyone else."

Once they left, she turned to Bethany, shaking her head. "Some boys never grow up."

"I have another load," Bethany said. "Should I wait another day?"

"Whatever for? You go on back home, and I'll alert the boys that you're returning with more stuff."

Since Bethany had stacked all the boxes by the door in her foyer, she loaded the rest in a matter of minutes. When she pulled up in front of the community center, the door flung open, and out walked Howard, Claude . . . and Pete.

"Pamela called and told me to hurry up," he explained. "She said you were a damsel in distress, so I needed to step up to the plate and become your knight in shining armor."

"Interesting way to put it." Bethany unlocked the hatch and took the first box off the top.

Pete immediately grabbed it from her. "Oh, no, ya don't. Let the guys take care of this." He nodded toward the corner of the building, where Pamela stood, watching with eagle eyes. He leaned over and whispered, "I know you're capable of helping unload, but please go stand by her and keep her out of our way."

"Whatever you say." She bit back a laugh as she joined Pamela. "You really didn't have to call Pete. There's not all that much to unload."

"Since when do you get to tell me what I don't have to do?" Pamela asked. "There are some liberties I can take as the president of the garden club, and I fully intend to do it."

Bethany knew there was no point in arguing with Pamela, because it would wind up in a battle she could never win. So she took a tiny step away and watched as Pete, Claude, and Howard finished carrying the last of the boxes inside. Each time she saw Pete, she felt another piece of her shield chipping away. His limitless generosity warmed her from the inside out, and she always felt as though he liked her just the way she was.

"Want me to set everything out?" Pete asked. Claude and Howard had already gone over to their table and resumed their checkers game.

"No," Pamela said. "You've done what we needed, so you can run along with Bethany now." She looked at Bethany. "Unless you have more loads."

"Not now," Bethany replied. "But I will when I do my final run-through in the house."

"After you're done, we can separate things according to what we'll do with them. I've decided that only the higher value collectibles will go as prizes . . . and maybe some of the handmade quilts. The other stuff can go in our garden club booth, along with the jams and jellies from the Pink Geranium and gardening starter sets Naomi is putting together."

"Does my mother know about this?" Bethany asked, half joking but knowing Pamela often assumed things.

"Yes, of course, she does." Pamela scowled. "She volunteered. Why would you even ask such a silly question?"

Bethany started to reply, but Pete spoke up. "Maybe I can come up with something from my family's business."

"Your dad already did. He's giving away some fancy faucets."

Bethany thought that was odd, but Pete nodded. "We received a shipment of faucets we didn't order. When I called to ship them back, I found out the company was going out of business, and they said to just keep them."

Pamela folded her arms. "I wondered about that. After all, faucets are such odd things to donate." She smiled at Pete. "But I'm sure someone will want them."

"These are very unusual, with ornamental scrollwork."

"More difficult to clean, I'm sure, but that won't matter to some folks who like fancy things." She fluttered her pastel fingernails in the air, and that was when Bethany caught sight of the glistening jewels on the tips. "I'm a much more basic person. Very down-to-earth and not fussy at all."

Bethany noticed Pete's lips twitching. He cut a quick glance in her direction, and even without a comment, she knew his thoughts lined up with hers.

Pamela scowled as she walked around the table. "Hey, I just noticed something. We're missing a few things." She patted an empty spot on the end. "I'd just emptied one of the boxes right here."

Bethany joined her and looked everything over. "Where's that stack of quilts my mother-in-law made?" She leaned around and glanced at the other side of the table. "And the hand-painted ceramic vase I brought in the last load?" Panic welled in her chest.

Howard waved his hands around to get their attention. "Don't get all worked up, ladies. I put some of the valuable things in the kitchen where we can lock them up until the rummage sale."

"Oh." Pamela made a face. "I suppose that's okay. Just don't do that again unless you let me know first."

Bethany shut her eyes and took a deep breath. *Lord, give me the strength to let go of the clutter and the cobwebs in my life.*

Chapter 15

As Pete finished unloading Bethany's car and carrying boxes into the community center, he took a few quick glances at Bethany. She seemed different—more relaxed and with a sense of resolve he hadn't noticed before. She even looked at him differently.

"Thanks again, Pete," she said, jolting him from his thoughts. "I better get back home now and let you go back to whatever you were doing before Pamela called. I'm really sorry about the interruption."

He shook his head. "No, I'm glad she called. I always enjoy helping out wherever I can."

They stood in the circular drop-off section of the driveway, gazing into each other's eyes. When he squinted, he thought he might even detect a smidge of attraction, but he suspected that was only wishful thinking on his part.

Bethany tilted her head with a questioning gaze. "Why are you looking at me like that?"

He sucked in a breath and smiled. "The sun's in my eyes." He left out the fact that seeing her brightened his day more than the sun ever could. "Since we're done now, I probably need to get going. Tomorrow comes early in the plumbing business."

"No, that's fine. I need to leave too. See you soon." She didn't budge, making his heart pound even harder than it was.

"You'll be at church on Sunday, won't you?"

She nodded. "Yes, of course, I will. You know I never miss church."

"Just making sure." He grinned, and when she smiled back at him, it hit him hard. There was more than just an attraction between them. He was in love with this girl and probably always had been.

He stood in the driveway and watched Bethany as she pulled away and drove toward her house. The sound of footsteps approaching from behind caught his attention, and he spun around in time to see Andy walking toward him.

"Still haven't told her, have you?" Andy asked.

Pete thought hard but couldn't imagine what Andy was talking about. "Huh?"

"You know, told her what's really going on with you."

"What's going on with me?"

Andy let out a hearty chuckle. "That you're head over heels."

"What makes you say—?"

"It's obvious, son. Anyone who sees the way you look at her knows you're hopelessly in love with Bethany, but you don't know what to do about it."

This was really weird. If he'd been that obvious to Andy, he wondered how big of a fool he'd made of himself to everyone else in town. "I don't know about that. Bethany and I have been friends practically all of our lives. I used to hang out with her and Charlie."

"Yes, but things change." Andy tipped his head toward Pete and studied him from beneath his heavy eyebrows. "Look at Pamela and me. No one ever would have thought she and I would be a logical match, but we've been together for a good while."

Pete knew about Andy's first wife's death and what a deep funk Andy had been in. For a number of years, everyone in town had been afraid of Andy because he was such an angry man after the car wreck. He'd even stopped going to church, until Pamela became a widow, and he saw she needed someone who understood.

Andy placed his hand on the side of the building and leaned into it. "And those people would have been right if we'd gotten together when we were younger. It took age and maturity for us to see each other's value."

"So you're saying that's the case with Bethany and me?"

"No, not really, because I think you've seen her value far longer than even you care to admit. Now it's time for her to see you as a possible suitor."

Pete had no idea what to say next. He couldn't deny Andy's observation, because he'd be lying. But he also didn't want to admit how he felt about Bethany, since it seemed pointless and maybe even hopeless. Even if Bethany felt the same attraction, it didn't mean she could ever love him.

"Andy! There you are!" The sound of Pamela's voice was music to Pete's ears. "I've been waiting for you for the past half hour."

"Sorry." Andy gave Pete a conspiratorial smile and turned back to Pamela with his arms outstretched. "Pete and I have been having a little man-to-man talk."

Pamela walked into his open arms but narrowed her gaze at Pete and turned back to Andy. "Anything I need to know about?"

"Nope." Andy gave her a hug, and then took her by the hand and pulled her to his side. "So why don't you and I go on our date and let this fella do whatever he needs to do?"

"See ya." Pete waved and took off toward his truck. He could hear Pamela asking one question after another about Pete as he walked away, but all Andy did was grunt one-word replies.

Bethany couldn't sleep, so she got out of bed and turned on the light. Her bedroom was packed with almost as many knick-knacks as she'd removed from the living room. A handmade quilt lay folded at the foot of her bed, but another huge stack rested atop the chair in the corner of the room. In the opposite corner, a laundry basket filled with some of Ashley's old stuffed animals added to the cluttered appearance. The things she had in the living room held memories, but the ones in her bedroom were closer to her heart. Maybe she shouldn't get rid of these so quickly.

Naomi's words about her things being a fire hazard rang through her head, and Bethany realized her mother was right. Then she thought about Aunt Mary's advice to pack most of her things away and rotate them. She pondered that idea for a moment and finally decided that was exactly what she'd do first thing in the morning. At least it would be out of sight, and she'd be able to dust the baseboards to satisfy Naomi.

On Friday morning, Bethany awoke with a crick in her neck, sore forearms, and her head swimming with a running list of all she needed to do. She sat up momentarily, but flopped back down and stared up at the ceiling. It could wait.

She'd barely rolled over when the phone rang. As tempting as it was to let it ring and check for messages later, she decided to answer it. She stood up, squinted down at the caller ID screen, and picked it up.

"Hey, Mom. It's early. Is everything okay?"

"You're normally up by now." Naomi sighed. "Just because I called you at eight, you assume there's a problem?"

Bethany rubbed the sleepiness from her eyes. "Well, yes."

"Did you know Pamela sprained her ankle yesterday?"

"No," Bethany replied. "I saw her late in the afternoon, and she looked fine to me."

"It happened when she stepped down off the curb at the community center. I heard you were there too."

"I was." Bethany thought back on her last conversation with Pamela. "Must have happened after I left. Any idea how she did it?"

"She said she was so busy running around, she lost her footing and slipped."

"You talked to her?" Bethany thought about Pamela directing the guys as they unloaded her car. She didn't see Pamela running around much.

"Yeah, that's how I knew to call you. The doctor told her to stay off her feet for a couple of weeks."

"I can't imagine Pamela staying off her feet for a couple of hours, let alone weeks."

"Apparently, she's in quite a bit of pain, so she just might obey the doctor's orders this time. At any rate, she's worried about this festival running without her."

"I thought Gina was in charge of it." Bethany thought for a moment. "Did I miss something?"

"No, you're right. Gina is in charge, but Pamela's worried, because the Maples family hasn't been in Bloomfield long and Gina might get lost in the mess of planning."

"She's perfectly capable of running it," Bethany argued.

"Of course she is, but you know how Pamela can be. I told her not to worry, though, because you could be Gina's right-hand woman."

Bethany had to bite back her annoyance at her mother for not asking first before volunteering her. She cleared her throat. "Mo-om."

"Calm down, girlie. Before you get all wigged out about my telling Pamela you'd help, I spoke to Gina, and she said she has everything under control. She won't need you to do anything more than what you're already doing."

Bethany was still annoyed, but it was too early to argue. "I'll call Gina later."

"You don't have to. She's coming over here in about an hour so we can strategize."

"Then why didn't you tell Pamela you'd be the go-to person if Gina needed help?"

Naomi laughed. "You know how Pamela is where I'm concerned. She'd forget about her sprained ankle and zip over here on crutches. No, I care too much about her well-being to put her in that position."

As convoluted as it sounded, Bethany understood. "Tell you what. After I have some breakfast, I'll come over and help."

"Skip the breakfast. I have a bowl of fruit and some fresh-baked muffins."

"What kind?"

Naomi hesitated. "Apple banana."

"And?" Bethany grinned as she waited.

Naomi made a clicking sound with her tongue. "Okay, so I added a few things."

"Like what?"

"Zucchini and carrots."

Bethany laughed. "Yum. I'll arrive hungry."

"Good girl. See you in a little while."

After Bethany hung up, she realized what her mother had just done. If Naomi had flat-out invited Bethany to come for a strategy meeting, Bethany would probably have found an excuse not to go. But being the expert schemer, Naomi had turned things around and set up Bethany to think it was her idea. At least there would be a reward of apple-banana-zucchini-carrot muffins. Her mouth watered.

Bethany arrived at her mother's place carrying a tote filled with a notebook, pens, and a small, hand-carved jewelry box for Gina. Her mother-in-law had received it for her charitable service, and Bethany kept it, thinking Ashley might want it someday. But the box looked more like something Gina would appreciate than Ashley.

Naomi greeted her with a hug and kiss on the cheek. "There's coffee in the kitchen."

Gina came up and gave her a squeeze. "You two are such sweethearts to help me with this." She glanced down at the box in Bethany's hand, and her eyes widened. "Oh, pretty."

Bethany smiled and handed it to her. "I'm glad you like it. I brought it for you."

"For me?" Gina didn't even try to hide her delight. "You don't have to give me presents."

"I really want you to have it."

Before Gina could argue, Naomi spoke up. "Just take it, Gina. We need to get moving on the plans."

"Thank you both so much," Gina said as she accepted the box.

"We're the ones who should be thanking you," Naomi said. "So what can we do to help?"

Gina blurted out a series of jobs that still needed to get done before she finally stopped talking. "I am so sorry. I don't know what I'd do without you, but I sound so bossy."

Naomi cackled. "No one can out-boss me. I'm the champ."

"I didn't mean—" Gina looked stricken.

"I know, I know. We're happy to do it, aren't we, Bethany?" Naomi nudged Bethany in the side.

"Yes, of course."

The three women maneuvered around each other while filling their coffee cups in Naomi's tiny kitchen. Then they settled down at the dining room table with a basket of muffins in the middle. Gina reached for one first. "I hope you don't think I'm rude, but ever since I first walked in and smelled the delicious aroma, I've been dying to have one." As she took a bite, her eyes fluttered. "Oh, my."

Naomi chuckled and gestured for Bethany to help herself. "I made these the way you like them, sweetie—with extra molasses."

Bethany finished her first muffin quickly, grabbed another, and placed it on her plate. "Excellent as always."

Gina lifted her pen, but before she could say a word, someone knocked at the door. Naomi glanced curiously at Bethany. "No one ever stops by at this hour unannounced. I wonder who it could be?"

"Are you saying this isn't a setup?" Bethany turned her head and looked suspiciously at her mother.

Naomi lifted both hands and shook her head. "I have no idea what you're talking about, young lady. Honestly, I have no idea who's at the door."

"There's only one way to find out," Bethany said as she got up and went to the door. Before she opened it, she heard a squawking parrot, and her heart sank.

There stood Pamela and Andy, and dangling from Andy's hand was a birdcage with a very unhappy Murray glaring back at her. "Knock knock . . . *squawk* . . . who's there . . ."

"Pamela?" Bethany glanced down at Pamela's ankle and saw the swelling above the bandage. She had her arm linked in Andy's, with the other holding a crutch. "I'm sorry about your ankle."

Naomi didn't waste a second before joining them at the door. "Oh, no. What are you doing here?"

"Oh, no . . . *squawk* . . . it's that bird again."

Pamela tottered away from Andy as she pointed. "Aren't you gonna invite us in?"

"Yes, of course." Naomi stepped back as she turned to Bethany and made a face. "Where are our manners?"

Pamela half hopped and half hobbled into the living room. She got to the closest chair and flopped down into it. "You need to consider moving a little closer to the parking lot, Naomi. That's a long hike."

"So what are you doing here?" Naomi asked again, this time with more obvious annoyance in her voice.

"We saw Jeremy in town. He told us Gina was here planning the festival."

Bethany turned around and saw that Gina remained sitting at the dining room table, a look on her face as guilty as the one on Andy's. Her questioning glance to Gina was met with a shrug.

"We have everything under control," Naomi said. "So if you have better things to do, as I'm sure you do, being president of the garden club and having to nurse your injury and all, you don't have to stick around." She pointed to Pamela's bandaged leg. "Besides, you should probably be at home with your foot propped up."

"That's ridiculous." Pamela waved her hands, showing off a fresh manicure, featuring a lime-green background with a different spring flower painted on each nail. "What could be more important than this?" She leaned around to face Gina. "So what have you planned so far?"

Gina cleared her throat and smiled, obviously trying to regain her composure, but Bethany could see her hands shaking as she tucked a stray strand of hair behind her ear. "So far, we have deposits from a dozen artists who want to rent booths." She cleared her throat. "But they want to know if we can add an inclement weather clause to the contracts."

"Deposits? Contracts?" Pamela looked confused. "We've never required deposits or contracts before."

Naomi stepped up. "We know that, but since this is a new festival, we thought it would be a good idea to make sure people didn't change their minds at the last minute and back down on us."

"Oh." Pamela appeared to ponder the thought before nodding. "I suppose that's a good idea."

"It's a great idea and a smart business plan, and you know it, Pamela." Naomi folded her arms and glared down at her friend and nemesis. "Gina is an excellent chairperson. She has lists for everything, including each act in the parade. She even has it broken down into how many floats, marching bands, cars, and other acts to make sure we have balance."

"Floats?" Pamela looked over at Gina. "You have floats?"

Gina nodded, and this time her lips quivered. "I hope that's okay. All the clubs at the high school loved the idea when I spoke at their assembly."

"You spoke at the high school assembly?" For the first time Bethany could remember, Pamela looked baffled.

Naomi laughed. "You're starting to sound like a parrot."

"Parrots rock . . . *squawk* . . . parrots rock."

Naomi glared at Murray. "Some parrots rock, but you are a bad birdie."

Murray hung his head. "Bad birdie . . . *squawk* . . . bad birdie."

"So what can I do to help?" Pamela asked.

"Absolutely nothing," Naomi replied. "Except maybe take care of yourself so you can heal up before the festival. I'd hate for you to do too much now and be laid up during the big event."

Using the crutch, Pamela wriggled back up to a standing position. "Well, since I'm not needed here, let's go home, Andy."

Murray ruffled his feathers and caused the cage to rattle. "Home is where the heart is . . . *squawk*!"

Bethany wasn't sure, but she thought Pamela might have growled at Murray. He burrowed his head down into his neck and grew quiet.

After they left, Gina looked concerned. "Is Pamela mad about something? I hope I didn't—"

Naomi shook her head. "Don't worry. It's just hard for someone like her to get used to someone else being in charge."

"I don't want her to think I'm trying to take her place."

"Nah, stop worrying. Now tell me what you have going on, and I'll show you what you have to do next."

Gina shot a look of amusement in Bethany's direction. Bethany had to turn around to keep from laughing.

Chapter 16

"I can't believe they've done all that without consulting me first," Pamela said as she slid into the passenger seat of Andy's car. "I mean, why didn't they at least call and ask if it was okay?"

Andy shook his head, put Murray's cage and her crutch into the backseat, and went around to the driver's side. As he got in, Pamela studied his features for some sign of his opinion. As usual, rock solid Andy never let any emotion pass through his expression. Maybe if she could get a good look at his eyes.

She leaned over and stared straight into his eyes. He pulled back. "What on earth are you doing?" He buckled his seat belt. "I can't drive with you in my face like that."

She flopped back, folded her arms, and turned back to Andy. "Do you think I'm a control freak?"

He grinned as he reached for her hand and squeezed it. "Maybe a little."

She pulled her hand back and inspected her nails. "I just want to make sure everything goes as it should. I hate leaving things to chance."

"Or someone else."

Pamela cast a questioning glance his way. "What?"

"You don't want to risk leaving things to someone else, because you don't think they can do a job as well as you can."

She shrugged. "Maybe they can't."

He turned the key in the ignition and looked at her with a sternness she hadn't noticed in him in a long time. "Or maybe they can, but that's inconsequential. Sometimes you just need to let go, Pamela. Let others take responsibility."

"But what if they make mistakes?"

Andy shrugged. "They probably will, but you have to let people figure out how to do things without you always pulling the strings."

Her chest felt heavy. "It's hard."

"I know," Andy said. "You and I are so alike on this, which is why I think we get along so well."

That brought some comfort to Pamela. At least Andy was comparing her to someone she admired.

"There's another thing I'm struggling with." She had to reposition her leg to keep her sprained ankle from cramping.

Andy turned to face her as he slowed down. "What's that?"

"How am I going to deal with my lack of mobility?" She cast a wistful glance in Andy's direction, and he gave her a sympathetic smile in return. "I still want to help out some at the festival. After all, even though it's a rather crazy idea and a labor-intensive way to get a couple of middle-aged people to fall in love, I'm ultimately responsible."

"I know it's hard." Andy patted her hand. "But it's only for a couple of weeks. The doc said as long as you're careful and stay off your feet, you can walk on it then."

"Two weeks is an awful long time." She looked out the window as they approached her house. "What's that all over my yard?"

Andy slowed the car down even more. "Your guess is as good as mine."

"Is that toilet paper?"

"Certainly looks like it," Andy replied.

"What's happening to our beautiful, safe Bloomfield? Are we becoming like the rest of the world? I've always felt safe in my home."

Andy shook his head. "I don't think an occasional papering of the lawn makes Bloomfield any less safe. It's just a childish prank."

"But it's so annoying and creates unnecessary work for the victim."

"Just be glad that's all you're a victim of." Andy cast a reassuring glance toward Pamela and smiled. "It could be a lot worse."

Pamela closed her eyes for a moment before opening them to get a better look. Toilet paper covered the shrubs, hung from the trees, and dotted half her lawn. At least whoever rolled the yard left her prize rosebushes alone.

"Why would anyone do such a horrible thing?"

Andy pulled into her driveway and stopped. "I'll clean it all up, but first let me help you to the front porch swing."

Pamela's eyes stung with tears over Andy's sweetness. Few people saw this side of him, and she was actually okay with that. To know that he reserved tender moments for her warmed her heart.

He cleaned the yard while she watched. Every few minutes, the temptation to hop up and help washed over her. But every time she made so much as a sound, Andy told her to stay put.

"Sit down, Miss Pamela," he said firmly as he pointed. "I don't want you making your ankle worse."

"I know, but I can pick out some of the paper from the bushes by the porch."

"No." His gaze leveled with hers, so she backed down. "Just stay right there and look pretty for me, okay?"

She leaned back and smiled. "Okay, if you insist."

"Pretty girl ... *squawk* ... pretty girl." Murray let out a wolf whistle that Pamela was sure could be heard a block away.

She shook her head and laughed. "You silly bird."

"Silly bird, funny bird . . . ha-ha-ha." Murray turned his head toward her. *"Squawk!"*

"All right," Andy said with a chuckle. "Calm down you two."

"It's not me, it's Murray."

"Blaming the bird now? Pamela, that's so not like you."

She shrugged and let out an uncharacteristic giggle. "Says who?" All the pain she'd felt earlier had subsided, and now she felt as giddy as a schoolgirl. Maybe she should take Andy's advice and let others deal with the responsibility. It sure did feel good to kick back a little while.

Andy filled two large trash bags with toilet paper. "Looks like they unloaded an entire case of the stuff. If we find out who did this, I'm sure their parents will have a thing or two to say about it."

"Are you saying you're gonna tattle?" Pamela tilted her head and smiled.

"You bet. They need to suffer the consequences." He lifted an eyebrow and gave her a comical look. "We don't want them to progress to bigger crimes, like soaping windows and chalking up the sidewalks, now do we?" He made a face. "Or worse, putting bubbles in the fountain on the town square."

Pamela sighed. Andy's take-charge attitude mixed with humor elevated him even higher in her eyes, creating an over-whelming desire to kiss him.

She lifted her finger and crooked it in a gesture for him to join her. "Come here, big fella."

"Hey, big fella . . . *squawk* . . . hey, big fella."

"Close your eyes, Murray, because I'm gonna kiss your daddy."

Andy plopped down beside Pamela, wrapped his arms around her, and gave her a kiss that curled her toes. When she opened her eyes, the look on his face let her know he planned to do it again. And he did.

Murray squawked and made his own smooching sounds.

Chapter 17

Bethany met Gina in front of Bloomfield Books first thing Saturday morning, according to plan. They'd asked Naomi to join them, but she bowed out, saying she was happy the younger folks were taking some of the responsibility.

"You don't think Naomi's upset, do you?" Gina asked. "I didn't mean to be so forceful with my opinions about how this should be done. I'm afraid I can be rather dictatorial if given too much authority." She made a comical face. "I don't want to come across . . . well, you know . . ."

Bethany smiled. "Yes, I do know, but don't worry about that. The only way people will pay attention around this town is to assert yourself."

"Like Pamela does?" Gina crinkled her nose, and they both broke into a fit of laughter. "She's amazing, though, and Lacy adores her."

After Bethany caught her breath, she nodded. "Exactly. You never see her worrying about upsetting anyone, do you? And she pretty much gets what she wants."

"Including the title of president of the garden club. Did you know she told me she can see me running the garden club someday?"

"I can too."

Gina tilted her head. "She told me to watch her in action and learn."

"I think you're a natural leader."

"Really?" Before giving Bethany a chance to reply, Gina leaned around her and glanced up the street. "Why don't you start on this side of the street, and I'll take the other side? That way, we can keep track of what's going on, and if it doesn't work, we can figure out something else."

"Oh, it'll work," Bethany assured her. She admired Gina's take-charge demeanor. Gina had the ability to lead without offending. Perhaps Pamela should watch her instead of the other way around.

"Let's get going. Jeremy needs to help Brad Henderson this afternoon around two, and I promised him I'd be back to take care of Lacy before he leaves." She sighed. "Or I suppose I could call one of the many grandmothers in Bloomfield for help."

"I'm sure my mother would love watching Lacy, but you don't have to do that. We'll be done long before then." Bethany took the stack of flyers and waved. "See you later."

As Bethany walked into each store and presented the managers or owners with flyers about the new Welcome to Bloomfield Festival, she was rewarded with smiles. "I wonder why we never thought of that before," the hardware store owner said. "My wife likes the rummage sale, but I'm not into looking at other people's junk." He nodded as he read the flyer. "But this is something I'll participate in. Tell you what. I'll donate a toolbox equipped with all the essentials for a prize."

"Wonderful! I'll let Gina know. She's the coordinator."

"What? Pamela let someone else take charge?" He chuckled. "I reckon it's time to pass the baton to someone else. Pamela, now that's one smart woman. She'll be a tough act to follow. Got any more flyers I can hand out?"

Bethany left some with him and promised to return with more. As she walked out of the hardware store, she spotted Gina across the street and gave her a thumbs-up. An hour later, they were both out of flyers.

"Wow, you weren't kidding about this working. This sure is a festival-loving town." Gina's eyes widened in amazement. "Not a single person turned me down."

"I just hope the actual event is as successful as passing out the flyers," Bethany said. "Pamela said she really stuck her neck out with the mayor, and if it doesn't work she'll have egg on her face."

Gina giggled. "I'm sure Pamela can handle whatever happens. Oh, by the way, I have three different people who want to provide the ponies for the children's pony ride if we have nice weather. I'm not sure what to do."

"That's a question for Pamela or my mom."

Gina nodded. "If we have as good of a turnout as we think we might, perhaps I should sign up all three of them and put them in different locations. That way, the kids won't have to wait too long for their rides, and none of the pony people will get their feelings hurt."

"Sounds like an excellent plan to me. My mother used to say more is always better. You fit into Bloomfield even better than I do."

"I've already told you we love it here."

Bethany loved it, too, but she still didn't feel as though she fit in. She'd always had Charlie with her when they were younger, and she relied on him for their social life, both in Bloomfield and after they moved away. With Charlie gone and Ashley away at school, she risked turning into a hermit if she didn't live near people who would force her to interact with them now and then.

Andy pulled up to the curb in front of Gina and Bethany and rolled down his window. "Hey there, ladies. How's it going?"

"Good!" Gina waved her hand in the air. "Everyone is super excited about the festival."

"Nice job!" Amusement twitched at the corners of Andy's lips. "Pamela said to tell you two she wants to treat you both to lunch at the Pink Geranium when you're done."

Gina waved. "Sounds great. Tell her we'll be there in about half an hour."

He waved back and sped off. Bethany stared after Andy's car.

"What's wrong?" Gina asked.

"Nothing. I'm just having a moment." Bethany didn't want to alarm her friend, but she suspected Pamela might have something up her sleeve. She'd never seen the garden club president summon anyone without having an ulterior motive. All of Pamela's moves were well calculated, and the timing of her invitation pointed in that direction.

"I'm sorry." Gina sighed. "Back to what I was saying, moving here was the best thing we could have done."

Bethany smiled. "I agree for our sake. Your family fits in so well, and you're such an asset to the garden club. As my mom would say, we needed an infusion of some fresh blood."

Gina's lips quivered into a half smile as she tilted her head and looked at Bethany. "Has anyone told you why we came?"

Bethany thought back. "Doesn't it have something to do with Jeremy finding work here?"

"Yes, but that's only after Lacy and I discovered it. Someone gave us a flyer about what a wonderful place Bloomfield was to raise a family. Jeremy had lost his job and was working out of town. He was gone more than he was home." She swallowed hard. "I was so lonely, and Lacy clung to me. I think she was afraid I'd leave. Not only did I feel sorry for myself, I was sad for our daughter. I've never been one to dwell on sadness, so one day I up and decided that Lacy and I should take a road trip and check out Bloomfield to see if it was as nice as the flyer said it was. Your mother sealed the deal."

"I heard about those flyers, and I wondered what they were thinking." Bethany paused. "Obviously they work, and that's a good thing, right?" She lifted one of the flyers. "Even if only one person decides to visit for the festival, that's one person who wouldn't have come before. So where does my mother come into the picture?"

"I asked around about where to worship. We met your mother at church, and then everything fell into place."

"I did hear that Mom instigated your move into Sherry's old family home."

"She did!" Gina laughed. "I think Sherry was as blindsided as we were, but after she thought about it, she was happy to let us rent from her. And it's the perfect place for us. Now that Sherry and Brad are engaged, she's decided to sell us the house when we're ready."

Everything was working so well for both Gina and Sherry. Bethany wanted just a fraction of their joy, but she wasn't sure if that could ever happen again.

Caroline greeted them at the door as they entered The Pink Geranium Tea Room. "Right this way, ladies. Pamela's at her favorite table waiting for you."

When Bethany glanced up, she spotted Pamela right away, wearing an out-of-season, wide-brimmed straw hat with a big pink bow on one side and a multicolored floral arrangement on the other. The pastel green-and-white-striped wall behind her provided the perfect backdrop to show off her flamboyant blooms.

Pamela fluttered her pink fingernails that matched the bow on her hat and gestured toward the other two chairs. "Have a seat. I was starving, and I didn't know what you wanted, so I went ahead and ordered a variety platter of sandwiches." She nodded toward the three-tiered sandwich stand. "Help yourself and order whatever soup you want."

Gina cut an amused glance in Bethany's direction. "I'll just have whatever you think is good."

Pamela leaned toward her. "No, you'll have whatever you like. Everything here is delicious."

"Oh." Gina glanced at the menu the server placed in front of her. "Last time I was here, I had the vegetable. I think I'll have tomato basil today."

"Same here." Bethany glanced up at the server, who nodded and smiled. "And I'd like some peach tea."

"Yum." Gina took a sip from her water glass. "I'll have some too."

Pamela tipped her head to one side. "Well, if it isn't Tweedledee and Tweedledum."

Gina's eyes widened. "What?"

Pamela's lips slanted into a mock smirk. "Where one goes, the other follows."

"She—" Bethany began before Gina gave her a gentle kick beneath the table.

"I've never heard that before," Gina said.

Pamela waved her hands around and laughed. "I'm just being funny. You do understand that, don't you?"

"Oh, yes, of course." Gina leaned back and let out a nervous giggle.

"Some people around here take me entirely too seriously. I'm actually a very laid-back, humor-loving person."

When silence fell, Bethany thought it might be a good idea to let Pamela know what they'd been up to. "We delivered flyers to all the businesses on Main Street for the festival."

Pamela smiled conspiratorially. "Did that old mean man at the tack store tell you to get lost?"

"No," Gina said. "In fact, he seemed happy to take the flyers."

"Don't be surprised to see them in the garbage can outside his store later. He hates the garden club."

Bethany doubted that. She suspected Mr. Potter was so

jealous about Pamela being cozy with Andy, he couldn't control his bad manners when she was around. According to what she'd heard, shortly after Pamela's husband had passed away, Mr. Potter had made it known to everyone at the church that he planned to be the next man in her life. Then Andy came along and ruined it for him.

Pamela snapped her fingers in front of Bethany's face, making Bethany jump. "You always go off into your own little world."

"Sorry." Bethany gave her an apologetic look.

"What all do you have planned for publicity?"

"Um . . . flyers and . . ." Bethany glanced at Gina. "I thought we might see if we can get some of the businesses in nearby towns to hand out flyers."

"No, no, no, no, no." Pamela shook her head as she wagged an index finger. "That will never do. Remember, this is a promotion to help persuade people to leave wherever they live and take up residence in Bloomfield." She leaned back and scowled. "I can't imagine business people in other towns being willing to hand out those flyers. You have to be a little more discreet than that."

"Maybe the businesses will want to move too," Gina said.

"I seriously doubt it." Pamela gave Gina a dismissive look. "In fact, I think it's rather naïve to even think such a thought."

Bethany saw Gina purse her lips, so she came up with something else to keep the conversation moving. "Radio spots would be good."

This time, Pamela nodded. "Yes, that's what I was thinking. Call around and get some prices so we can get board approval to spend the money."

It was no secret the only approval anyone needed was Pamela's for the Bloomfield Garden Club to spend money, but Bethany knew they still had to go through the motions. "I'll do that first thing Monday."

"Ya know," Gina began. "I really don't think we'll have a problem handing out flyers in other towns." She glanced at

Bethany and smiled. "That is, if we agree to do something for them in exchange."

"Like what?" Pamela asked.

"Maybe give them a discount on a booth at our festival."

"A discount, huh?" Pamela squinted for a moment. "Hey, I like that." She slowly nodded as she grinned at Gina. "You're a smart girl. And who knows? Maybe the business people will decide they like Bloomfield so much they'll want to move here too."

Gina looked confused. "That's what I was say—"

"Hey, ladies. Andy said I could find you here."

Bethany glanced up and spotted Pete standing in front of the table, his thumbs hooked in his belt loops, a goofy grin on his face. The blend of masculinity and kindness standing before her made her head spin. And the stirring she felt in her chest caught her breath and rendered her speechless.

Pete hadn't been in the Pink Geranium in years. Considering the tearoom was a place with pastel walls and napkins to match, lace everywhere, and girly food, there wasn't much reason for him to frequent it, except when he needed to talk to his favorite woman. Naomi had given him a pair of tickets to the latest drama production at the high school with an unstated understanding he'd ask Bethany to join him. Since it was tonight, he didn't have time to waste. She'd made sure he knew they were having lunch with Pamela.

He sure hoped it wasn't a mistake coming here and interrupting Bethany's lunch with friends. Based on the look on her face, she didn't mind, and from the looks of what was left on the table, they were probably finishing up.

"Do you want to go to the play at the high school with me tonight?" he asked Bethany.

"Sounds like fun," Pamela said before Bethany had a chance to reply. "They're doing *Arsenic and Old Lace*."

"That's what Naomi said." Pete turned to Bethany. "I think the last time Bloomfield High School put on that play was when we were there."

Bethany nodded and cleared her throat. "Remember when Mrs. Blankenship made us see it for a grade?"

He laughed. "Yeah, and we all grumbled. But ya know, it turned out to be one of the funniest productions I've ever seen."

Gina looked baffled. "What's this *Arson and Lace*? A play about some sort of fancy person who sets fires?"

Everyone at the table laughed, including Pamela, who reached out and placed her hand on Gina's arm. "No, dear. It's *Arsenic and Old Lace*, a story about a couple of little old ladies who poison men with arsenic."

"Really?" Gina's forehead crinkled. "Sounds kind of bizarre."

"Yes." Pamela smiled at Bethany and Pete before turning back to Gina. "It will leave you in stitches."

Now Gina looked more confused than ever. "You think it's funny they poison men?"

Pamela nodded. "That's what I said."

"How can that be funny?"

Pete exchanged another conspiratorial glance with Pamela and then Bethany. "Why don't you and Jeremy come along with us and find out for yourself?"

A wistful look washed over Gina's face. "I would, but Lacy—"

Pamela cleared her throat. "I would love to watch that darling little girl of yours so you and your sweet husband can enjoy a double date."

Gina's mouth formed into a crooked grin, and she nodded. "Another reason to love this place. Back home, if my mom was busy, I would have been on the phone for hours looking for a babysitter. Here, all I have to do is act like I want to do something, and I get offers."

Pamela pointed to Gina's handbag. "Give Jeremy a call to make sure he's interested. If not, I'll talk to him."

Pete looked at Bethany and knew she was thinking the same thing he was—that Pamela left nothing to chance. She wanted to be right there, making sure everything happened as she thought it should, and she wasn't willing to settle for anything else.

While Gina called Jeremy, Pete studied the relationship between Bethany and Pamela. He knew many people didn't care for Pamela, even though they respected her ability to get things done. However, he saw more than respect flowing between the two women—at the moment, at least—an almost we're-in-this-together sort of camaraderie. He wondered if Naomi had anything to do with this.

Gina slipped the phone back into the side of her purse and grinned. "He said yes! We're going if we can get tickets."

Pamela whipped a stack of cardboard tickets out of her bag, removed two, and handed them to Gina. Then she turned to Pete, who gave her a curious look. "What?" Her gaze darted toward Bethany and then back to Pete. "I always get a few extras for garden club giveaways."

"Oh, I wouldn't want to take them if they're for—" Gina reached for her purse.

Pamela held up a hand. "Nonsense. This is exactly what they're for. Now go enjoy yourselves tonight." Pamela stood. "I need to run now. I promised Andy I'd help him look for new window treatments for his sunroom." She made a clicking sound with her tongue. "He actually thought he could slap a bunch of blinds on his windows and be done with it. Where is that man's sense of style?" She shook her head and laughed. "Good thing he has me to set him straight, or his place would look like an institution."

"I can only imagine what you'd say about my apartment," Pete said.

Pamela lifted an eyebrow. "Want me to come take a look at it? I can make any place look like home."

He laughed. "No, but thanks. I'm hardly ever there, so it doesn't matter."

She clicked her tongue and shook her head. "That's what you men don't seem to understand. Home should be your sanctuary— a place that makes you happy."

She might have a point, Pete thought. He bobbed his head. "Maybe I'll think about getting a few things to spruce it up a bit."

Pamela gave him a placating smile. "Okay, you do that. In the meantime, I'll leave the three of you to discuss plans for tonight." She took a couple slow, wobbly steps toward the door before turning around. "Oh, by the way, I've already paid for lunch, so you don't have to worry about it."

Both Bethany and Gina thanked Pamela in unison. After she left, Pete saw a visible release in tension.

"Did you ladies have fun?" he asked.

Gina nodded. "Actually, we did." She told him about their morning spent distributing flyers and then having lunch with Pamela to give a recap. "She wants to know every single last detail, but I think that's probably good since she's the president."

Pete saw Bethany's forced smile. He cleared his throat. "I need to run, but let me know if there's anything I can do to help out with this festival."

Bethany nodded, but Gina held up a finger. "Ya know, there is one thing you can do." She leaned over and pulled a small stack of flyers from her tote. "You can have your workers hand these out during their service calls." The firm tone of her voice showed she expected nothing less than agreement, so he took them. As he walked out of the Pink Geranium, he pondered the idea that Gina just might eventually give Pamela a run for her money one of these days. She came across softer and more gracious, but he detected a steely determination beneath the surface.

Chapter 18

Bethany and Pete had just found their seats in the high school auditorium when they spotted Pamela on the other side of the aisle waving.

"Over here," Pamela said. "We saved seats."

Pete looked puzzled. "I thought Pamela was watching Lacy."

Bethany laughed. "She managed to get my mom to do it instead. I think she wanted to keep an eye on all of us here."

Pete leaned down and whispered, "Do you want to go over there or not?"

Bethany thought for a moment and shrugged. "We might as well join them. No point in hurting anyone's feelings."

Pete made a mock sad-puppy face. "I don't think it would hurt anyone's feelings if we sat somewhere else."

"But Gina and Jeremy are over there." Bethany gave him an apologetic look. "They're still sort of new to Bloomfield, and I don't want them to think we're not friendly."

Pete tilted his head. "They know we're friendly."

"Yeah, but—"

A slow grin of understanding spread across his lips. "You really want to sit with them, don't you?"

"Yes."

"Okay, let's go." Pete took her by the hand and led the way toward the large group from the church and garden club. "Looks like most of the gang's here."

Bethany appreciated the fact that Pete didn't mind giving in and doing what she wanted without kicking up a fuss.

Once they were seated, Pamela straightened her shoulders and lifted her hands. "Let's everyone say a prayer for the kids who'll be performing tonight." She glanced around. "You can say silent prayers, but be very specific that everyone remembers their parts."

The fact that Pamela's control never ceased, even for silent prayers, wasn't lost on Bethany. She started to bow her head but opened one eye to see what Pete was doing. His wide grin and wink before he bowed his head made her smile.

As they watched the high school kids play the parts of people older than anyone on the stage or in the audience, Bethany relaxed and allowed herself to enjoy sitting with friends she'd known most of her life. They weren't perfect, but they all cared about each other.

Every once in a while, Bethany leaned around to gauge Gina and Jeremy's reaction to the play. Gina seemed to enjoy the production more than anyone else. The story of *Arsenic and Old Lace* obviously caught her off guard. She laughed so hard Bethany had to reach into her handbag for a tissue. Gina accepted it, dabbed at her eyes, and continued laughing. Jeremy kept shaking his head as the women plied the elderly men with tainted elderberry wine. By the time the play was over, Gina had little makeup left on her eyes and cheeks.

"That was one of the funniest things I've ever seen," Gina said. "The kids were great. How often do they put on a play?"

"They generally present a couple of plays a year," Pamela said. "I try to show my support by attending."

Gina nodded. "I fully intend to do that too. How do I buy season tickets?"

"Just ask me," Pamela said with a wink. "I always have extras."

Once they walked outside to the parking lot, Pamela gestured for everyone to listen. "Why don't we all head on over to Sonic and get something yummy to drink?"

Andy shook his head. "You know we can't do that. Murray's been by himself too long as it is."

Pamela opened her mouth, but before saying anything, clamped it shut. She issued a clipped nod and shrugged. Everyone understood she knew better than to argue when Murray was involved.

Pete walked Bethany to his truck. "We don't have to worry about Murray, so would you like to go somewhere?"

Bethany wanted to, but shook her head. "I don't think so. We have church in the morning, and I'm pretty tired from handing out all those flyers this morning." More than anything, she needed some time alone to regroup, even though the temptation to prolong her date with Pete was tempting. All this social stuff wore her out.

"Maybe lunch after church then?" The hopeful look on his face touched her heart.

She smiled and nodded yes. "That sounds good."

"Want me to pick you up for church? No point in taking two cars, since we're going to . . . hang out afterward."

The more time Bethany spent with Pete, the more she could see herself in a relationship with him, but then his words about never settling down with one woman continued to ring through her head. Panic welled in Bethany's chest, but she forced herself to accept his words at face value. After all, it wasn't as though he expected her to commit to a long-term relationship. It was just

lunch with an old friend—albeit a friend who kept chipping away
at her heart.

The next morning, Bethany crawled out of bed before the alarm
went off. She'd fallen asleep fairly easily, but she awoke at the
crack of dawn with a smile on her face and a memory of Pete
looking into her eyes as they stood on her doorstep. He looked
like he wanted to kiss her but wasn't sure if it was appropriate. So
she'd done the only thing she could think of—stand on her tiptoes
and plant a kiss on his cheek. She then turned around, unlocked
her door, and waved good-bye as she closed it. She had stood
silent as she listened for him to pull away.

Now she wondered what it would have been like to share a
kiss that involved his lips on hers and his arms around her. She
shuddered. Even the thought gave her a feeling of disloyalty to
Charlie.

She'd just turned on the coffee pot when the phone rang. It
was Naomi.

"Hey, Mom. What do you need?"

Naomi snickered. "So you think just because I called I need
something?"

"Well, do you?"

A brief pause was all Bethany needed to know her answer.
"There is one thing," Naomi said. "My car wouldn't start last
night, so I wondered if you'd mind picking me up for church this
morning. I figured I could have it towed to the mechanic first
thing tomorrow."

"I'll need to call Pete and let him know," Bethany said.

"Why do you have to do that?"

Bethany took a deep breath and slowly let it out. She really
didn't want her mother to assume anything that wasn't there,
but she didn't exactly have a choice at the moment. "Pete offered

to pick me up for church, because we're going out for lunch afterward."

"Oh?"

"Yes, but I'm sure he'll understand if I call and change plans. He's very understanding."

"Yes, I know he is," Naomi said. "I better run and get ready then."

Bethany hung up, poured her coffee, and sat down at the table with it. She glanced up at the clock and figured it was a tad too early to call anyone, so she'd wait at least an hour or so to call Pete.

The next time her phone rang, she was surprised to hear her mother's voice again. "Never mind picking me up. I'm riding over with some friends from the Village."

"Are you sure? I really don't mind."

"And ruin your chance for . . . I mean . . . your plans with Pete? I don't think so. Besides, I have some things to discuss with my friends."

"Like what?"

"Normal stuff. You know, garden club business and the vegetable garden and the festival and a few other things."

"Right." Bethany smiled. "Okay, I'll see you at church then."

"But don't feel like you and Pete have to sit with me."

"Okay, I won't." Bethany hung up still smiling. Her mother was so obvious it was hilarious. And Bethany was reminded that Naomi didn't miss a single opportunity to scheme.

Pete reached out to ring Bethany's doorbell, but she yanked open the front door before he had a chance.

"I heard your truck in the driveway," she explained.

"You look mighty happy." Pete stood on Bethany's porch, unable to take his eyes off of her. "I hope it has something to do with me."

"Oh, trust me it does. You know I've always enjoyed hanging out with you." Bethany stepped back to let him in. "Just wait until I tell you about my mother."

As she relayed the information about how Naomi had called to ask for a ride but shifted gears after she found out Bethany was going to church with him, Pete's heart sank. He realized Bethany was more amused about her mother's behavior than she was happy to spend time with him.

"We can swing out to the Village and pick her up. I don't mind."

"I know you don't," Bethany said, as she looked up at him with her twinkling blue eyes. "But I know her well enough to know she wouldn't even consider that as an option. She's trying way too hard to get me out and about with my old friends."

"Is that a bad thing?" Pete stopped and looked down at Bethany.

Her smile faded momentarily as she shook her head. "No, not at all. It's just I don't appreciate being manipulated by my mother." She paused. "Do you?"

"No, of course not. At least not by my mother."

"Or mine." Bethany giggled. "So why don't we behave totally scandalous and sit next to my mom in church?"

Pete couldn't help but laugh. "Knowing Naomi, she just might get up and move."

"Not if you sit next to her. She would never want to risk hurting your feelings."

Bethany picked up her purse and strode toward the door. Pete followed right behind her, glancing around and noticing how much less clutter remained in the house. Bethany had obviously worked hard on clearing things out.

"You're devious," he said, as they slid into his truck.

"You like that about me, don't you?" She cast a devilish smile in his direction, making him laugh again.

"Oh, yeah. The more you scheme, the more attractive you are." He winked and started the engine.

"My mom and Pamela must be gorgeous if that's the case."

He thought about it and nodded. "You know, for women their age, they're really pretty."

Bethany thought about the difference between her mother's and Pamela's ages and realized that might have been part of the problem between the two older women. Naomi had always liked being in charge, and the only time Bethany had ever seen her defer to someone else was if the other person was her age or older. Pamela was a good twenty years younger than Naomi.

"Whatcha thinkin'?" Pete asked as he drove toward the church.

Bethany fidgeted with her purse strap. "I'm trying to sort out a few things."

"I noticed how much work you've done in your house."

She stilled and looked at him. "What do you think?"

He wasn't sure how to answer, so he simply smiled and said, "Looks good. So how do you feel?"

"Much better."

"I thought you might."

She nodded. "Maybe that's how it works. Clear away the physical clutter, and the mental clutter fades away."

"Could be." He pulled up to a stoplight and turned to face her. "If that's the case, I should be in good shape mentally."

"Why?"

"My apartment has absolutely no clutter."

"How do you do that?"

He shrugged. "I don't have much stuff."

After he turned his attention back to driving, he noticed her studying him in his peripheral vision.

"Is that because you don't like stuff, or is it to keep your place neat and tidy?"

"I never put all that much thought into it. I have the basics—a couch, a TV, and an end table in the living room. My bedroom has a bed, a nightstand, and a dresser."

"Is that all?"

"Yup. That's it for the furniture. Add a few dishes, some clothes, and a couple pairs of shoes, and that's all I own. I don't need anything else."

"How about pictures?"

He pointed to his head. "I have all the pictures I need in here."

"No wonder you think my place is a mess."

"C'mon, Bethany, I never said that." He pulled into the church parking lot. "I just—"

Bethany lifted her hand. "Okay, let's end this discussion. I didn't mean to put you on the defensive, but I'm afraid I have." She opened her own door before turning to look at him. "Are you ready to face my mom and her coconspirator?"

"Ready as I'll ever be. Let's go."

The church was packed when they arrived, so there were few places left for them to sit. Naomi generally sat toward the front, so Bethany led Pete down the aisle. When she spotted her mother, she pointed. "They're over there. You go first so it won't be so obvious."

He took her by the hand and led the way toward the pew. Naomi glanced up first, and then Pamela turned to face them. "You barely made it on time," Naomi said.

Pete waited for Bethany to sit before he eased down beside her. Naomi leaned over, grinned, and waved.

"Hi, Mom."

"It's about time you two got here," Pamela said, as she leaned around Naomi. Andy visibly elbowed her in the side, so she turned and scowled at him before plastering a smile back on her face. "But why would you want to sit with us old folks?"

Pete leaned over. "You're not that much older than us, Pamela, so watch what you say."

Pamela started to respond, but Andy took hold of her shoulders and turned her around to face the front. Naomi pretended not to notice, but Bethany was fully aware her mother didn't miss a thing. She never did.

Throughout the service, Bethany felt the current flowing between her and Pete as their elbows touched. Since there were so many people in the sanctuary, they shared a hymnal, obviously to Naomi's delight. Occasionally, Bethany caught her mother openly observing them and looking satisfied.

After the benediction, Naomi whispered something into Pete's ear, and his face instantly turned bright red. Bethany didn't want to embarrass him further, so she decided to wait until they were safely in his truck before asking what her mother had said.

Chapter 19

"Why did you keep jabbing me in the ribs?" Pamela folded her arms and glared at Andy as they stood by his car in the church parking lot.

Andy shrugged. "I thought it might be best to keep quiet and let things happen on their own for a change."

"Oh, yeah?" She tipped her head to one side, holding his gaze. "So you think things *just happen* on their own?"

He nodded. "If you let them."

"What if nothing happens?" She glared at him, tipped her head, and folded her arms in a challenging stance.

He broke his gaze to unlock the car door and let Pamela slide in. "Then it's not meant to be." Before she had a chance to respond, he closed the door and went around to his side.

She wanted so badly to give Bethany and Pete a little prod in the right direction, but Andy's constant elbow nudges kept her from doing what she did best. He obviously didn't understand how relationships worked. Romance between two people who were eager to fall in love was easy. However, when one was shy and the other afraid, the whole game changed.

"By the way, we're having some firefighters come over to the fire hall from other stations in the region, so I wondered if you could take Murray for the afternoon," Andy said as he pulled up in front of Pamela's house. "But I'll understand if you can't." He sighed. "I just wish people would try to get to know him."

"Stop trying to make people feel sorry for you and him." She sighed as she turned toward Andy. "For how long?" She didn't mind parrot-sitting Murray for a few hours, but the bird's constant demands wore on her after a while.

"Someone can come pick him up before dinner."

"Want me to take him to the fire hall later?" That way, she could make sure she wasn't stuck longer than planned.

"If you don't mind. That sure would make things easier. So you'll do it?"

She nodded. "Of course. You know I will."

"Good. I'll drop him off on the way to work." He started to walk away but stopped and turned to face Pamela. "You're an amazing woman, which is why I appreciate you so much, but there are times when . . ." He glanced around before looking back at her. "I'm not so sure you know when to stop."

"What are you talking about?" Pamela felt her lips twitch. Most of the time, she and Andy got along fine, but now, his strange comment made her nervous.

"You know." He waved his arms. "Bethany and Pete. They seem to be doing okay without your interference."

She rolled her eyes. "Their relationship is going nowhere."

"It might be moving slowly, but . . ." Andy lifted an eyebrow. "Maybe that's how it's supposed to be."

She shuddered to think how his way of thinking would never work. "I don't think so. I think—"

Andy touched Pamela's lips with the tip of his fingers. "Wanna know what I think? I think we should end this conversation before one of us says something we'll regret."

"I promise I'll be careful what I say to either of them. Heaven knows, those two are as skittish as all get-out. But I find it hard to just sit back and let them miss an opportunity at real love." Pamela opened the car door. "I've known Bethany most of her life, and she's never been one to go after what she wants. Her hesitation is part of the problem, and from what I've seen, Pete isn't any better."

"It must work for her. She married Charlie," Andy reminded her. "I'm not so sure about Pete, though."

"It worked for Bethany in the past only because Charlie was aggressive, and he was willing to take chances. Pete has never been married, and he's still with the family business. I'm not saying there's anything wrong with either of those things, but I do think it's pretty telling about his lack of initiative."

Andy didn't say a word. He just shook his head.

Three hours later, Pamela found herself talking to Murray as he sat on his perch in her kitchen. "So do you think I'm a busybody?"

Murray stared back at her but didn't answer.

"Don't start the silent treatment now—not when I really need you. Talk to me, Murray. Am I meddling too much in Bethany and Pete's business?"

"Takin' care of business . . . *squawk* . . . Takin' care of business." He bobbed his head and squawked a few more times.

"See? That's what I'm talkin' about. You agree with me, don't you?" She went to the refrigerator to get Murray a treat. When she came back, she shoved a carrot stick through the wires of the cage. "You're being good today."

Murray let out a loud wolf whistle, making Pamela laugh. She poured herself a cup of coffee from the morning's brew, stuck it in the microwave, and then leaned against the counter to wait for it to heat up. Murray scooted across his perch until he was as close to Pamela as he could get in his cage.

When the microwave beeped, Murray fluttered his wings, bobbed his head, and jumped around the cage. "Fire, fire . . . *squawk* . . . Get moving, everyone! Fire."

Pamela pulled her coffee from the microwave, set it on the counter, and leaned over to talk to the bird. "Murray, you spend way too much time at the fire hall. I need to talk with your daddy about that."

"Daddy loves his precious little birdie . . . *squawk* . . . Daddy loves his precious little birdie." Murray tilted his head and gave her an innocent look. "Daddy loves . . . " Murray stopped mid-sentence and didn't even bother to squawk. Pamela leaned over and looked at him to make sure he was okay. She jumped when he let out one of his ear-piercing squawks.

She laughed. "Don't scare me like that."

"Scary bird . . . *squawk*!"

"You're right," Pamela agreed. "Very scary." She smiled down at Murray. "And yes, your daddy does love you . . . very much." She dumped two heaping teaspoons of sugar and at least as much cream into her coffee. As she took a sip, she imagined Andy telling Murray how much he loved him, and that warmed her heart.

"Maybe I can watch you a little more often." Pamela paused for a reaction from Murray, but quickly realized how silly that was. "You're actually pretty good company."

"Company's here . . . *squawk*! Answer the door, dummy."

Pamela chuckled. "At least you're good company until you say something like that." She glanced up at the clock and thought about how she'd normally be out and about after church, but she actually didn't mind spending time at home with Andy's bird. In fact, she found it rather comforting. "We might as well figure out what to do with the rest of our day."

She sat down at the table with the phone and pondered who she should call and invite over. Naomi immediately came to mind, so she punched in the number she knew by heart. No answer. Next on her list was Sherry, but as she thought might be the case, Sherry and

Brad had plans. She scanned her list of garden club members until she got to the end with the listing of new people. Gina! Perfect!

"I've got Andy's bird for a few hours, and I thought you and your sweet little family might enjoy coming over for a snack this afternoon. I'm sure Lacy would enjoy Murray."

"Actually," Gina said slowly. "Lacy is scared to death of that bird."

"Why on earth would she be afraid of Murray? He's harmless . . . well, he is until someone tries to grab him."

"Maybe so, but they got off to a bad start. The first time we ever saw him, Sherry was bird-sitting him, and he was in the card shop. He let out one of his loud noises, and that shook Lacy up pretty bad."

"That's all the more reason you should bring her over," Pamela said. "We can help them make friends."

Some noise in the background caught Gina's attention. "Let me call you back, okay? Jeremy needs me for something real quick."

After Pamela hung up, loneliness flooded her heart, and she felt as though every ounce of breath had been sucked from her lungs. It had been many years since her husband had passed, but every once in a while, something happened that reminded her how much she missed him. She got up from the table, dumped the rest of her coffee in the sink, and turned to face Murray.

"So what would you like to do?"

"Murray wants candy . . . *squawk*!"

"Spoiled rotten, that's what you are." Pamela got Murray a couple more carrots. "You may have two. That's all."

"That's all, folks! *Squawk*!"

"Maybe we should work on teaching you some new words." Pamela smiled at her brilliant idea. "Andy will be so surprised." She planted her fist on her hip and thought about what to teach Murray. "I know. Let's try this." She leaned over and said, "Repeat after me. 'Yes, ma'am, anything you say.'"

Murray stared at her, his beak closed, his wings flat by his sides.

"C'mon, Murray, you can do this. Say, 'Yes, ma'am, anything you say.'"

She spoke slowly, hoping Murray would pick up the words. She leaned down and repeated the sentence, but he didn't even open his beak.

"Hmm. I wonder how many times I have to say it before you catch on." She walked back and forth in front of his cage. "Yes, ma'am, anything you say; yes, ma'am, anything you say . . ."

Pamela repeated the phrase over and over until she got tired of hearing her own voice. Finally, she sighed. This was pointless.

She was about to carry Murray into another room for a change of scenery when Gina called. "Jeremy said he thought it would be an excellent idea to bring Lacy over to see Murray. He doesn't want her to be so afraid of a bird, and he thinks it would be a good idea to let them gradually get to know each other."

"Wonderful! When can you come?"

Gina laughed. "We're standing on your porch right now."

As soon as Pamela dropped the phone into the receiver, she hurried toward the door. Gina was the only person Pamela knew beside herself who didn't see any point in waiting. That was why Pamela intended to groom her for garden club presidency. Sherry had already said she wasn't interested, and someone had to do it.

She flung the door open, and there stood Lacy looking cuter than ever. "Is Murray here?" the little girl asked, her voice quivering.

"Yes, come on in." Pamela stepped back to let Lacy and her parents inside. "He's in the kitchen, so let's go see him."

Lacy hesitated until Gina nodded and gave her a gentle shove. "Go on. He won't hurt you, will he, Miss Pamela?"

"Of course not. Besides, he's in his cage."

As soon as they entered the kitchen, Pamela realized she'd

spoken too soon. Murray's cage door hung open, and he was nowhere in sight. Her heart sank.

"Where are you, Murray?" Panic rose in her chest as she skittered around the kitchen, looking high and low for the mischievous bird, while Lacy wedged herself between her parents.

Jeremy squatted down beside his daughter. "Lacy, sweetie, I'm gonna help Miss Pamela find Murray and put him back in his cage. Stay right here with Mommy, okay?"

"Come out, Murray. I'll give you some candy if you do."

A rustling sound from the indention above the cabinets caught everyone's attention. "Murray wants candy . . . *squawk* . . . Murray wants candy!"

Pamela pulled the carrots out of the refrigerator again and pointed to the cage. "You'll get some candy if you're a good boy. Now come down from there and go back to your perch."

"Murray wants candy!"

"I told you I would give you some if you behave." She slid a carrot stick into the cage and pointed again. "Now go on in there and get your candy."

He bobbed his head, stepped side-to-side, and flapped his wings. Pamela held her breath as he lifted off the cabinet and flew down and into the cage, jarred the wire door, and pounced on the carrot stick.

"Good boy." She slammed the cage door shut and brushed her hands together. "Would you like some more candy, Murray?"

"Yes, ma'am, anything you say . . . *squawk*! Yes, ma'am!"

Jeremy chuckled. "Smart bird."

Chapter 20

Bethany drove home after spending Sunday afternoon at Pete's stark apartment. He wasn't kidding when he said he had few possessions. Until seeing his place, she thought she'd done a good job of clearing out the clutter. But now, as she walked through her own house and compared it to Pete's, she realized she still had too much. The thought of how they could be good for each other flitted through her head, until she reminded herself of his commitment to bachelorhood.

She put down her purse on the hall table and entered the living room, where photos remained lined up on the built-in bookshelves. She lifted one and studied it. She remembered seeing this frame the first time she ever stepped foot in Charlie's parents' house, but she had no idea who the people were. She carefully placed it face down on the coffee table and moved on to the next picture.

An hour later, she'd removed all but three framed pictures from the shelf—one of Charlie's family when he was a boy; one of her and Charlie's wedding; and another of her, Charlie, and Ashley. The rest of the pictures could be stored in the attic.

After wrapping the delicate frames in tissue and loading them in a box, she started on another shelf filled with curios—one she'd overlooked during her last round of cleaning. After living with it a while, everything had become invisible. She sighed. Between her mother-in-law's ceramic pieces and her own vacation souvenirs, she was able to fill two more boxes. She sneezed.

A knock sounded at the door, so she stopped to see who it was. Her mother stood there grinning. "I thought you might need some company."

Bethany smiled and gestured for her mother to enter the house. "You did? Or are you curious about how my day went with Pete?"

Instead of answering, Naomi walked around looking at the area Bethany had just cleared. "You've been busy, haven't you? Where are your dust rags? These dust bunnies are prolific, and they'll run you out of the house if you don't do something about them quickly."

Arguing and defending herself wouldn't do a bit of good, so Bethany pulled a couple of rags from the hall closet. "I'm doing this in stages."

"So I see." Naomi pointed to one end of the shelf. "You start over there, and I'll take this one. By the way, speaking of your day with Pete, how was it?"

"Good. We grilled hamburgers in the courtyard at his apartment complex."

"That's nice, but you didn't answer my question. How was it?" Naomi stopped dusting and stared at Bethany as she waited for an answer.

"The hamburger was delicious."

Naomi let out a groan. "Bethany, stop evading my question. Did you and Pete have a chance to talk about anything?"

Bethany shrugged. It was fun watching her mother work so hard for information. "We talked about all kinds of stuff."

"Like what?"

"Plumbing and the garden club and the festival and . . ." Bethany grinned. "Is that what you're asking?"

"What do you think?" Naomi narrowed her eyes. "Got anything to drink? This dust is clogging my throat."

Bethany knew it was a ploy to change the setting. Naomi had always said the best place to find out anything you wanted to know about someone was sitting at the kitchen table. Fortunately, Bethany knew her mother well, and besides, there wasn't anything earth-shattering to discuss. She'd spent most of her time with Pete dancing around the topics she'd already mentioned to Naomi, and when either of them strayed to more personal topics, the other pulled the conversation back to safety.

The instant they sat down with glasses of lemonade, Naomi looked Bethany in the eye. "Did you kiss?"

Hunch confirmed. "Um . . ." Awkward. "Yes."

Naomi leaned back and grinned. "Was it a good one?"

"Mom!" Bethany tilted her head forward and gave her mother a hooded look. "I'm not sure how to answer that, and besides, it's none of your business."

"I'm your mother. I've been married and given birth to four children. I changed your diapers when you were little. Nothing should embarrass you around me."

Bethany laughed at her mother's tactics. Annoying but creative.

Naomi frowned. "I can't help it if I want my children to be happy."

"What makes you think I need Pete to kiss me in order to be happy?"

Naomi shrugged. "I don't know. Maybe it's just that I'm worried about you becoming one of those people who never leave the house. You can develop agoraphobia."

Bethany choked on her lemonade. "I am not becoming agoraphobic."

"That's because I'm not letting it happen."

Bethany held up her hands. "Stop worrying about me. I'm just fine. I'm removing the clutter, and I'm getting out almost every day. I'm at church on Sunday, and I'm involved with the festival committee. What more do you want?"

Naomi nodded. "Yes, you're getting out, and at least that's a start. But what about Pete?"

"Let me decide what to do with my own relationships."

"But I want—"

"This isn't about you and what you want, Mom." Bethany hated cutting her mother off, but the conversation was having the opposite effect Naomi had intended. It made Bethany want to hide and not give folks in Bloomfield so much to talk about, but it was time to stand up to people, starting with her mother. As long as she continued seeing Pete, she knew their gums would flap.

"Okay, I get it." Naomi stared at the table in silence for a moment.

Bethany placed her hand on top of her mother's. "I know you love me, and you want what's best for me, but let me decide what that is, okay?"

Naomi lifted her head, jutted out her chin, and looked Bethany in the eye. "Okay."

Her mother's voice cracked, belying the stoic face she wore. Bethany had to glance away to keep her mom from seeing the tears that had begun to form in her eyes.

Naomi shuddered and cleared her throat. "How are things going with the festival promotion?"

"Good." Bethany grinned. "Putting Gina in charge as coordinator was an excellent move. That woman has more energy than anyone I've ever seen."

"She reminds me of someone, but I can't put my finger on who that is."

"Pamela?"

Naomi's eyebrows shot up. "That's it! She reminds me of

Pamela when she was much younger." She chuckled. "And that daughter of hers is following in her footsteps."

"That's not a bad thing," Bethany said. "At least not for the garden club."

"True. It's good to know we'll always have someone ready to take charge."

"Now back to the festival. We already have enough booths reserved to put on a decent festival if the weather is nice. Anything from now on is gravy."

"The garden club's booth will be the biggest, right?" Naomi gave her a hopeful glance. "And it's indoors?"

"Yes, of course." Bethany knew how important that was to her mother and all the other people who'd been in the organization for decades. "They . . . I mean *we'll* have a strong presence, and we won't have to worry about bad weather."

Naomi nodded. "Now we need to move into high gear since the festival is less than a month away. And to think this all started with what I thought was a cockamamie plan to get Pamela off my back about growing the town." She chuckled as she stood. "I better get on home. I have Zumba for Seniors first thing in the morning, so I have to get up mighty early."

The next morning, Bethany finished another round of de-cluttering. This time, she felt joy surge with every item she removed from her house. She loaded up her SUV and drove everything to the community center that was now abuzz with festival activity. Following in Pamela's footsteps, Gina had enlisted the aid of some of the folks who hung around playing board games. The grin on Howard's face as he followed Gina around gave away the fact that he'd transferred his ardent admiration for Pamela to Gina, and he would do just about anything she asked him to.

Bethany managed to pull Claude and Marvin away from the chess table to help her unload the boxes. Howard took it upon himself to be second-in-charge.

"Put it over there, guys." He pointed to the farthest table. "We have to make sure there's plenty of room for everything else."

Claude opened his mouth, but Marvin shook his head, and he closed it. Of the three, Marvin was the oldest, and he apparently had the wisdom to know when to argue and when to fold. At least that was the case this time.

It took them less than half an hour to unload the SUV and categorize Bethany's contributions on the tables, thanks to the system Gina had set up. That woman could definitely give Pamela some competition in the leadership department. Bethany was sure it didn't hurt that Gina was drop-dead gorgeous and sweet to people when they offered their help. These guys would clearly do their best to move heaven and earth if she asked them to.

Out of the corner of her eye, Bethany noticed Howard and Claude inspecting some of her most recently donated items. Claude mentioned that his sister collected Hummels, but Howard seemed more interested in the handmade objects. Marvin stood back, his arms folded, looking at everything spread out on the tables.

Gina came up to Bethany and whispered, "Do I need to keep an eye on these guys? Pamela says we're missing some things."

Bethany had known Howard, Claude, and Marvin all of her life, and she'd never heard any of them accused of dishonesty. "I don't think it's them. Maybe we need to find a place to lock up the most valuable things. There's not enough room in the cabinets here."

Gina nodded. "I agree. I asked the mayor for a room in City Hall, but he said no one in Bloomfield is dishonest and not to worry about it."

Bethany laughed. "Of course, he'd say that. In case you haven't noticed, he's more of an ambassador than a realist."

"I wonder . . ." Gina walked around the table, paused, and tapped her chin. "Nah, never mind."

"What?"

Gina contorted her mouth. "We have a closet where we can store some of it. Jeremy wanted to add shelves and turn it into a toy closet for Lacy, but that can wait until after the festival is over."

"That sounds like a good idea," Bethany said. "But you should probably discuss it with Jeremy first."

"In the meantime, if you really think those guys are honest, I can ask them to guard the loot."

Bethany laughed. "They'll do anything for you, but be prepared for them to trip over each other to report what they saw."

"Yeah, I know, right?" Gina grinned. "I think it's very sweet, but sometimes they try so hard to be helpful that they get in the way."

A week had passed since Pete spent the day with Bethany, and he still couldn't get her response to his apartment out of his mind. She didn't say a word, but her expression told him everything he needed to know about what she thought. From the way her eyes slowly squinted and her jaw tightened as she walked through the apartment made him wish he'd taken her someplace else. She hated the way his place looked, and her reaction mattered to him more than he thought it would.

He stood in the center of the living room and slowly turned around, taking it all in. He couldn't say he blamed Bethany. The apartment looked downright sterile. There wasn't a single item that identified him or said anything about who he was.

Deep down, Pete was a sensitive guy, but if an alien stopped by for a visit, he'd think Pete was cold and not the least bit sentimental. Maybe he'd pick up a few things from the festival to liven up the place a tad. There was always an excellent selection of decorations at the garden club rummage sale booth. He had no idea where to start, but he didn't want to ask Bethany, since she was the one he wanted to impress. So he called his mother.

She chuckled. "Why wouldn't you get Bethany to help you out? I'm sure she'd love it."

"I want to surprise her."

"Okay, let me think about it. In fact, I might even have a few things put away in the attic."

He groaned. "Not Granny's junk. That stuff looks like it came from a little old lady's house."

"That's because it did." His mother paused. "Okay, we can go shopping for some frames and some nice prints of fishing or something else you like. I'll make you a couple of throw pillows for your couch."

"Let me pick out the fabric," he said. "I want it to look manly."

"I'm all for fixing up your apartment, Pete, but I don't think it'll make that much difference in how Bethany feels about you."

Now that she mentioned it, he realized Mom was probably right, but he'd already decided it would make him feel better about coming home to his apartment. As it was, even after living there a few years, he still didn't have a sense of belonging. But until now, he didn't much care.

"Would you like me to get a few frames and put some of your old class pictures in them?" she asked.

"No, I'll do that. I don't want pictures of me, but one of you and Dad would be nice."

She giggled. "That's sweet of you, but you don't have to do that."

"I know, but I want something that makes me smile, and seeing your pretty face will definitely do that."

Another giggle escaped on her end of the phone line. "I have one of your father and me at last year's Fourth of July celebration."

"Perfect! And I'll go through some of the pictures from school and find one with a bunch of my buddies." He glanced at his watch. "Gotta run, Mom. See you soon?"

"Yes, I'll be in the office in the morning. I'm doing payroll this week."

The bookkeeper was on vacation, and his mother knew the office better than anyone, so she always filled in when they were short-staffed. After they hung up, Pete thought about what else he could do to make the most visual impact on his place. Then he remembered some of the things Bethany had reluctantly donated. That's where he'd start shopping during the festival, and he'd make sure to pick up something he knew she liked.

Bethany hadn't been to a garden club meeting in a while, but when Gina asked, she didn't want to say no. So she agreed that it would be fun to ride together.

Gina called from Bethany's driveway. "I'm here."

"Be right out." She grabbed her purse and coat on her way out the door. When she got to Gina's car, she saw the humongous portable file box on the backseat. "Looks like you're ready for anything."

"I'm nervous," Gina said. "Pamela wants me to give a detailed report, and I'm afraid I'll leave something out."

Bethany laughed. "I don't think you have a thing to worry about. You seem to have everything under control."

Gina sighed as she backed out of the driveway. "I sure hope so. This is such a big project for my first, and I certainly don't want to blow it."

When they arrived at the meeting, the roar in the community center drowned out individual conversations. She headed toward the back of the room, but Naomi approached, took her by the arm, and led her closer to the front. As she glanced around the massive space, she saw that Sherry's gaze had settled on her.

"I'll go sit with Sherry, if you don't mind," Bethany said.

Naomi glanced over her shoulder. "Of course, I don't mind. I think it's a good idea to socialize with more folks close to your own age." Her voice lowered. "I've been a little concerned about Sherry. She tends to hang out with us old biddies, and that's not healthy for someone her age."

"Stop worrying so much about everyone."

Naomi shrugged. "I can't help it. It's the mother hen coming out."

Bethany left her mother, crossed the room, and slid into the seat beside Sherry. "I have to admit, I feel like a fish out of water here. Did you know I didn't inherit any of my mother's green thumb genes?"

"I'm not exactly the best gardener either," Sherry admitted. "If it weren't for your mother, I probably wouldn't even be allowed in the garden club."

Bethany knew this about Sherry, which she found comforting at the moment. "I think tonight's meeting will be mostly about the festival."

"It's *all* about the festival. You should see Pamela's notes."

"That bad, huh?" Bethany sighed. "At least it'll all be over soon."

A squawking sound came from the back of the room, announcing Pamela and Andy's entrance with Murray. "One of these days, someone's going to start charging that bird for membership. He seems to have as much to say as anyone here."

Chapter 21

By the time Sunday rolled around, everyone in the garden club felt confident that the festival would run smoothly after Gina's thorough and entertaining presentation. Even Pamela was impressed. On her way out, Naomi had asked Bethany to pick her up for church on Sunday.

"This place is packed." Bethany glanced around the church, looking for enough room in a pew for herself and Naomi. The one where Naomi normally sat was taken.

"Pastor Brunswick's on vacation, so John's preaching the sermon today." Naomi pointed to a pew behind a group of teenagers who'd uncharacteristically clustered toward the front of the church. "Why don't we sit over there?"

Bethany nodded. It made sense that with popular youth pastor John Currey, preaching, the kids would sit up front to show their support. When he first arrived in town, the girls swooned over his dimpled good looks, and the guys respected him for his athleticism. The youth attendance in the church had been dwindling before he came, but once he started his programs, youth membership skyrocketed. Now they continued to have steady growth.

The sermon was on accepting change during the different phases of life. As he related 2 Corinthians 5:17 to accepting the change that comes from faith and being new in Christ, Bethany pondered what it meant to her. She'd been a Christian ever since she could remember, but she still felt cleansed as she experienced change that the Lord had inspired. She opened her Bible to the verse John had quoted and read it again. *Therefore, if anyone is in Christ, the new creation has come: The old has gone, the new is here!*

Those powerful words sent goose bumps over her entire body. Change could come in so many different forms and to different degrees based on where each person was in her faith; there was no doubt the Lord was working on her. She closed her eyes and inhaled a deep breath. When she opened her eyes, she saw her mother watching her, a look of understanding written on her face.

After the service, Naomi tugged at Bethany. "I need to get home right away."

"Can you give me a minute to talk to John and let him know what a great sermon he preached?"

Naomi shook her head. "No. We need to leave now. You can call him later."

Bethany looked longingly at the line that had formed. John smiled at all the folks who wanted to shake his hand and offer their gratitude, but she wouldn't be one of them.

"Okay, let's go." Bethany reached into her handbag, pulled out the keys, and took off after Naomi.

All the way to the Village, Naomi fidgeted, first with the hem of her top and then with the handle of her handbag. Something was up, but Bethany knew if her mother didn't want to talk about it, there was nothing she could do.

When they came within sight of the Village entrance, Naomi cleared her throat. "I have a favor to ask."

Okay, here it comes, Bethany thought. "What's that?"

"I need a ride someplace. Can you wait for me to grab something?"

Bethany laughed. "Where do you need to go, and what do you need to grab? I can help."

"Never mind that. Will you wait for me?" Naomi glared at her daughter with annoyance.

"Okay. Do you need some help?" Bethany pulled the car into the driveway closest to her mother's apartment and stopped.

"No." Naomi got out, leaned over, and pointed her finger. "Wait right here. Don't go anywhere."

As Bethany waited, she pondered what could possibly be going on. Naomi definitely had something up her sleeve, but she couldn't imagine what it could be.

♡ ♡

Pete thought his mother acted strange all during church. He kept glancing over at her, but she never looked him in the eye until he started to leave. "Stop by the house on your way home," she said. "I have something for you."

He didn't have anything else to do, so he nodded. He figured she'd probably gathered some items to decorate his apartment. Even if he didn't want to use them, there was no point in hurting her feelings since she'd gone to the trouble. Besides, she'd probably ask him to stay for lunch, and he was hungry.

She finally met his gaze, offered a shaky smile, and then quickly glanced away. "I better run. See you in a few minutes."

"I'll be there." Pete stood on the church steps and watched his mother skitter toward the car where his dad stood waiting for her.

"That sure was invigorating." The sound of John's voice behind him caught his attention. When he turned around, he saw the youth pastor smiling at him. "I love working with the youth, but it's nice to step out of my comfort zone once in a while and preach to the whole congregation."

"You did a great job," Pete said as he ambled toward John. "No one would ever guess you were outside your comfort zone."

John chuckled. "You can't even imagine how far outside it I was. Have I ever told you how shy I was when I was a teenager?"

"I had no idea."

John nodded and shoved his hands deeper into his pockets. "Maybe that's one of the reasons I do so well with kids. I understand what they're going through, so when they come to me, I relate my own experiences."

Pete nodded. "And that's what you did with the sermon today, isn't it?"

"Yes, that's the only way I can preach. I have to feel it." He pulled a hand out of his pocket and touched his chest. "And man, did I ever feel it."

As they chatted for the next half hour, Pete realized John could have been talking about him too. As a teenager he'd been shy in certain situations, particularly with girls, but now he considered himself a reserved adult—something he assumed was the transformation of shyness. He wondered, though, if he never had taken the steps to get out of his own comfort zone, and all he'd done was rename the way he related to people.

John finally glanced at his watch. "I need to head on out. Let's get together sometime, like for pizza or something."

"Sounds good." As John turned to leave, Pete headed toward his truck. If he didn't hurry, his mother would wonder if he'd changed his mind and start calling his cell.

He'd barely started the engine when his phone rang. He glanced at the number. Yup. It was his mom.

"Where are you?"

"Still at the church. I have to stop by my apartment for a minute, but I'll be there as soon as I can."

He heard voices in the background, and none of them sounded like his dad. "Who all is there?"

"See you in a few minutes, Pete. Hurry up." *Click.*

At least he knew his hunch was correct. Mom was up to something, only it wasn't what he initially suspected. It involved other people, most likely Bethany, but he wouldn't find out for sure until he got there. He'd gotten used to the scheming, and Bethany seemed to find it amusing, so he wasn't worried.

The second he turned onto his parents' street, he spotted several familiar looking cars—one of them Bethany's. He smiled as he scanned the different vehicles and thought he recognized Andy's, John Currey's, and Brad Henderson's. His mother should have told him she was having a party.

He parked as close as he could and sat in his car for a moment to pray. *Lord, You're obviously working on me. Please help me understand whatever it is. You know how hardheaded I can be.* Pete opened his eyes and sighed. Time to go face whatever his mom had planned.

As he drew closer to the house, he could hear squawking, and then suddenly, as he stepped up onto the porch, a loud thudding sound. "Don't open the door!" Andy's voice boomed, stopping Pete in his tracks.

He wasn't about to open the door after that, so he scooted over toward the big picture window and peeked into the dining room. Murray sat perched on top of his mother's china cabinet, and Pete's mom stood below, with hands folded and her face scrunched in concern, while Andy reached up toward Murray with a carrot stick.

Andy caught sight of Pete and motioned for him to go away. Pete decided he'd probably be safe going around to the back of the house and letting himself in through the kitchen.

With all the stealth he could muster, Pete opened the back door barely wide enough to slip in, and he quickly closed it. As he tiptoed toward the commotion, he noticed one person hanging back right outside the dining room.

"Bethany?" he whispered. "What happened?"

"Your mother was showing something to Pamela in the china cabinet, and next thing I know, Murray flew into the dining room with them. Your mom sort of freaked out when he got close to her china, and that's when things got crazy."

Pete thought for a moment. "Maybe I can do something." Yesterday he would have hung back and worried that he might be overstepping his boundaries, but after the sermon, he figured the time had come to step out of his comfort zone.

He walked right into the dining room, went up to his mother, placed his hand on her shoulder, and said, "Andy and I can take care of this. You and everyone else go on into the kitchen."

"But—"

Pete gently took her by the arm and pulled until she went on her own. He motioned to the crowd. "C'mon, everyone. There are way too many people in here, and it'll make it that much harder to corral Murray."

Pamela gave him a curious look but followed his lead, gesturing for everyone else to do the same. Less than a minute later, Pete was back in the dining room with Andy and his bird.

"Good job getting everyone out of here. All that commotion made things worse." Andy handed Pete a bag of carrots.

"I saw that." Pete glanced up at Murray whose head bobbed as he stepped side-to-side on top of the china cabinet. "Looks like he's still a bit anxious."

"Maybe you can lure him down. All the noise frightened Murray, and I couldn't get everyone to leave us alone." Andy rubbed his shoulder. "Been holding my arm up so long it's starting to creak."

Pete nodded as he pulled out a carrot and extended it toward Murray. "Want a carrot, Murray?"

Andy cleared his throat. "Ask him if he wants candy."

"But—"

"Go ahead." Andy nodded toward his bird. "He'll probably take it."

Pete turned back and looked Murray in the eye. "Want some candy?"

Murray's sidestepping and head bobbing quickened. "Murray wants candy . . . *squawk* . . . Murray wants candy."

"Then here ya go. I have just what Murray wants."

Andy nudged Pete. "Slowly pull the carrot stick toward you so he'll get close enough for us to get him down."

A noise erupted from the doorway, causing Murray to flap his wings and skitter to the other side of the cabinet. Andy scowled, but Pete used his free hand to motion everyone to back away.

He started over, trying to lure Murray down. Andy remained right by his side, still occasionally rubbing and working his shoulder. Pete knew it was up to him, so he had to be persistent.

"Murray wants candy . . . *squawk* . . . Murray wants candy."

"Then come and get it," Pete said as he showed Murray the carrot stick and slowly pulled it closer.

"Come and get it, folks . . . *squawk* . . . while supplies last."

Pete cast a curious glance in Andy's direction. Andy nodded. "He likes commercials."

Murray studied the carrot, bobbed his head a few more times, and trotted closer to the edge. Pete held his breath as Murray's beak came toward the carrot. He wasn't sure if he should grab Murray with the other hand or pull the carrot a little closer.

"Don't make any sudden moves," Andy whispered. "You've almost got him."

Now Pete knew why Andy's shoulder was sore. He resisted the urge to relax his arm since Murray was so close to getting the carrot.

"Talk really nicely to him. He likes sweet talk."

"Sweet talk?"

"Yeah. Tell him how handsome he is."

Pete glanced down at Andy and saw he was serious. "Okay, I'll give that a try." He wiggled the carrot in front of Murray. "Come and get your . . . candy, you handsome fella."

"Hello, handsome . . . *squawk* . . . lookin' good." Murray paused and then let out a human-sounding sigh. "Keeps you fresh all day."

"What?" Pete nearly dropped the carrot when he looked back down at Murray's master.

Andy gestured for Pete to turn back around. "I already told you; it's those commercials."

Pete couldn't help but laugh. "Murray, do you watch too much TV?" He wiggled the carrot again. The ridiculousness of the situation had diffused some of the tension in Pete's shoulder.

"Change the channel . . . *squawk*!" Murray grabbed the carrot, flapped his wings, and hopped down onto Pete's shoulder. "Murray wants candy!"

"Hold still," Andy whispered as he slowly reached for Murray. "Got him!"

Applause erupted from the other room, until Pete glared at all the faces in the doorway. "Hold it down, people. You'll scare him."

Once Andy put Murray back into his cage, everyone joined them in the dining room. Pete glanced around until his gaze settled on Bethany, and when he saw her smiling, he felt as though all was right in the world.

"Good job, son," Pete's dad said. "I thought your mother might have a heart attack with that bird prancing around on top of her best dishes."

Pete looked at Andy who bent over the cage and made silly baby talk to his bird. He turned back to his dad. "Maybe we need to give them some privacy."

Andy straightened and shook his head. "That's not necessary. I think it's time for Murray and me to make our exit." He glanced at Pamela. "Want to come with us, or would you like me to come back and get you later?"

"I'll take her home later if she wants to stick around," Pete said.

Andy's chin jutted, and he squared his shoulders. "I said I'd come back and get her. She came with me, and she can leave with me."

"I really don't mind."

"But I do." Andy stared him down as he lifted the birdcage. Pete suspected he might be worried about losing Pamela over his bad-boy bird's antics.

Bethany couldn't believe what she saw—two grown men arguing over who would take Pamela home. She leaned over to see Pamela's reaction, and she wasn't surprised at the woman's smile of satisfaction.

"Now boys, you don't have to fight over me. Pete, I appreciate your offer, but Andy's right. He can come back and pick me up since it was his idea to bring Murray here in the first place." She shook her head as she glared at Andy. "You know he's okay with a few people, but he's such a bad bird in crowds."

Murray squawked. "Bad birdie."

"That's right, Murray." Pamela turned and shook her finger at him. "And I'm going to have a long talk with you later."

"Yes, ma'am, anything you say . . . *squawk!*"

Murray hung his head and lifted his wing to cover his face. Bethany had to bite the insides of her cheeks to keep from laughing, until she noticed Pamela glaring at her.

With all the finger-shaking, Bethany wanted to hide for fear she'd be next. But she wasn't. Pamela walked Andy and Murray out to the car, leaving everyone inside to rehash the Murray incident as though it affected the universe.

Pete sidled up beside her. "It sure doesn't take much to get people riled around here, does it?" He grinned. "No telling what folks would do if something really bad happened."

The sight of another car pulling to a stop outside the window grabbed their attention. Pete leaned over to see who it was. "It's Bailey. Looks like we made the news." He squinted. "I wonder how she found out."

"Oh, I'm sure someone here might have called." Bethany chuckled as she glanced around at all the guilty faces. "Maybe even more than one person, but I bet Bailey's thrilled to cover this story." She made a face. "Not."

"Oh, Bailey's a trooper. We all know she's a better reporter than what she has to cover, but she seems to take it in stride."

Yes, that was one of the things Bethany appreciated about Bailey. "I'll let her in."

Over the next hour, guests took their turns relaying their side of the Murray story to Bailey McCullough, reporter for the *Bloomfield Gazette*. She once worked as a hard news reporter for a larger newspaper before moving back to Bloomfield to be with family. Now she was the society columnist and covered stories the senior reporter didn't want. Bethany wasn't sure where this event fit, but she suspected somewhere in the middle.

At first, Bailey appeared amused during the interviews, but by the time she got to Bethany and Pete, her amusement had turned into obvious annoyance.

"So you're the hero of the day," she said sarcastically.

Pete expelled a breath in a half-laugh, half-frustrated sort of way. "Not exactly hero. More like the only person who didn't mind risking getting pecked by a delinquent bird."

Bailey stopped writing, glanced up at Pete, and then turned to Bethany. The corners of her lips twitched, and when Bethany smiled back, she giggled. Bethany joined her, and they both laughed so hard tears ran down their cheeks.

Chapter 22

Pamela kissed Andy on the cheek. "I'll call you when I'm ready to leave," she said. "You really need to stop forcing Murray on people who don't appreciate him."

"What am I supposed to do?" He gave her a helpless look.

"Let's put our heads together and figure out a solution. We can't continue like this." She sighed. "It's hard to believe it'll take two of us to outsmart a bird with bad social skills."

"I'm starting to think I should find him a better home."

"No." Pamela shook her head. "You can't do any such thing. He might be annoying, but deep down, you love that bird."

Andy frowned and tilted his head. "You're right. He isn't a bad bird, except when he doesn't get the attention he wants."

Pamela shrugged and gestured toward the Sprocketts' house. "Which is any time he's in a crowd."

Andy nodded. "True." Murray squawked. "I guess I better get on home so he can watch his shows. That'll calm him down."

"Oh, brother." She turned to head back inside the house, but Andy took hold of her arm and spun her around. "What?"

"Pamela . . ." The look on Andy's face was different, almost fearful. "I know this is a rather odd place and time, but I wondered . . ."

She swallowed hard as she realized something big was about to happen. "What did you wonder?"

"You and I . . . well, we've been together for quite some time now, and we're not exactly teenagers, and—" He cut off his sentence and grimaced. "Would you consider marr—"

She lifted her fingers to his lips to him. "You were right, Andy. This is definitely not the place and time, so let's table that thought until later."

He smiled and let out a sigh of relief. She was fully aware they were both straddling the line of wanting to make their relationship permanent and fearful of making a mistake. Something so monumental as a lifelong plan deserved a conversation they didn't have time for at the moment.

"Let me know when you're ready to go home."

"I will."

"I'm sorry about Murray."

"I know." Pamela stepped back from the car and watched Andy pull away. He'd never been good with timing, something she found endearing. That was one more reason they were good together.

As his car turned the corner, she thought about Murray's misbehavior in public. He was actually a good companion one-on-one. She wondered how much of the problem was Murray's and how much was Andy's fault for giving in. Seriously? Making sure a mouthy parrot didn't miss his favorite TV shows would make any stranger wonder about Andy's sanity.

Pamela walked up the sidewalk and paused before opening the front door. No telling how many people witnessed her talk with Andy and whether they guessed about what had almost happened. She'd lived in Bloomfield long enough to know that no one minded their own business. Maybe one of these days she'd discuss that in one of the garden club meetings. She might even consider hiring an etiquette expert to come in.

As she took her first step inside, the noise from the kitchen at the back of the house let her know no one had watched from the window as she'd suspected. In an odd sort of way, she resented their lack of curiosity. After all, Murray had livened up the party.

Before rejoining the group, she darted into the dining room and checked herself out in the buffet mirror. Her hair still held its shape, but her lipstick had feathered a bit in the creases of her mouth. She reached into her purse and refreshed it.

The instant she joined the people in the kitchen, folks pounced on her, wanting to know if Andy and Murray were okay. What she suspected they really wanted to know was if she and Andy were getting along.

"Oh, Andy's just fine, but Murray might be in trouble." She turned to Bailey. "Did you have a chance to talk to everyone else yet?"

Bailey nodded and patted the tote that hung from her shoulder. "Yep. I got it all here."

"Okay, now I can tell you what I know."

Bailey smiled. "Thanks, but I have what I need. As it is, most won't even make it into the article."

Disappointment swelled in Pamela's chest. She hadn't been interviewed, even though she was closer to Murray than anyone else in the house. She walked away so no one would see her sulking, but Bailey followed and tugged at her arm.

"I changed my mind. I would like to ask you a few questions a little bit later." Bailey smiled as she spoke in a lowered voice. "But first, why don't you get something to eat? After that craziness, I bet you're half starved."

Oh, so that was it. Bailey was just being considerate. She grinned back at the reporter. "Thanks, I'll do that."

As always, there was so much food in Gertie's kitchen, it overflowed from the island to the countertops. Some people sat at the kitchen table, but since it was unseasonably warm, a few of them had carried their plates out to the picnic table in the backyard.

"How about the blessing?" Pamela asked.

"Pete said it." Bethany grinned with pride as Pete stood behind her with a red face.

Pamela stared at Bethany and Pete as they looked at each other before quickly glancing away. She never ceased to be amazed by how adults acted like teenagers when they were about to fall in love.

Chapter 23

Bethany noticed something different about Pamela after she left Andy outside. Her demeanor was more subdued, and she didn't have an answer for everything. She hoped Pamela was all right.

"Isn't this delicious?" Bethany asked.

Pamela shrugged. "Food's always good here."

Wow. Something had definitely happened. Maybe she should try another approach.

"I'm looking forward to the festival."

Pamela lifted an eyebrow and snorted. "Are you really? I mean, won't it be difficult to see people walking off with all that stuff you used to hoard?"

In spite of the harshness of the comment, relief flooded Bethany to know Pamela hadn't lost all of her spunk. "I'm over that. In fact, I feel free now that I don't have it taking up so much space in my house."

Pamela's eyes narrowed, as she looked Bethany in the eye. When she opened her mouth, Bethany braced herself for another dig.

"I think I'll get some dessert now," Pamela said. She glanced at Bethany's dessert plate that still had some of the remnants of cherry pie and chocolate cake. "Which was better?"

"I'm more of a pie person, so I liked the cherry pie."

Pamela pulled away. "Then I'll get the chocolate cake."

All was right in Bloomfield. Whatever had bugged Pamela when she first came back inside had obviously faded.

Now that almost everyone had finished eating, the conversations grew louder. Lacy ran around with another little girl—her cousin Kelsey—who was staying with Gina and Jeremy for the weekend. Any doubts Bethany might have had about moving back to Bloomfield were now replaced with the joy of family and friends who loved each other in spite of quirks and disagreements.

Naomi's voice startled Bethany. "Having fun?"

Bethany nodded. "This is really nice, and it brings back so many memories."

"Of Charlie?"

"A little." Bethany met her mother's gaze. "But more than anything, of hanging out with friends, eating Mrs. Sprockett out of house and home, and watching the dynamics of so many different but wonderful personalities coming together like this."

"You've always been observant." Naomi chuckled. "Even back in the day when you were a cheerleader, I noticed you standing back quite a bit and watching others. There were times I thought you might even become a writer."

"I'll stick to writing in my journal." She grimaced. "Those people were probably right. I might have been shy."

Naomi shook her head. "I don't even like that word. Shy. What does it really mean?" She paused. "When people say the word, it's usually a negative jab. Why can't people accept that not everyone is a blowhard?" Her gaze darted to Pamela, but it didn't linger. She turned back to Bethany. "I've never seen you cower or be afraid to talk to people, so I definitely wouldn't call you shy."

Bethany started to tell her mother there were times she

inwardly cowered, but Pete appeared and grinned at Naomi. "Now that the commotion has died down, this is quite nice," he remarked. "It reminds me of being a teenager again."

"Why that's exactly what Bethany just said." Naomi took each of them by the arm and pulled them closer together. "So why don't the two of you reminisce, and I'll go see what kind of trouble I can start with someone else?"

Pete and Bethany both laughed as Naomi sauntered toward Pamela. "Your mom's hilarious."

Bethany tilted a look up at Pete. "Even more so when she's with Pamela. You should see them go at it during garden club meetings. Talk about competitive."

"Pamela needs to listen to Naomi's words of wisdom."

Bethany shrugged. "They both get things done in their own ways."

Pete opened his mouth, but before anything came out, Lacy and her cousin plowed right into his backside. He leaned over and tousled their hair. "Whoa there, girls. You need to be more careful indoors." He squatted down to their level. "Why don't we go outside and play?"

Lacy jumped up and down, clapping her hands, and her cousin followed. Gina gave him the thumbs-up, so he took both of them by their hands and guided them toward the back door.

Once the three of them left the kitchen, Gina stepped over to Bethany. "It's so much easier being a parent here than it was back home. We had my mom and dad, but that was about it. Everything was up to Jeremy and me . . ." She grimaced. "But mostly me the last few months with him away at work most of the time."

Bethany nodded. "People here are always up to helping you with your kids, including telling you what to do."

Gina laughed. "Yes, I've noticed, but I really don't mind. Since Lacy's my only child—so far at least—I don't exactly have the experience some of these women have after raising three or four children and all their grandkids."

Bethany wasn't so sure she'd be as agreeable as Gina. "My mom adores Lacy. Having her here has taken quite a bit of pressure off me."

Gina pursed her lips as though trying to hold back something, but she obviously couldn't for long. "Naomi still hopes you'll have more kids."

"Not gonna happen," Bethany replied. "Ashley's in college, and that would be too much of a spread."

Gina smiled but didn't say another word about children. Instead, she pointed to Jeremy. "Look at my husband. He's happier living in Bloomfield than I've ever seen him before. We'd given up hope that we'd ever own a home, and when he lost his job, we even wondered if we'd be able to move out of my parents' place. Thanks to the wonderful people in Bloomfield, all our dreams are finally coming true." She glanced down before looking back up with a demure expression. "We're even talking about making Lacy a big sister."

Bethany glanced at Gina's abdomen. "Soon?"

Gina laughed and touched Bethany's arm. "No, I'm not pregnant yet. I promise you'll know when I am. We'll shout it from the rooftops when it happens."

"Another Bloomfield citizen!" Bethany grinned. "You realize it'll make Pamela ecstatic."

"Oh, trust me, I know. In fact, she's been asking me when we're going to have more kids ever since we signed the lease on Sherry's house. I thought she and Naomi would get into a cat fight over it, until I told Naomi that I really didn't mind." She shrugged. "I'm flattered that anyone would care so much."

That was another difference between Bethany and Gina. Bethany wanted people to back off, while Gina didn't seem to mind people sticking their noses into her business.

Pete entertained the little girls out in the backyard while the adults inside helped clean up. Bethany had a good time chatting with her friends. It made her realize what she had been missing.

The quickly approaching festival weekend had everyone running around town getting ready. Although most events in Bloomfield had a welcoming element, this one centered around bringing in new people. Everyone felt pressured to make sure it happened. Gina had geared up into full-on Pamela mode, while Bethany used her stress to create more buzz.

"You're turning into a human dynamo," Naomi said. "I never saw this coming." She laughed. "Too bad I didn't know you were so high energy, or I would've tapped into it a long time ago."

"This is a one-shot time," Bethany admitted. "I just don't want to let anyone down."

"You get that from me." Naomi chuckled. "People-pleaser— that's what I am."

Bethany tilted her head and gave her mother a "you're kidding" look. "Right."

Naomi pretended to be hurt. "I am. So what do you want me to do next?"

"You have a choice." Bethany held up an envelope. "I've e-mailed this radio spot to all the surrounding towns, but only two said they'd use it. So I figured if I took the scripts there in person, they'd have a harder time ignoring me or turning me down." She reached into the plastic bin on the floor of her foyer. "I also need to distribute more flyers to local merchants, so take your pick. Day trip out of town, or running up and down Main Street."

Naomi's mouth twisted as she looked back and forth between her options. Finally, she reached for the envelope. "I haven't left Bloomfield in a while, so why don't I go see how the rest of the world lives?"

That was exactly what Bethany hoped Naomi would do. Although Bethany was willing to visit the radio stations, it made her uncomfortable asking for something, particularly since

Pamela had changed her mind and didn't want her to spend garden club money.

Bethany smiled. "I have some pots of African violets to hand out."

Naomi's eyes lit up. "Ooh, that'll be even more fun. I love giving presents. In fact, I have some cookies in the freezer I was saving for a special occasion. Can't get any more special than this."

"Then come on. Let's go out to the sunroom, and I'll put the plants in a box for you."

It took them ten minutes to load Naomi's car with enough potted African violets to leave two at each radio station. After Naomi drove away, Bethany surveyed the rest of her promotional materials. She'd hired some teenagers in her neighborhood to post handbills, so she had little left to do. Still, she felt somewhat out of sorts as she realized there was always more she could do.

Pete called. "Need me for anything? Heavy lifting? Moving stuff? Venting?"

Bethany grinned. "I'll probably need you for at least one of those things, but I'm not sure what yet."

"Okay, call when you know. I'll have my phone on me at all times."

After they hung up, she reflected on the differences between Pete and Charlie, who'd been more take-charge but not as accommodating. They had a good Christian marriage, though, and that was what really mattered.

Bethany carried the boxes of flyers to the foyer and transferred the first one to her car. When she got back inside, Ashley called.

"Good news, Mom. I'll be able to come home for the weekend of the festival. Let me know if you need anything."

"Thanks, sweetie. I'm sure I'll have plenty for you to do."

"Oh, and there's one more thing. There's this guy . . . and . . . well . . ." She cleared her throat. "Do you mind if I bring him home with me?"

A strange jolt shot through Bethany. Ashley had dated a few boys back in high school, but Bethany had known all of them and most of the time, she knew their families as well. "That would be fine." As her voice came out, she realized she didn't sound sincere. "I'd love that."

"Are you sure? I don't want to burden you, but he's really sweet, and I already told him about the festival, and he said it sounds like fun, and he'll be really helpful, and . . ."

Bethany laughed. "I'm positive. It'll be nice to meet someone new."

Ashley's tone softened. "Mom, he's really a great guy. His name's Eric."

Bethany realized she'd been so caught up in her own life, she hadn't spoken to Ashley in a while, so she walked into the living room and sat down. "Where did you meet him?"

"The campus chapel. After church one morning, I lingered to pray for you."

"You prayed for me?"

"Yes," Ashley said. "You've been so stressed lately, and I thought you needed prayer more than anyone. Anyway, when I turned around, there he was, looking at me. It was strange, almost as though we knew each other, but I'd never seen him before in my life."

"Was he at the church service?"

"Yes. He normally goes to the community church in town, but his car was in the shop over the weekend, so he walked to the campus service that Sunday."

They chatted about all the things Ashley liked about Eric. Then silence fell between them—a familiar silence that made Bethany's insides twist into a knot.

"What are you not saying?" Bethany asked.

"Mom . . ." Ashley took a deep breath and slowly blew it out. "We're serious. I really love him."

"But you've only known him—"

"Four months, but it's one of those things that feels right."

"Why didn't you say something earlier?"

She heard Ashley take a deep breath, so she braced herself for something she didn't want to hear. "Because I didn't want to make you feel bad after losing Dad. You've been so lonely."

"Is that why you haven't called lately?"

"Yes."

Bethany didn't want to say anything she'd regret later, so she paused to gather her thoughts. "I'm sure this relationship feels right, and I'm not saying you shouldn't see him. It's just that you don't need to lose your head over someone based on feelings you have at such an early stage of your relationship. If he's the right guy for you, he'll still be there when you graduate."

Ashley let out a nervous laugh. "What do you think I'm going to do? It's not like we're running off and eloping or anything."

Relief flooded Bethany. "Then what are you trying to tell me?"

"I just wanted to tell you about him, since he's coming home with me. Can I not do that anymore?"

"Of course you can talk to me." Bethany hoped she hadn't bruised her relationship with Ashley. "And I'm sorry I overreacted."

"No, I'm the one who should apologize since I haven't called you in a while."

Bethany felt the tension fade. "The phone works both ways. Let's make an effort to talk more often."

"Sounds good. Anyway, I gotta run. Eric is picking me up in a few minutes. See you next weekend."

Bethany hung up the phone, feeling as though she'd been hit by a tornado. She and Ashley had always been close and able to talk about anything. Had her loneliness been that obvious?

She squeezed her eyes shut. *Lord, I pray for guidance with my daughter and in my relationship with Pete. I'm obviously missing some things that should have been obvious. Help me to be more discerning about the people in my life.*

Chapter 24

Aunt Mary showed up a half hour early to pick up Bethany on the first official day of the festival. As soon as Bethany opened the door, Aunt Mary darted inside and shivered. "It's so cold out there."

"I hope that doesn't keep people away." Dread filled Bethany. All the hard work she'd put into promotion wouldn't make an ounce of difference if it was too cold to walk around outdoors.

"It's supposed to warm up by noon." Aunt Mary put her arm around Bethany and gave her a squeeze. "Don't worry, though. No one will blame you." She pointed heavenward. "It's all in the Lord's hands. Besides, in the big scheme of life, what does this one itty-bitty festival really matter?"

"I know. It's just that . . ." How could she explain the need to accomplish something she could take credit for without sounding like it was all about her?

"Don't worry, sweetie. I want to take you to breakfast before we get started. That should warm you right up and make you feel better," Aunt Mary said. "So hurry up."

Bethany laughed. "You should have told me you were doing this. I have to finish putting on my makeup, clean the kitchen, and change clothes again."

"Do the makeup, but leave the rest." Aunt Mary waved her hand just like Naomi did to make a point. "Your clothes look just fine, and you can clean the kitchen later. It'll be there when you get back."

Bethany opened her mouth to argue, but when she saw the look of determination on Aunt Mary's face, she decided to go along. Her mother had always said some things weren't worth arguing about, even though Bethany knew her mother would argue any point if she thought she had even a smidge of a chance to get in the last word.

"You've worked so hard promoting the festival," Aunt Mary said. "You deserve a break."

"I don't know if I deserve it, but I do appreciate breakfast."

Aunt Mary pointed to the front of the house. "Whose car is that in your driveway?"

"Ashley's boyfriend's."

Aunt Mary's face lit up. "Ashley's here? With her boyfriend?" She was so excited her voice came out in a squeal.

Bethany nodded and laughed. "They came to support me."

"As they should." Aunt Mary sighed as she clasped her hands beneath her chin. "So how is this guy? Do you like him?"

"He seems nice, but we haven't had much of a chance to talk. They got in late last night. Good thing I moved all the junk out of the third bedroom, or he'd be sleeping on the couch."

Mary nodded. "All the more reason to keep your life clutter free."

Bethany agreed. "I have to admit I really do feel better now. I have more energy than ever."

"Does that mean you'll get out more?" Aunt Mary's eyebrows rose.

"Probably." Bethany glanced at her reflection in the foyer mirror and frowned. "Are you sure this outfit is okay?"

"It's perfect." Aunt Mary gave her another once-over. "Casual but pulled together. Not too fussy."

"You sound like one of the fashion experts on TV."

Aunt Mary chuckled. "I missed my calling. Which would you rather have? Something small from Dunkin' Donuts or a full breakfast from the Pink Geranium?"

Bethany shrugged. "You pick. I don't really care."

"Pink Geranium it is. Since I'm not sure how long I'll be in town, I might as well get my fill of the best breakfast on the planet."

Aunt Mary drove and found a parking place close to the Old Towne Inn. "After we eat, I'll help you finish setting up the booth. Naomi said you volunteered to do that."

Bethany nodded. "That's right. And I'm even working a shift later this afternoon. I'm sort of hoping to see who buys all those collectibles I donated."

"You're not gonna try to talk folks out of buying them, are you?" Aunt Mary asked.

"No, of course not. I'm just curious."

"Does it really matter? After all, if someone is willing to pay the price for them, I'm sure they'll go to a good home. Pamela told us not to sell them cheap." Aunt Mary placed her arm about Bethany as they walked into the Old Towne Inn. "I'm starving."

At the door of the Pink Geranium, Aunt Mary stopped in her tracks. "Well, look at that. The whole gang's here." She gently turned Bethany around to face her. "I wanted to talk to you about something, but I'm not sure we'll have time with all the commotion."

"What do you want to talk about?"

"I really wanted to discuss my plans, but I don't think I'll have much of a chance later. After the festival is over, I'm going back to get things in order so I can move home to Bloomfield."

"For good?"

Aunt Mary smiled. "Yes, I think so."

"That's so exciting!"

"Now that I've had a chance to talk with Andy, I feel much better about moving back here. In an odd sort of way, I'll be picking up where I left off and starting all over at the same time." She gestured toward the dining room. "We're making quite a spectacle of ourselves, so we best go on in. And by the way, you're the first person I've told, so please don't bring it up. I plan to talk to Naomi right before I leave. I don't want her to be tempted to go with me. If she helps, it'll take twice as long."

Bethany nodded as she glanced around and saw most of the active members of the garden club seated at several tables in the Pink Geranium, all of them watching her and Aunt Mary. From the far corner of the dining room, her mom lifted her hand and wiggled her fingers to get their attention. Pamela sat across the table from her.

"Naomi didn't tell me she would be here," Aunt Mary said. "But then she didn't say she wouldn't either. Do you want to join them?"

Bethany glanced at her mom and then turned back to her aunt. "Sure. Did you mention that we might come?"

Aunt Mary nodded as they made their way across the crowded dining room. "I said I was taking you to breakfast, so I'm sure she assumed this would be the place."

"We just ordered a basket of pastries," Pamela said as she lifted her hand for the server. "We need two more coffees."

"I'll take regular tea," Aunt Mary said. "How about you, Bethany?"

"Coffee's fine."

Pamela gave Mary a self-satisfied grin before turning to Bethany. "So are you ready for the big day?"

"As ready as I can be, I guess."

Pamela propped her elbows on the table, folded her hands, and rested her chin on them as she looked at Bethany. "Your mother tells me you're planning to become more active with the garden club. Do you want to run for office?"

Bethany shot her mother a panicked look. Naomi turned

and glared at Pamela. "I told you not to say anything. And don't go putting my daughter to work so fast. Let her get her feet wet first." She cast a sheepish glance in Bethany's direction. "I don't want to scare her away."

Pamela bobbed her head and leaned toward Naomi. "It's not like she hasn't been working her tail off for this festiv—"

Aunt Mary lifted her hands to get their attention. "Ladies, this is not the time or place to get into a debate about what Bethany should or shouldn't do. The garden club has been here longer than any of us, and it'll be here long after we're gone. Bethany can do pretty much whatever she wants, and it won't make all that much difference . . ." She tipped her head toward Pamela. "To anyone." Then she turned to Naomi. "Understand?"

Naomi's eyes widened, and she nodded. Pamela took a little longer, but she finally removed her elbows from the table and glanced down.

Whoa. If Bethany hadn't seen it for herself, she never would have believed anyone could quiet both Naomi and Pamela in a matter of seconds.

With a serene smile on her lips, Aunt Mary turned back to Bethany. "So did you want some fruit or maybe an omelet?"

"An omelet would be good."

Aunt Mary gave the order to the server and leaned back in her seat. "Isn't this nice, all of us here, with a full day of fun ahead?" Sweetness dripped from her voice.

"Very nice," Naomi replied, a gleam in her eye as she looked at her sister. "Great idea to start the festival like this." Then she turned to Pamela. "Too bad some people can't behave."

Pamela scowled. "Are you insinuating—?"

Again, Mary lifted her hands. "What did I say a few minutes ago, ladies? We will behave today, if for no other reason but to appear like a friendly town to all the folks who'll be here for the festival."

"That's right," Naomi said directly to Pamela. "And don't you forget that either."

It took every bit of self-restraint for Bethany not to laugh. When the omelet arrived, Bethany sank her fork into the fluffy yellow exterior and watched as the cheese and vegetables oozed from the center. The aroma of a blend of cheese, onions, and peppers made her mouth water. Perfect as always.

"Mmm." Aunt Mary's eyes glazed over as she took her first bite. "Delish."

Bethany enjoyed everything about her breakfast, but she'd always enjoyed the Pink Geranium where everything was fresh-baked and cooked with love by people she'd known all of her life. Naomi always said the reason everything was wonderful at the Pink Geranium and the Old Towne Inn was that Caroline had found her calling and allowed the Lord to direct her.

"If you do that, you can't go wrong," Naomi told her children. "You won't be any good at anything if you don't pay attention to where the Lord leads you."

Pamela finally finished her breakfast. She stood and dropped her pink napkin on the table. "It was nice having breakfast with you, ladies." Then she looked directly at Bethany. "Now that you've got your house de-cluttered, it's time to work on your wardrobe. I can help you with that." She smiled and nodded toward Aunt Mary. "Nice to see you too, Mary. Have a wonderful day."

Bethany blinked as she watched Pamela leave the Pink Geranium. Aunt Mary remained silent, until Bethany turned and looked at her.

"Do I look that bad?" Bethany asked. "I thought you said—"

Aunt Mary shook her head. "That was totally uncalled for."

"Do you agree with her? Is my wardrobe really horrible?"

"Well . . . not exactly horrible." Aunt Mary tightened her lips and glanced away before finally nodding. "It wouldn't hurt to update it a bit."

"But you told me not to change clothes. In fact, you said I looked fine just as I was."

Aunt Mary gave her an apologetic look. "Your clothes are okay, but you can do so much better, dear. You're a beautiful woman, so I have no idea why you try to hide behind such . . ." She looked Bethany up and down. "Behind such matronly clothes."

"What do you think I should wear?" Bethany's voice cracked.

"Something more stylish, maybe?" She scrunched her face. "I wish Pamela hadn't started this. I want you to have a good time this weekend."

"I will." Bethany leaned back in her chair, still numb from Pamela's comment.

"Maybe we can go shopping again while I'm here, only this time for clothes." Aunt Mary comically wiggled her eyebrows. "Unless you'd rather go with Pamela. I'm sure she can help you pick out some interesting outfits."

An image of fluttery chiffon angel sleeves, high heels with rhinestones, and floppy hats flitted through Bethany's thoughts, and she shuddered. "No thanks."

"And we really don't have to do a major overhaul. Just maybe pick up a few stylish tops and some accessories to freshen things up a bit." Aunt Mary laughed. "Pamela probably has other ideas, like a bunch of sequined tops, maybe a few hats, and . . ." She pointed to her fingernails. "Lots of glitter."

"That's beyond wrong." Bethany made a face.

Aunt Mary laughed. "I think you'd look cute in a turquoise V-neck top with a silver necklace and some hoop earrings. You can wear that with any neutral pants or skirt."

That didn't sound too bad. "Okay. I'll give it a whirl if you'll go with me."

As they got up to leave, Bethany couldn't help but feel self-conscious. When people looked at them, she wondered if they saw her as a dowdy woman who didn't know how to dress. Now that she thought about it, she realized even her mother's wardrobe was more stylish than hers. Yes, it was time to make a few more changes.

By the time they arrived at the garden club booth, a small crowd had formed on the sidewalk on both sides of Main Street, waiting for the parade. It had warmed up enough for some people to shed their scarves and heavy coats. *Thank You, Lord.*

Bethany saw the boxes full of sale items had been delivered as she'd asked, so all she and her aunt needed to do was pull them out and find ways to display them. Fortunately, Aunt Mary knew how to arrange her treasures to show them off. She stacked boxes to create tiers and then covered them with scarves and doilies.

"Wow." Bethany took a step back. "This looks good."

Aunt Mary nodded toward the sound of the marching band moving into position. "Why don't we go watch the parade?"

Bethany nodded and pulled her purse from beneath the table. "I really missed parades after I left Bloomfield."

"I know, and that's too bad. Parades make me feel like a kid again. I'll never forget the time I brought you to your first parade here on Main Street. Your father was on the city council, and our whole family was so proud of him and your mother as they rode in a convertible, waving to the crowd like dignitaries."

Bethany had her own personal flashback of her parents' involvement in Bloomfield events. By the time she'd come along, her dad had been deeply involved in city politics. Between his position and her mother being the president of the Bloomfield Garden Club, they were like royalty ruling over the town. Whatever they wanted they got, so it was a good thing they never did anything without praying first.

"Oh look!" Aunt Mary pointed to something behind Bethany. "Here comes Pete."

Bethany turned and saw Pete walking full-speed toward them, and right behind him were Ashley and Eric. After all that talk about her clothes, she wanted to make herself invisible. She wondered if Ashley was embarrassed by how she dressed. Bethany had never thought about it before.

"This is turning out to be quite the event," Pete said, grinning.

"The mayor can't believe we have so many people visiting for the festival and parade. Did you know all the hotel rooms in town are booked?"

Another reason to be thankful for the weather that continued to warm up. "That's nice." Bethany glanced down at her sneakers and wished she'd thought to buy some newer, more fashionable shoes for the event.

"Bethany?" Pete's voice cracked. "Is everything okay?"

When she glanced up at Pete, she saw the look of concern on his face. Ashley and Eric stood off to the side looking puzzled.

She nodded. "Everything is just fine. I'm glad we have so many people here."

Aunt Mary went over to Ashley. "Introduce me to your young man." Before her niece had a chance to say a word, Aunt Mary extended her hand. "Hi, I'm Mary, Ashley's great-aunt. You must be Eric."

When Bethany looked at her daughter, she didn't see an ounce of embarrassment on her face. Instead, she noticed pride.

Eric shook hands with Aunt Mary and answered one question after another. After the inquisition wound down, he chuckled. "I can see why Ashley loves it here so much."

The look he gave Ashley brought a flush to Bethany's cheeks. These kids were obviously in love. She should have known something was up when Ashley had stopped calling. When Bethany called her, she always had to go. And she hadn't been home since shortly after she'd met Eric. At least Ashley had chosen a guy who didn't shy away from anyone, which was a good thing, because she saw Naomi and Pamela bearing down on them. And he seemed to take his Christian faith seriously.

With her normal flourish, Pamela's smile widened, and she gestured with her long fingernails, now painted a royal purple and tipped in silver. "Didn't your mother do a wonderful job promoting this festival?" she asked Ashley, but before giving her a chance to answer, she turned to Eric. "I'm Pamela Jasper, president of the Bloomfield Garden Club. It's nice to have so many young people interested in moving to our fabulous town. Will you be next?"

Naomi grunted. "Back off, Pamela. Eric is in college, and he didn't say he was moving here."

Pamela tilted her head and gave Naomi a mock glare with her lips pooched out and her eyes comically wide. "But he didn't say he wasn't, did he?"

Eric laughed. "This is a beautiful town, ladies. Maybe after I graduate, I might consider Bloomfield . . . that is, if I can find a job here." He smiled down at Ashley, who grinned back with open adoration.

"No problem," Pamela said. "Just let me know when you're ready, and I'll see what I can do."

Eric smiled at Ashley and winked. She nuzzled closer to his side.

Pete leaned over and whispered, "Isn't young love sweet?"

Bethany paused and nodded. "Yes, very sweet." She glanced over at Pete and suspected he wasn't sure what to say to her with Ashley standing there. Even though Charlie had been gone a while, even Bethany thought Ashley might still harbor thoughts that no one else should be with her.

As the high school band marched closer, Bethany felt tiny prickles of excitement. She'd watched many parades on this very street in her past, but this was the first time she'd been so actively involved in the process of making it happen. The joy from seeing the results of her hard work made her giddy.

"Having fun?" Pete asked. He'd shoved his hands in his pockets, but he remained right beside her.

She nodded. "The parade has barely started, and it's already the best I've ever seen."

Aunt Mary laughed. "That's because you know what goes into making one successful." She shielded her eyes and looked around at the crowd. "Oh, there's Gina and her family."

Bethany looked across the street and made eye contact with Gina, who waved. Lacy sat atop Jeremy's shoulders, clapping to the beat of the drums as the band approached the corner. When they stopped and did a short dance formation on the street in front of her, Lacy's eyes lit up, flooding Bethany with memories of Ashley at that age.

After the band moved on, one of the colorful tissue-stuffed high school floats followed. Bethany stood transfixed, watching more floats, the mayor and his city council riding in convertibles, clowns carrying balloons, and other acts as they made their way past her.

"Wow! I think that's the best parade I've ever seen," Pete said as the final float turned the corner. "And we've had some good ones here in Bloomfield."

Gina ran across the street toward them. "This is so much fun! Bloomfield is the best place in the entire world!"

Pete laughed at Gina's enthusiasm. Living in Bloomfield all of his life, he sometimes wondered if the reason he liked it so much was because he had nothing to compare it to. Gina's enthusiasm confirmed this place truly was a wonderful town.

"I agree," Eric said as he stepped forward, still holding on to Ashley's hand. "I've only been in town since last night, but I can feel something different here. It's really special." He winked at Ashley. "A feeling of being in a Norman Rockwell painting."

Gina's eyes lit up. "Yes! That's totally it. The first time I stepped foot in Bloomfield, I felt as though I'd been transported to a different time and place." She grinned at Eric. "You absolutely have to move here after you finish college. There's no place like it."

Eric chuckled. "There are several factors to consider, but I'll definitely put it high on my list."

Pete noticed Bethany squirming. It had to be difficult to see her only child with a serious love interest, especially since she didn't know much about him. Maybe he could help.

"So, Eric, where are you from?"

"Chicago. We have parades there, but they're nothing like this."

"Chicago, huh?" Pete had been there once, but he didn't know enough to talk about it intelligently. "I've never lived anywhere but Bloomfield. I bet living in the big city is quite a bit different."

Eric nodded. "Really different. My folks used to live in the city, but they moved to the suburbs when I was in elementary school."

"You do go to church, don't you?" Pamela asked.

Pete wished Pamela wouldn't be so aggressive, but Eric handled himself quite well. Eric nodded.

"Yes, ma'am. My family attends a small church close to our neighborhood. At college, I go to a church in town most of the time, but when I can't, I go to the campus chapel." He grinned down at Ashley who held onto his arm. "That's how the Lord brought Ashley and me together."

"That's so sweet." Pamela's beatific smile almost made Pete laugh. "Church is the best place to meet the person you want to spend your life with."

Pete almost choked when she said that. He looked down at Bethany, and he saw she was just as shocked.

"No one's talking about a lifetime commitment, Pamela," Mary said.

Pamela grunted. "Maybe that's the problem with everyone. You're all too afraid to say what's on your mind."

Pete wanted to gag Pamela, until he caught the exchanged glance between Ashley and Eric. Something was going on, and apparently, until now, Pamela had been the only one to see it . . . or at least the only one willing to mention it.

Chapter 25

Gina gestured toward the town square, where throngs of people had begun to gather. "C'mon, everyone. The mayor is about to make a proclamation."

"Daddy, what's a proc-lation?" Lacy asked as Jeremy lowered her to the ground.

"It's a type of announcement."

"Nouncement?" Lacy still looked confused, but she grew quiet.

Bethany noticed that Pete appeared amused. "She's cute, isn't she?"

He nodded. "Yes, very cute."

Before Bethany could say anything else, Naomi tugged on her arm. "Let's go join the mayor on the stage. He wants the committee up there with him. I think he wants to call each of us up to the podium and give us something."

To her surprise, Bethany enjoyed being front and center, and as the mayor handed her a certificate for being an outstanding citizen of Bloomfield, her insides swelled with pride. She scanned the crowd for Pete, and when she finally spotted him, she grinned. He waved and gave her a thumbs-up and a wide grin.

The mayor drew his speech to a close. "And now, ladies and gentlemen, I want to thank the rest of the folks of this beautiful town and welcome all our visitors to Bloomfield. Don't forget to stop off at the visitor's booth by the courthouse before you leave. I'll be there with the rest of the city council, and we'll be happy to answer your questions . . ." He chuckled. "And hug a few babies." He made a shooing gesture. "Now go have yourselves some fun!"

"Hey, Bethany," Sherry hollered after she stepped down off the stage to join Pete. "I have something I'd like for you to take a look at. I'm not sure if you can use it in the booth, so I want your opinion."

"Sure, I'll be right there." She gave Pete an apologetic look. "Looks like I'll be super busy all day."

"That's fine. I think I'll go help out with one of the pony rides." He sounded disappointed.

"Maybe we can have dinner later."

Pete shook his head. "I heard the mayor has something special in mind for the committee before the folk band plays."

Bethany had forgotten all about the folk group. Gina tried her best to contract Peter, Paul, and Mary, but the group was booked throughout the rest of the season. The folk tour wasn't playing anywhere near Bloomfield, but she'd managed to find a regional group that had a decent following.

She went over to see what Sherry wanted. After Sherry thanked her, Bethany enjoyed the sense of pride, knowing her opinion was valued. Yes, she was definitely experiencing a change, and it felt wonderful.

In the past when she was a child and later when she visited, Bethany had walked up and down Main Street, stopping off at booths, perusing shelves of handcrafted items, and munching on hotdogs and bear claws. But today, she was so busy working the garden club booth, helping Gina, and answering questions, she didn't have time for anything else. And she loved every single minute of it.

Bethany's mom approached her midway through her final shift for the day at the booth. "Looks like all your hard work paid off. Thanks to your promotion, we have more people visiting than ever. I'm so proud of you I could pop."

"Thanks, Nao—" Bethany caught herself. "Thanks, Mom. I learned most of what I know from you."

"That's utter nonsense." Naomi tried to pretend she wasn't flattered, but the flush in her cheeks showed otherwise. "I have to admit I'm surprised we had such a good turnout. Nothing against anything you did, but we have so many festivals, you would think folks would get sick of them."

"Are you sick of them?" Bethany challenged.

"No, but don't tell Pamela. I actually enjoy a good festival." Naomi chuckled. "It makes me feel young again."

"You act younger than most people half your age," Bethany said.

Naomi chuckled, but a serious look quickly crossed her face. "So what do you think of Ashley's young man?"

"He seems nice." Bethany darted her gaze away.

"But?" Naomi took hold of Bethany's shoulders and turned her around to face her. "What's wrong?"

Bethany shrugged. "I like him, and you know how much I adore Ashley, but I feel sort of . . . well . . ."

"Left out?" Naomi asked.

"Yes, I guess you can say that. Why didn't I know about Eric before the phone call?"

Naomi laughed. "Maybe because at this place in her life, telling you everything isn't as important as the experience itself."

"Did I do that to you?"

Naomi's chest rose and fell as she pondered the question. "Not like this, because you never moved out until you and

Charlie got married. But I still felt as though you pushed me away sometime during your late teen years."

"I'm so sorry. I had no idea."

"No need to apologize, sweetie. It happens. It's normal. I'm sure I did it too. Now try to enjoy the rest of the festival and stop worrying about your relationship with Ashley, because it's as wonderful as ever. She loves you, or she wouldn't have brought her guy home to meet you."

"Good point." Bethany nodded. "I am having a great time."

"And you do realize that vacation you've been talking about taking with Ashley might not happen, right?"

Bethany frowned. "I don't think—"

"Good." Naomi grinned. "Do yourself a favor, and keep on not thinking. You've had so many excuses to put what you really want on hold for so long, you don't know what to do, so you think."

"Huh?" Bethany looked at her mother who'd resorted to talking in circles.

Naomi tilted her head back and laughed. "You know exactly what I'm talking about." Her expression grew more serious. "Didn't know getting involved would be this much fun, did you?"

"No, but I do now, and I intend to get out even more after the festival."

Naomi grinned. "Good girl. I'll see you a little later at the mayor's dinner."

"Oh, where is that?"

"Inside City Hall. He's having it catered by the Pink Geranium." Naomi wiggled her eyebrows. "After all the fuss he made about having too many festivals, we're surprised he's springing for the whole thing out of his own pocket. Pamela told me he likes to kick up an argument to make us think he's doing us a big favor. I'm starting to think she may be right about way more than I realized."

Bethany had the sense not to openly agree with her mother.

Instead, she chose to change the subject. "I'm so relieved we had good weather."

"Yup. I looked up the weather on the Internet, and it looks like we might have some light flurries next week."

"Hey, Bethany! I need your help!" Bethany glanced up and spotted Gina across the street, waving her arms. "Do you have a minute?"

"Go on and give her a hand," Naomi said. "We can talk later."

Bethany took off to help Gina settle a dispute between two different vendors who'd claimed the same space. Then another disaster beckoned, and they were off to deal with that. Nothing was critical, but solving even the minutest problems gave Bethany a stronger sense of belonging and being needed.

"This is so amazing," Gina said when they finally had a moment to catch their breath. "I have never felt so much a part of anything in my life. It's like . . ." She looked around and turned back to Bethany with her arms out. "I finally belong."

"I feel the same way."

Gina tilted her head and gave her a curious look. "Seriously? You're from here. How can you say that?"

Bethany shrugged. "I know, but until now, I always felt like I was on the outside looking in."

Gina opened her mouth, but the mayor approached and said some of the city council members wanted to talk to them. They agreed to chat more later.

The dinner with the mayor and city council solidified something Bethany already knew—that the town relied on all the hard work of the Bloomfield Garden Club. In spite of the few sputterings about too many festivals, everyone seemed happy with the turnout.

By the end of the day, Bethany was exhausted, but in a good way. She looked around for Pete, but he'd obviously gone on home. That was fine, though. She needed to get some rest. Tomorrow morning, she had church, and then the festival would be back in full swing at noon. She'd promised to help out at the booth until closing, and if it went anything like the first day, Gina would need her.

On Sunday morning, Pete spotted Bethany as soon as he walked into the church, but she was busy chatting with a group of garden club members, and he didn't want to interrupt. Ever since getting involved with the festival committee, she'd been busier than he'd ever seen her. And happier too.

The quiet Bethany Hanahan had blossomed into a smiley, bubbly version of her old self, and as difficult as it was for Pete to watch from afar at times, it brought him great joy to see her thrive like this. Her sadness after Charlie passed broke his heart. Now he faced a conundrum he didn't know how to handle. Since she obviously enjoyed hanging out and staying busy with her garden club pals, should he keep his distance and not interfere? Or should he try to join in and risk getting in the way or annoying her?

Pete had headed toward the opposite side of the church when he heard his name. An out-of-breath Naomi approached him. "Where do you think you're going, young man?"

"Over there." He pointed to a half-empty pew.

"Oh, no ya don't." She grabbed him by the arm and pulled him toward Bethany. "I don't want you sitting all by yourself when you can sit with Bethany."

"But she'll probably want to sit with her friends."

"Nope. She wants to sit with you."

"Did she say—?"

Naomi silenced him with one of her head-tilted glares. "I've known my daughter since before she was born, and I know what she wants before she does." She gave him a gentle push in Bethany's direction. "So go on and sit with her."

Pete hesitated until Pamela joined them. "You heard the woman." She wiggled her fingers toward Bethany. "Go on before it's too late."

Naomi cackled. "Too late for what?"

Pamela scowled at Naomi. "Church is going to start soon, and if he stands around waiting much longer, he'll have to sit in the back."

Naomi leaned and looked at the people who'd crowded around them. "Pete, I'm not trying to tell you what to do, unlike some people I know." She darted a quick glance at Pamela. "But if you want to sit with my daughter, go on. Or if you'd rather, you can sit with me." She laughed. "Now that could set some tongues to waggin', couldn't it?"

Pamela grunted and took off toward Andy who'd just walked in. Suddenly, Pete took Naomi by the hand and pulled her toward Bethany. "We'll both go sit with her."

Naomi grinned. "Atta boy. I like seeing this take-charge side of you."

Chapter 26

Since most people at church planned to attend the festival afterward, the pastor kept his sermon short. Immediately after the benediction, he lifted a piece of paper from the podium.

"Pamela Jasper has informed me the garden club booth is selling out fast, so if you want any of the collectibles or handmade items, you need to act soon. If you want some of the jams and jellies that have already sold out, you can place your order at the Pink Geranium." He folded the paper, put it in his pocket, and added, "And I'll be happy to see anyone who wants to stop by the church booth. We'll be handing out CDs, DVDs, and information about our programs for children, youth, and adults."

Bethany glanced at Pete who'd surprised her and sat down right before the service started. Her mother, no doubt, had pushed him. She liked the fact that he'd joined her, but she wished he'd taken the initiative on his own. As things were, she wondered how much of his attention came from his own desire to be with her and how much was the result of not knowing how to say no to Naomi.

"I really need to run," Bethany said. "There is so much to do, and I don't want to neglect my responsibility."

A sly smile curved the corner of Naomi's lips as they all stood to leave. "Pete, why don't you go help Bethany at the garden club booth?"

"I'm sure he has better things to do," Bethany said.

"I really don't mind helping." Pete shoved his hands deep into his pockets and glanced back and forth between Bethany and Naomi. "That is, if you want me there."

"Of course she wants you there." Naomi scooted out into the main aisle and waved over her shoulder as she turned and scurried off.

"I am so sorry," Bethany said. "My mother knows what she wants, and she forgets to ask if that's okay with everyone else, whether they're involved or not."

Pete's expression momentarily flipped to dismay before he caught himself. "She's a sweet woman. I'm sure she doesn't mean any harm."

"Of course not. You really don't have to help. We have everything under control." Bethany wanted him to argue with her, but his hesitation said more than words ever could.

He slowly shook his head as he took a step back. "Maybe I better let you go work the booth with your pals. I think I'll see if the pastor needs me to help hand out literature at the church booth. I'm pretty sure he can use the extra hands."

Bethany's heart sank as she nodded. "You're probably right. See you around later. Stop by if things get slow."

She stood transfixed to one spot as she watched Pete wander out the side door of the church. Memories of the fun she'd had yesterday faded a bit.

"Why'd you go and do that?" Pamela's voice startled her.

Bethany spun around. "Do what?"

"Let him get away." Pamela gave some semblance of a smile, but it quickly faded as she shook her head. "Why is it you young people are so afraid to go after what you want? After all you've been through, I would think you'd grab hold of the reins and make sure you jumped on your own personal path to happiness."

Somehow, that made sense to Bethany, but she didn't have an answer. "Pete said he wants to help the pastor."

Pamela rolled her eyes. "No, he doesn't. He just told you that, hoping you'd argue with him and beg him to be with you."

"Beg him?"

Pamela snorted. "You're still young, but you're not a school-girl, Bethany. You know how guys think."

Bethany frowned. "I'm afraid I don't."

"Well then, let me teach you. I would have thought Naomi would have done that by now." She planted her hand in the middle of Bethany's back and guided her toward the door. "I'll go to the garden club booth with you and hang out for a few minutes, but at some point, you'll have to do this on your own."

"Where's Andy?"

"I told him to run along and hang out with some of his fire-man buddies."

"Did he leave Murray at home?"

Pamela made a face. "Yes, and that means he can't stick around long. I have a feeling he'll want me to take turns bird-sitting, but that's not something you need to worry about."

As they walked down Main Street, Pamela lectured Bethany on the inner workings of a man's brain. "They want to feel needed, but they will not go where they don't think they're wanted."

Now Bethany was confused. "I told him he could go with me."

Pamela shook her head. "I was listening, and that wasn't exactly how it went. You acted like you really didn't care what he did."

"But the pastor needs his—"

"No, he doesn't. The pastor is perfectly capable of getting his own crew to hand stuff out. In fact, look over there." Pamela pointed her bright red fingernail toward the church booth on the corner, where Pete and several other men from the church stood around talking. "They already have too many people working there, and they don't have anything to do but talk to each other."

"Oh." Bethany slowed her pace. "So maybe if he comes by later, I can let him know I want him to stay."

"You can do that," Pamela said, "or you can go over there right now and tell him you really need him."

"Now?" Bethany's insides churned at the thought of approaching him in front of so many people. What if he said no, or worse went along with her but didn't want to?

Pamela looked at the church booth, tapped one of her fingernails on her chin, and made a face. "I suppose that could be rather awkward for a shy girl. Maybe you shouldn't."

Bethany didn't like the idea of getting rejected in front of an audience, but she absolutely hated being called shy, especially now that she was coming back out of her shell. "Okay, I'll do it. What's the worst that can happen, right?"

"Exactly." Pamela smiled. "Now go break a leg."

Bethany shoved her damp hands into her coat pockets and walked straight toward the church booth. Pete's back was to her, but Jeremy nodded and said something that caused him to turn around. The smile on Pete's face completely rocked her world and made everything else around them invisible.

"Pete, I would really like for you to help me . . . I mean, I really need you to help out at the garden club booth . . ." She cleared her throat that had tightened with nerves. "That is, if the pastor doesn't mind."

His eyes crinkled as he grinned. "I'm sure he doesn't mind. Let me tell them where I'm going, and I'll be right there."

She nodded, turned, and scurried back to where Pamela stood watching and grinning. "There now, that wasn't so bad, was it?"

Bethany shook her head. "Now I need to go to the booth and find something for him to do so I won't look like a liar."

"Whatever are you talking about?"

"I said I needed him to help me."

Pamela nodded. "No problem. Bailey is supposed to work with you, but I have another job for her. We don't want anyone to work alone, so that solves your problem."

There was nothing Bethany could do now but go to her duty station at the garden club booth in the community center. As she walked past covered booths, she thought about how Pamela and her mother always managed to show up in time to make things happen the way they wanted. She wondered if she'd ever be like that, and then she shuddered. For Ashley's sake, she'd work hard not to be.

Claude and Howard had put away their game table, but they hovered over the spot where they spent most of their days. As soon as they saw her, they smiled and waved. Claude whispered something to Howard before walking over to her.

"Need any help?" he asked.

"You've been pretty wonderful, but I don't need you today. I have all the help—" She noticed his attention diverted to something behind her, so she stopped talking and turned around in time to see Pete heading in their direction.

"I take it he's the help you're talking about?" Claude chuckled and wiggled his eyebrows. "Do I sense romance in the air?"

Bethany's cheeks heated up. "Thanks for the offer."

"No problem." Claude waved to Pete and returned to his spot by Howard. He whispered something to his friend, and they both looked at her and laughed. Bethany's cheeks flamed even hotter.

Pete followed Bethany's lead and helped her uncover the tables and rearrange items to fill in the empty spots. Every now and then their hands touched. Pete wanted nothing more than to pull her into an embrace and let her know how good they could be together. But he wasn't sure she was ready, and he didn't want an audience.

As the crowd grew, Bethany's smile widened. Her obvious joy delighted his heart. He knew being part of something bigger than herself was exactly what she needed. Too bad he hadn't been the one to show her.

All afternoon, they stayed busy replacing items from the boxes beneath the table. "Where did all this stuff come from?"

She tilted her head and gave him a sweet, puppy-dog look. "More than half from my house."

Pete gave her what he hoped was a sympathetic look. He'd forgotten to look at the clock, so he didn't realize they were nearing the end of the festival until Howard approached them and said, "How much do you want for everything you've got left?"

Bethany walked over to Pete's side. "Everything?"

Howard nodded. "Yeah, I'd like my wife to pick out a few things she likes, and then I can take the rest of them down to the V.F.W. hall for their rummage sale this spring. Last time I asked my wife to give me some of her useless things to donate, she just about took my head off." He shrugged. "So I reckon bringing her something nice from here will be like a peace offering."

"Peace and love . . . *squawk* . . . peace and love."

Everyone turned toward the sound of Murray by the door. Howard groaned. "Oh, no, not that bird again."

"Oh no . . . *squawk*! It's that bird again."

Pete leaned toward Bethany. "I sure hope Andy stays with him this time. I'd hate for Murray to get loose right now. There's so many people here we might never catch him."

"Don't you worry," Andy bellowed from twenty feet away. "I put a twist tie on the cage door. It'll take Murray a long time to figure it out."

"What's wrong with a lock that he'll never figure out?" Howard asked. "I don't wanna hear how sensitive Murray is. He's a bird, not a kid."

Andy widened his eyes and lifted his finger to his lips in a shushing gesture. "Don't tell him that."

"Murray wants candy . . . *squawk* . . . Murray wants candy."

Pete groaned and whispered, "I'm surprised Pamela puts up with that noise."

"I know." Bethany smiled up at him. "Me too. And speaking of Pamela, look who's coming this way."

Pete glanced up and spotted Pamela strutting directly toward the table, looking around in confusion. "Where is everything?"

"We sold most of it," Bethany replied.

Howard jumped in. "And the rest of it is mine, as soon as someone tells me how much I owe so I can pay and get outta here."

"Three hundred dollars," Pamela said without batting her false eyelashes. "Still want it?"

Howard frowned. "That's a tad more than I expected."

Pamela shrugged and turned her back on him. "We'll get more than that if we keep the booth open another hour, so take it or leave it."

Howard dug his hand in his pockets and pulled out the rattiest looking wallet Pete had ever seen. "Okay, Miss Pamela. Three hundred dollars it is. You drive a hard bargain."

"It's a very good deal, and you know it." She stuck her hand out.

He shrugged. "I reckon you're right. It'll make the missus happy, and that's priceless."

"You bet it is." Pamela glanced over her shoulder at Bethany, winked, and turned back to Howard. "If you want to claim what's left, you'll need to pay now. There's quite a crowd still working their way in this direction."

Howard chuckled and extracted three one-hundred dollar bills. "Here ya go. Now maybe Bethany and her nice fella wouldn't mind helping me pack this stuff up in those boxes over there. I'll get Claude to help me load it in the minivan my wife insisted we get to haul the grandkids around when they visit." He snorted. "We only see 'em once a year, so I might as well get some use outta that bus."

Pete watched Pamela's earbobs bounce as she flitted from one person to the next in the community center while Andy stood next to the birdcage he'd propped on the chair by the door. If he'd been Andy, he probably wouldn't have taken such a chance being that close to where Murray could escape for good. Given the parrot's history, it could happen.

Bethany couldn't remember a time when she'd been so exhausted. Strange thing about it, though, she didn't realize how much her feet hurt until she got home and sat down.

She flopped back on the couch and wished she'd taken a rain check on dinner with Pete. At least they were going to Bert's Barbecue and not The Fancy Schmantzy. She wouldn't have to dress up.

After resting for a half hour, she managed to pull herself up off the couch and head for her bathroom to get ready. By the time she combed her hair and reapplied her lipstick, the doorbell rang.

She opened the door to Pete's grinning face. Just the sight of him energized her.

"Ready?" he asked.

She raised her palms. "As ready as I can be after such a long afternoon. Aren't you exhausted?"

He slowly nodded. "I have to admit, I am. I'm not used to talking to so many customers."

"Me neither. I worked a little bit of retail during the holidays when Ashley was little, and that just about did me in, but in a way, today was worse."

Pete looked at her but didn't say anything. Even after he

helped her into his truck and got in on the other side, he remained silent.

She sighed. "Part of my exhaustion is emotional. Watching people walk away with things I've had in my house for so long took a lot out of me."

"I can imagine."

"I know Naomi and Pamela think it was the best thing to do, but I'm not so sure Charlie's mom would appreciate it."

Pete reached for her hand and squeezed it. "Belva was a smart and kind woman. I'm sure she'd be happy to see you happy."

"That's true." Bethany leaned her head back and closed her eyes. "I promised Gina I'd help her with the wrap-up tomorrow, and then Sherry has asked me to help her with her wedding plans. This promises to be a busy week for me."

She glanced at Pete, who didn't comment. However, she could tell something bothered him.

"Are you okay?" she asked.

He nodded. "Oh, yeah. I'm just fine and dandy."

Chapter 27

The next few weeks were a whirlwind for Bethany. Between getting together with friends and garden club meetings, she had little time to relax. To her continued surprise, she found her involvement invigorating, even though it was exhausting.

"Having fun?" Naomi asked after the garden club meeting.

Bethany nodded. "Yes, very much. In fact, I think I might be catching the gardening bug."

"Good girl."

"I might even try to resurrect my mother-in-law's gardens."

"Just remember, you don't have to do it all at once. Start with one small garden, and after you're comfortable with managing that, enlarge it. Once you have that one like you want it, move on to the next."

Bethany agreed. "I thought I'd start with a few flowers on either side of the front sidewalk."

"Petunias will look mighty pretty there. They're easy to grow, and they come in a variety of colors."

"I like petunias, but I also think some vinca would be pretty."

Naomi shrugged. "Then do petunias and vinca. They're both pretty hardy, and they look nice together."

If someone had told Bethany a few years ago she'd be talking about gardening, she would have thought they'd lost their minds.

Gina had said the same thing—that once she moved to Bloomfield and started attending garden club meetings, she suddenly had the itch to plant some flowers. Her small flower bed had grown into a massive explosion of color that took over practically her entire front yard. She'd even gotten Lacy involved by having her plant some things in pots on the porch. Gina called her daughter the future president of the Bloomfield Garden Club. Pamela and Naomi gave Lacy so much attention, there was no doubt in Bethany's mind Gina was right.

"Did you hear a single word I just said?" Naomi had her hands on her hips as she stood in front of Bethany, scowling.

"Um, was it about planting both vinca and petunias?"

Naomi snorted. "Naw. I asked you when you last saw Pete."

"Oh." Bethany's cheeks flamed. "I haven't seen him much since the festival."

"And why not?"

Bethany shrugged. "I've been too busy."

"Then forget about planting flowers. You need to work on cultivating your relationships first. The flowers can be planted any time."

"But—"

"No *buts*, young lady." Naomi shook her finger at Bethany. "You need to decide whether you like Pete or you don't, because if you don't, there are plenty of women who will."

Bethany gasped. She'd never even thought about that. "I do like him. It's just that . . . well . . ."

"You're afraid, right?"

"Sort of."

"Either you are or you're not. There's no in between." Naomi took a step back. "Make up your mind quickly, or you just might completely miss out on the opportunity."

"If he's that fragile, I'm not interested." Had she just said that?

"Well!" Naomi took a step back, clearly stunned. "I guess you just told me."

Bethany sighed. As much as she hated to admit it, she meant it. She liked Pete quite a bit, but she wasn't willing to risk what they had by pushing too hard.

Pamela approached them. "Have you two had enough mother-daughter time? I don't want to interrupt anything."

Naomi snorted. "Since when?"

Instead of her usual retort, Pamela turned to Bethany and smiled. "How would you like to chair the yard-of-the-month committee?"

"Oh, don't do that to her," Naomi said. "My daughter needs to make friends, not enemies."

"Whatever are you saying, Naomi? Who says that job involves making enemies?"

"You know good and well how competitive people around this town are. If the award goes to Andy again, Winnie will get mad. And if Winnie gets it, Sylvia won't speak to her."

"Did I hear someone say my name?" Winnie asked.

Pamela nodded. "If Andy or Sylvia wins yard-of-the-month, will that make you mad?"

"No, of course not. I'll be happy for either of them."

"See?" Pamela said sweetly as she looked at Bethany.

Winnie laughed. "But I'll know if that happens that someone got the yards mixed up. Anyone would have to be blind not to see that my yard is prettier than either of those."

"See?" Naomi said in a mocking tone. "What did I say?"

Pamela scowled. "Oh, stop it, Naomi."

Bethany wanted to do more for the garden club, but she wasn't sure being in charge of such a controversial committee was the place to start. "Can you give me another job?"

"Yeah, like I said, don't stick her with something that'll win enemies right off the bat," Naomi said.

Pamela made a face at Naomi but quickly switched to a smile when she looked back at Bethany. "Sure, sweetie. Give me a few days, and I'll come up with something."

"Give her something good," Naomi ordered. "Like maybe the chairperson of the bake sale."

"I don't know." Pamela showed off her black-and-white striped fingernails as she tapped her chin. "We had problems with it last time, and besides, Helen's always been in charge of the bake sale."

"That's right," Helen piped up from behind. "I have been, and I'm ready to move on to something else. Just because I have a bakery doesn't mean I need to run that stup . . . I mean the annual bake sale."

Pamela lifted her arms and let them slap her sides as she lowered them. "Okay then, it's settled. Bethany, you're in charge of the bake sale. Helen, you're the chairperson of the yard-of-the-month award."

"I'm already the cochairman, along with Elsie," Helen reminded her. "At least for the time being."

"Okay, so you are. You get to keep your job." Pamela walked away, mumbling. "It's been a long day. I'm going home now."

Once Bethany was alone with her mother, she relaxed. "The first thing I need to do is get acclimated with the dynamics of the group."

Naomi grinned. "All you need to know is that if you want something, you have to make Pamela think it's her idea."

"Is that what you do?" Bethany asked.

"Afraid so. I tried to fight it when she first got elected president, but I don't have time for pointless battles I can't win, no matter how much energy I put into them. So I've learned the fine art of finessing my whims to make them hers."

The fact that Bethany was still learning from her mother

wasn't lost on her, but one thing bugged her. "Do you ever feel as though you're being deceptive?"

"No, I would never do anything I thought was deceptive. In fact, I think making Pamela happy is an honorable thing."

Bethany narrowed her eyes as she held her mother's gaze. "But the two of you still argue quite a bit."

Naomi chuckled. "Of course we do. She'd be suspicious if I didn't put up a good fight every now and then. That's how I keep the peace. I let the steam out in small puffs rather than let it explode all at once."

The following Saturday evening, Pete stopped off at his parents' house to check on them. His mom had supper waiting for him when he arrived.

"Smells good," he said as he bent over and kissed her on the cheek. "But I don't want you to think you have to cook for me every time I come over."

"You'll know something's wrong if I don't," she said with a smile. "C'mon, let's dig in. Your dad's starving."

"He didn't have to wait for me."

"Oh, yes, he did." She gestured toward the dining room. "It wouldn't be polite to start before our guest of honor arrived."

When Pete walked into the dining room, he saw his dad sitting at the head of the table, staring at the big baked chicken on the platter in front of him. His dad glanced up, grunted, and reached for the knife.

"Before you carve the chicken, let Pete say the blessing," his mother said.

Pete didn't look at his dad before bowing his head. No point keeping his dad waiting too much longer.

For the first few minutes, their conversation centered on food and the plumbing business. "Our end-of-year profit looks good,"

Pete said with pride. "Even after the new hires, we have more to invest back into the business."

His dad placed his fork on the plate, steepled his fingers, and took a deep breath. He glanced over at Pete's mom. "Should I tell him now?"

"Tell me what?"

"I wish you hadn't done that, Frank." His mom nodded. "But now that you've opened your mouth, you don't exactly have a choice."

Pete's dad took a deep breath, slowly let it out, and blurted, "I'm thinking about starting another business."

"Another business?" Pete frowned. "But why?"

His mom looked worried. "I told you it might not be a good idea to bring that up tonight, Frank."

"I don't see why now's not just as good a time as any to let our son know what I've wanted to do all my life."

"It's not—" she began before Pete held up his hands.

"Dad, I would like to know all about it."

His dad gave his mom a cursory glance before turning back to Pete. "As you know, I've always had a passion for trains. Last time your mother and I went on vacation, we stumbled upon this really cool model train shop. I felt like a kid again."

His mother nodded. "It took forever to pull him out of there."

"It was a store?" Pete asked. "As in a place where they sell model trains?"

"Yes, that's what's so cool about it. They sell everything related to trains—train cars, tracks, tunnels, magazines, remote controls . . . everything."

Pete had always known of his dad's passion. The only presents he'd ever gotten excited about were train related. And he'd subscribed to a model train hobby magazine for as long as Pete could remember.

"How profitable can a niche business like that be in such a small town?" Pete asked.

"Very. Train enthusiasts will travel a long way to see something new." His dad leaned back in his chair, cut a glance at his mom, and finally settled his gaze on Pete. "It'll be good for business all over Bloomfield. But there is one caveat."

"I wish you wouldn't discuss this now," his mother pleaded.

Pete frowned at her. "Please, Mom. I'd like to hear what Dad has to say."

His dad leaned forward and looked Pete in the eye. "I'll need some startup capital, and the only place I know to get that is from the plumbing business."

Pete's spirits fell. Sprockett Family Plumbing was doing extremely well, and they finally had enough money to replace their fleet of trucks. However, if his dad's business turned into a money drain, all the plumbing in the world wouldn't be able to plug it.

"Frank, maybe we should consider talking to someone at the bank."

Pete couldn't let his dad go outside the family when they had the capital he needed. "No, Mom, what Dad wants to do makes more sense. We have the money, and it's all in the family."

"But what if—?"

"No matter what, this is something Dad obviously wants, so I think we should find a way to make it happen." Pete's chest tightened, but he knew what he was saying was important to his dad.

When Pete turned back to face his dad, he saw more respect than he'd ever seen before. "Thank you, son. I think you'll be pleased once I get started."

Pete softly sighed. He'd planned to give his crew the good news they were getting new trucks soon. Now that would obviously have to wait.

"Why don't I come to your office on Monday, and we can discuss some of the details?" Before Pete could reply, his dad added, "And perhaps you can give me some advice on the business side.

I don't think it's any big secret that you're the businessman in the family."

"Frank . . ." Pete's mom looked at his dad with love. "I'm sure you're a fine businessman."

"I refuse to continue trying to fool anyone into thinking I am." Pete's dad turned toward him. "And you of all people could probably see right through to the fact that I hated the plumbing business."

Pete wasn't about to participate in this conversation. So he just sat there and listened.

His dad's expression intensified as he leaned forward. "But I'm passionate about trains. I figure the business angle can be learned, and between you and Abercrombie, I'll learn how to run a train shop."

"Abercrombie?" Pete asked.

"Yes, that's the name of the guy who owns that train shop I was telling you about. He said he'd give me all the information I need to get started, as long as I don't compete in his area. Apparently, there's a brotherhood among train shop owners, and they like to help each other out by sharing business info and referring folks to each other. They even have an advertising co-op."

Pete had to admit his dad's enthusiasm might carry him in the business. "It sounds like an interesting venture."

"I'd like to include you, son—that is, if you're interested. I can't think of anything more fun than a father and son running a train business together."

Pete didn't know where he'd find the time to participate, but with his dad so excited like this, he wasn't about to turn him down. He nodded. "It does sound like fun. I'll do what I can."

His dad leaned back and grinned. "This has to go down as one of the best days of my life." He grinned at Pete's mom. "See? I told you there was nothing to worry about."

Chapter 28

"Have you talked to Pete lately?" Naomi asked as she and Bethany walked toward the back of the church. "I saw him come in here, but he darted out so fast, I couldn't catch up with him."

"No, I haven't had much time to chat with him since the festival." Bethany had wondered if she'd said something to make him mad, but she wasn't about to tell her mother for fear Naomi would try to fix things that might not be broken.

Naomi looked worried. "Maybe one of us should call to make sure he's okay."

"I'm not calling him," Bethany said.

Naomi reached for her cell phone and turned it on. "Then I will."

"No, don't." Those words tumbled from Bethany's mouth before she could catch herself. "I mean, we don't need to bother him if he's busy."

"That's ridiculous. If he's too busy to talk to us, he's too busy." Naomi set her jaw in her take-no-prisoners way, letting Bethany know it was pointless to argue.

"Do what you think is right," Bethany said, "but I've got a bunch of garden club business to deal with right now, and—"

Naomi held up her hands to stop her. "Say no more. I understand."

"You do?"

"Yes, of course. I was there once." Naomi snickered. "I remember being president of the Bloomfield Garden Club. It was the third most important thing in my life—after faith and family, of course." She smiled. "I loved every minute of it, which is why I'm glad you're getting so involved. It made me feel useful. Important."

"So you're saying it wasn't important—?"

"No, of course not," Naomi interrupted. "In fact, it was very important. The garden club serves a big need in this town. If it weren't for us, our city council would have no idea what to do next. In case you haven't noticed, they lean quite heavily on our expertise in most matters." She made a face and laughed. "Including getting elected."

"So what are you saying?" Bethany asked.

Naomi grinned in silence for a few seconds. "Never mind. You go on about your garden club business and let me deal with Pete."

Bethany sighed. She was happy to work on garden club business. It was her mother's dealing with Pete that had her worried. No telling what that involved.

Over the next few days, Bethany worked on the upcoming bake sale, securing commitments from each garden club member. She was surprised that so many people had to be persuaded to contribute.

"Last time I brought two cakes to the sale, and neither of them sold," Lydia-Sue, a woman who rarely came to the meetings, admitted. "When I found out the reason, I said never again. Pamela put a seventy-five dollar price tag on one and sixty on the other.

I told her not to do that, but she claimed people would pay more since some of the money went to the children's unit at the hospital."

Bethany had to admit that was steep, even though the money was for a good cause. "What if I promise not to do that?"

"How much would you charge?"

Bethany shrugged. "I don't know. I guess that would be up to you."

Lydia-Sue grew quiet before finally clearing her throat. "I reckon I can support the cause one more time. After all, since you're new, I should give you a chance. If you promise to leave the price as I have it, I'll donate, but only one cake—at least until you prove yourself."

"That's fine." Bethany was happy for anything at this point. "I just appreciate anything you can do."

Another woman had the same reaction. "I wound up picking up all six dozen cookies I brought. They were good, but even I wouldn't pay the price Pamela put on them."

"If I let you price them, would you reconsider?" Bethany asked.

It took a little more arm-twisting to get an affirmative answer this time, but she managed to get a commitment of two-dozen cookies. Almost everyone who didn't regularly attend garden club meetings repeated this scenario. Those who did attend actually came to her with what they planned to bring, but with the same stipulation—that Pamela wasn't involved in the pricing.

The following Saturday, Pamela called Bethany. "So how are you coming along with the bake sale? Got anyone willing to donate anything after last year's fiasco?"

"Um . . . yes. Everyone I asked has agreed to donate something."

"You're kidding." Pamela's sounded shocked. "I'm surprised since we didn't even sell a quarter of what we had last year. People were furious when they had to bring everything home after all the trouble they went to, and every last one of them threatened to never contribute again. To be honest with you, I thought we might even have to cancel this year's sale. You must be a better salesperson than I realized." She paused. "What did you say to get them to participate?"

"I just told everyone they could put whatever price they wanted on it."

Pamela groaned. "That's a huge mistake. They have no idea what home baked treats are worth. You'll wind up doing a lot of work for very little."

"I don't mind." Bethany smiled. "In fact, I've really enjoyed working on the bake sale."

"Good. Just make sure you come up with a detailed report for the meeting. I like to have everything in the minutes."

After Bethany hung up, she sank down on the couch and thought about how difficult and demanding Pamela could be. Now that she saw things from the inside, she was surprised Naomi and Pamela ever worked together and got things done. Her mind drifted back to all the events that had transpired since she'd arrived back in Bloomfield. Too bad it had taken her this long to finally hit her stride in the community. At least she'd finally gotten involved.

She smiled as she thought about what she'd accomplished. Not only had the festival booth sales hit an all-time high, she heard rumors that several out-of-towners had spent some time looking at houses in town. And to top it off, her house was practically clutter-free.

♡ ♡

"Why don't you call Bethany and see if she'd like you to pick her up for church in the morning?" Pete's mother said. "I'm sure she'd love your company."

Pete shrugged. "I don't want to bug her too much. She's been busy lately and all . . ." He glanced up at her, smiled, and lowered his head. "The garden club really has her hopping."

His mother took a step in his direction and leaned toward him until he looked her in the eye. "The garden club is only a small part of her life. She needs more."

"Looks to me like her life is pretty full at the moment."

She shook her head. "I don't know what to do about you, Pete. It's almost as though you really don't want to be happy."

"What are you talking about? I'm very happy." He forced a smile and pointed to his lips. "See?"

"Right." She laughed. "So make me happy now and call Bethany."

Pete shook his head. "You sure do know how to turn things around."

"It's all that practice from having to outsmart you when you were a teenager." She gestured toward the kitchen. "Why don't you go on in there and call her? I'll stay out here and give you some privacy."

He whipped out his cell phone. "I'm only doing this for you."

"Good boy." She grinned. "Now go on into the kitchen. I'll make sure no one bothers you."

Pete chuckled as he made his way back to the kitchen. There wasn't anyone else in the house to bother him, unless Dad came home. But Pete doubted that would happen since his dad was out looking at space to rent for his new train shop. He was glad his dad finally had something to work on besides his mother's nerves.

He pressed Bethany's speed dial number and started preparing a message to leave. But she picked up in the middle of the first ring.

"Hey, I wondered if you needed a ride to church in the morning." The instant those words came out, Pete cringed. *Be smooth, man.* Like Charlie used to be.

"Sounds great!" Her voice lilted just like it did years ago. "I have so much to tell you. It'll be fun to catch up."

"Yeah . . . um . . ." Her response was so quick he didn't know what to say. "It will be. Maybe we can go somewhere afterward."

"Funny you should say that. Mom called me right before you did. She wanted to know if you and I would like to join her for lunch."

He rubbed the back of his neck. "I don't want to intrude."

"Don't be silly. I've intruded on your mom enough. Besides, Mom is the one who invited you, so you really won't be intruding."

Pete laughed. "If you're sure she doesn't mind."

"I'm positive. See you in the morning."

He hadn't even disconnected the call when his mother entered the kitchen grinning from ear to ear. "So did she say yes?"

He narrowed his gaze. "Did you and Naomi get together on this?"

She glanced away quickly. "Why don't you set the table so we can eat as soon as your dad gets home."

As Pete pulled three dishes down from the shelf and placed them on the table, he thought about how little he'd seen of Bethany lately and wondered if there ever would be a chance for the two of them to have a romantic relationship. She'd been so busy with her gardening club friends and enjoying her new zest for Bloomfield, he figured she didn't have room in her life for him. That bugged him to no end, but he didn't want their mothers forcing things. He wanted Bethany, but not if she didn't want him back. There was no getting around the fact that Charlie was the love of her life.

As soon as that thought hit Pete's mind, he nearly dropped the spoon he was holding. He still felt the competition from Charlie—long after Charlie had passed. Back in high school, Charlie was the one who made things happen, while Pete stood back and watched, admiring his friend for having so much spunk. By now, Pete realized the only reason he hadn't settled down with a woman was because Charlie had the only one he'd ever wanted. Now she was available, and the only thing holding him back was the memory of Charlie.

Chapter 29

Pamela stared down at Andy's bird. "Oh, for crying out loud. He's a bird. Don't worry about him so much."

Andy stood at the door and picked up Murray's cage. "So if you don't want to help me out, I reckon I'll just take my bird and go home."

"Stop it, Andy. I didn't say I wouldn't help. Come in and bring the bird with you."

Andy pouted. "Not if you're going to be mean to him."

Pamela rolled her eyes and shook her head. "Since when have I ever been mean to Murray? I'm always nice to him." She leaned over and looked the parrot in the eye. "Isn't that right, Murray?"

Murray stepped side-to-side, not looking back at Pamela.

"He's mad," Andy said. "He's been giving me the cold shoulder all morning."

"Did you give him some . . ." Pamela slowed down to clearly enunciate, ". . . candy?"

Andy set the cage on the table. "Did you hear that, Murray? Pamela asked if I gave you some candy."

Murray completely turned his back on them and faced the wall. No *Murray wants candy* or squawking.

Pamela took a step away and shook her head as she continued looking at the cage. "Yeah, I'm afraid there's definitely something wrong with him if he doesn't want candy."

"I think I might have offended him." Andy stuck his finger inside the cage, but Murray moved away. "He doesn't even want to nuzzle."

"That is bad." Pamela couldn't remember a time when Murray didn't lean his neck into Andy's finger. "I wonder what happened."

Andy shrugged. "He was fine this morning when we first got off duty at the fire hall. In fact, he chatted all the way home. I brought him inside, set him on the kitchen table, and made myself some breakfast."

"That sounds perfectly normal. Did you feed him then?"

"He ate some birdseed and an apple slice." Andy shook his head and blew out a breath. "I called the vet, but the office is closed until Monday. I don't think this is an emergency because he's eating."

"Yeah, I don't think a moody bird constitutes an emergency, and it doesn't sound like he's sick."

Andy and Pamela both leaned over and studied Murray. Finally, Pamela straightened up and took a step back. "Why don't I fix us some supper, and maybe we can come up with a solution."

"What're we having?" Andy lifted the birdcage off the table and placed it on the floor beside his chair.

"Stir fry." She pulled some vegetables from the crisper in the refrigerator. "Mind if I cut up some carrots for Murray?" She offered a sympathetic smile. "Just in case he drops the mood?"

Andy shrugged. "Sure, that's fine. Just not too much."

Pamela handed Andy a small bowl filled with sliced carrots and a celery stick. As she cooked, they chatted, and Murray didn't interrupt them—not even once.

As soon as she plated the food, she sat down next to Andy. He said the blessing, and they started eating immediately afterward. Murray hadn't touched any of the vegetables in his cage.

"Maybe he *is* sick." Pamela looked at Murray with concern. As annoying as his squawking was, she really did care about the little fella. "Murray, are you not feeling well?"

He let out a faint squawk and buried his head beneath his wing.

"Maybe he's depressed," Pamela said. "Has anything changed in his life?"

"Nope. In fact, he had a great time at the fire hall. It was Smitty's birthday, and he even joined in singing 'Happy Birthday.' All the guys thought it was funny that Murray can carry a tune better than I can."

"What else happened?"

"Nothing. We did the usual. Gag gifts, lots of jokes." Andy paused. "And then we ate cake."

Murray shuddered, hopped down off his perch, and stood on the floor of his cage—something Pamela had rarely seen him do. She looked up at Andy. "That all sounds normal, but as soon as you said cake, something happened." Murray shuddered again. "There's something about the word . . ." Pamela lifted her hand to shield her face from Murray and whispered, "Cake."

Andy frowned. "Let me go make a quick call." He headed toward the door to the hallway but stopped and turned around. "Mind if I leave you and Murray alone for a few minutes?"

"Don't be silly." Pamela waved him away. "We'll be just fine. Won't we, Murray? In fact, we might even have a party while you're gone."

The instant she said that, Murray hopped right back up on his perch and started dancing around and squawking. "Party like it's your birthday . . . *squawk!* Party down, boys."

Andy rushed back to Murray's cage. "What did you say?"

"He said, 'Party like it's your birthday.'"

"I know what he said." Andy looked back and forth between Pamela and Murray. "I've never heard him say that."

"Party like it's your birthday . . . *squawk!*"

Andy snapped his fingers. "Okay, that does it. I'm definitely calling Smitty. I need to find out what's going on."

Pamela nodded. "We'll wait right here for you, okay, Murray?"

Murray turned his back again and lowered his head. As Andy left the room, Pamela tried to think of what could make Murray act this way, but nothing made sense. Finally, after about five minutes, Andy returned.

"Well, I think I know what happened. Apparently, Smitty got such a kick out of making Murray talk, he rewarded him with chocolate."

Alarms went off in Pamela's head. "Isn't chocolate poisonous to animals?"

Andy nodded. "It is if they get too much, but the small amount Smitty fed him will only make him sick."

Pamela looked at Murray. "Are you sure? I mean, shouldn't we have his stomach pumped or something?"

"No. We just need to give him some time for it to go through his system."

"No more treats for you, Murray," Pamela said. "At least no cake."

"Murray wants candy . . . *squawk!*" His voice came out weak this time, and after his squawk, he shuddered.

"I hope he's okay," Pamela said. Why would anyone feed chocolate cake to a bird?

"He'll be fine." Andy shook his head. "According to Smitty, he only had a few bites. If I'd known that's what happened, I would never have brought him over here and worried you."

Pamela sighed with relief. "I'm glad you brought him."

"You are?" Andy's gaze gave her a tingle from the top of her head to the tips of her toes.

She nodded. "Yes. I really care about Murray's well-being.

I mean, he's just a bird, but there's definitely something special about him." Her mouth went dry as he watched her. "In fact, I'm wondering if it might be a good idea to call the emergency number for the vet right now . . . you know, just in case."

Andy laughed. "He'll be fine in a day or two." He looked at the bird. "Right, Murray?"

Murray didn't reply and continued to hang his head.

Pamela let out a sigh of relief. "I'm just glad it's nothing serious."

Andy closed the distance between them, tucked the tips of his fingers beneath her chin, and tilted her head up to face him. "You really do care, don't you?"

She nodded. "Yes, I do. Probably too much." The look Andy gave her caught her breath. Maybe one of these days they'd both be ready for marriage. In the meantime, she'd enjoy moments like this.

"Thank you." Andy gave her a feather-light kiss on the lips and looked back down into Murray's cage. "As for you, too bad you have a tummy ache, but that's what you get for being such a party animal."

"Party hearty . . . *squawk*!"

Chapter 30

Bethany settled into the pew with Pete on one side and her mother on the other. When she and Pete first walked in, he made a beeline for Naomi, who did her best to shoo them away. But Pete said he liked sitting there, so she finally relented.

As the pastor preached, Bethany stole an occasional glance at Pete, who remained steadfastly riveted to the sermon. She liked the feeling of being in church with Pete. The combination of romantic flutters and mutual respect let her know what they had was special.

Occasionally, Pete glanced down at her and smiled, warming her from the top of her head to the tips of her toes. During the hymns, her mom sang slightly off-key, which would have thrown Bethany off on the melody if Pete hadn't been such a strong tenor.

Naomi occasionally leaned forward, turned, and grinned as her gaze met Bethany's. After the service ended, her mom told them to take their time getting to her place since she still had to warm up the food.

"What would you like to do?" Pete asked once he and Bethany were alone.

"Would you mind driving around so I can look at gardens? I'm trying to decide what I want to plant in front of the house."

"I'll be happy to." Pete fell into step beside her as though they'd been together forever.

Pete drove, while Bethany jotted some notes on a pad she always kept in her purse. "I've always loved marigolds," she said. "They're so cheerful."

"Then why don't you plant them?"

She tapped her pen on her chin. "I probably will, but I'd like some contrasting color to go with them."

"Ya know, Bethany, the garden club is always looking for a new project. Why don't you ask them if they can help you?"

"That's a great idea." She noticed the pleased expression that flashed across his face. "I just might do that, but I still want to pick out everything."

Pete chuckled. "You might want to select your own group then. Otherwise, Pamela will take over."

"Or my mom." Bethany tapped the pencil on her notebook as she thought about who could help with her garden. "Gina has done such a terrific job, and we get along really well . . ."

"And I'm sure Sherry would enjoy helping," he added.

"Maybe Bailey too. She seems to be gardening more, and I don't think she'll be bossy." Bethany spotted another cluster of flowers in the yard of a garden club member. "There are so many different options of flowers and color combinations, but I'm starting to get a picture of how I want my first garden."

"I hope you know you can count on me to help."

"Yes, and I appreciate it."

"How about that?" he asked, pointing to a cluster of grape hyacinth around a mailbox.

"It's pretty, but I was thinking about petunias." She laughed.

"Actually, Mom and I talked about petunias and vinca, and I think that might be nice."

As they chatted about gardens, Bethany marveled at how comfortable she felt with Pete. Although she'd always enjoyed doing things with Charlie, he never would have discussed flowers, or even driven her around looking at them for that matter. He was more practical, so he would have brought up the cost of fuel.

"We don't have to keep driving around," Bethany said. "I don't want to use up all your gas."

He shrugged. "I hardly ever go anywhere during personal time, so I really don't mind." As he pulled up to a stop sign, he smiled at her. "Besides, I enjoy being with you and seeing you so cheerful."

Bethany sighed. For the first time in years, she really was happy. When Charlie got sick, and after he died, she felt as though her world had caved in on her. Since she moved back to Bloomfield, she now realized the clutter kept her in that dark, unhappy place.

"I really am happy right now—probably the happiest I've been since before Charlie got sick." She grinned at Pete. "And one of the reasons is I'm having such a good time with you."

His face lit up. "Really?"

She nodded. "Yes, really."

"I'd like to think I might have something to do with that."

"You definitely do." The sight of a burst of color across the street caught her eye. She pointed. "Hey, look at that garden. I wonder if I could do something so lavish."

He turned, looked at the asymmetrically shaped flower bed, and shrugged. "I don't see why not. It's just large clusters of flowers grouped together by color."

"Can you pull up closer so I can take a picture with my cell phone and jot down some notes?"

Pete maneuvered the car closer to the property with the flowers. Between the two of them, they managed to identify all but one type. "Since this is city property, I bet someone from the Bloomfield Garden Club will know what kind of flowers those are."

Bethany slapped her forehead. "Silly me. Mom will definitely know. In fact, I wouldn't be surprised if she planted them herself." She glanced at the clock on the dashboard. "I think we've given her enough time to heat up the food. Let's go on to her place now."

"Why don't you give her a call and tell her we're on our way?"

Naomi opened the door to her apartment before they had a chance to knock. "What took you so long?"

Bethany chuckled. "You said you needed time, so we drove around looking at flowers. Do you know what those purplish ones are over by the playground near City Hall?"

Her mom's forehead crinkled as she thought about it. "If you'd asked about the flowers near that playground by the Village, I could tell you, but Pamela led the group at the other playground. Let me give her a call, and I can find out."

Before Bethany had a chance to tell her she could wait, Naomi had her phone in hand and the number punched out. Pete winked as they listened to Naomi say "uh-huh" and "uh-uh" a few times. Finally, she hung up. "Those are ageratum. Easy to grow and very hardy." She cleared her throat. "Pamela said she isn't gonna be able to make the garden club meeting tomorrow night. She tried to call Sherry, but she couldn't get a hold of her. Do you know where she is?"

"I didn't see her at church," Bethany said. "I wonder if she's out of town."

Pete nodded. "She and Brad went to visit some old friends, and I don't think they'll be back for a few days."

"Oh, dear." Naomi shook her head. "Sherry's vice-president,

and she's supposed to lead the meetings when Pamela's not present. I won't be able to make the meeting, because I promised to watch Lacy so Gina can go. Jeremy's out of town." Naomi's frown deepened. "I have no idea who we can get to lead it. How about you, Bethany?"

"Me?" Bethany let out a nervous laugh. "I've only been to a few garden club meetings, so I don't think—"

Her mother waved around her hand. "Don't worry about thinking. You don't have to think. All you do is follow the agenda that I'm sure Pamela has already made."

Pete placed his hand on Bethany's shoulder. "I think you'll do an excellent job."

"Thanks." Bethany appreciated their votes of confidence, but this would be a huge leap for her. "Why can't Pamela be there?"

"She said Andy's bird is sick, and he has to work." Naomi stared at Bethany for a moment, not bothering to hide her amusement. "That bird. Before you leave, I'll call Pamela and ask if she has the agenda done. You can pick it up on your way home. That'll give you some time to look it over. If you have any questions, just call me, and I'll do my best to give you some pointers."

"Maybe you better ask Pamela if it's okay to do this."

"Oh, I'm sure it is. She said she wanted to groom you and Gina to be the next leaders of the Bloomfield Garden Club."

"Gina would—"

Naomi held up a hand. "Before you volunteer Gina, we've already got her lined up to lead the next meeting. I'd really like for you to do this . . . just this once." She paused and gave Bethany a pleading look. "For me."

Bethany glanced at Pete, who drew a little closer to her side, showing his support. "Okay, I'll do it."

Naomi pumped a fist. "Good girl. I knew you'd come through for me."

"But under one condition. You tell me everything I need to know."

"Yes, of course. That goes without saying." Naomi stepped toward the kitchen. "I have some enchiladas in the oven. You two have a seat, and I'll bring out the pan."

Bethany and Pete sat at the dining room table that had already been set for three. Good. At least there wouldn't be any surprise guests.

As soon as they were alone in the dining room, Pete looked her in the eye. "Don't worry. You'll do just fine."

She forced the old doubts to the back of her mind and nodded. "I'll do my best."

The look in his eye let her know he had much more than mutual respect for her. If they hadn't been in her mother's apartment, she suspected they'd be having a completely different type of conversation. More personal. Maybe even romantic. She rubbed her arms to tame the goose bumps.

A few minutes later, her mom joined them, placed the pan on the trivets in the center of the table, reached for Pete and Bethany's hands, and bowed her head. "Thank You, Jesus, for bringing my little girl and her guy here to eat with me on the Lord's Day. Bless this food as we enjoy each other's company. I pray You'll scoop up Bethany into your arms and carry her through the garden club meeting tomorrow night. Show her just how smart she really is." She paused and cleared her throat. "'Cause she certainly doesn't believe me when I tell her. Amen."

After Bethany said "Amen," she glanced over at Pete and saw he was trying hard to hide a smile. She had to look away to keep from laughing.

Naomi's eyes darted back and forth between Pete and Bethany and smiled. "You two are so cute together." She shoved a forkful of food into her mouth and slowly chewed.

Bethany had no idea what to say, so she followed her mother and took a bite. When Pete cleared his throat, she gave him her attention.

"Naomi, I'm happy you invited me over, but I'm not so sure Bethany likes it when you call me her guy."

Naomi put down her fork, propped her elbows up on the table, and leaned toward Bethany. "Only she can tell us that. How about it, Bethany? Do you like it when I call Pete your guy?"

"Nao-um . . . Mom, why are you doing this?"

"It's time somebody did. If folks left things up to you, nothing would ever happen." Naomi gave Pete an apologetic smile. "No offense, but this goes for you too. The two of you have known each other practically all your lives, so it's not like you have all that much to learn about each other."

"But—" Bethany began.

Naomi held up a finger. "I'm not finished. I've watched both of you when you didn't think anyone else was looking, and I can tell there's something special going on between you two. So why don't you just get past whatever issues you have and call yourselves a couple?"

"I . . . um . . ." Bethany looked at Pete and then back at her mother. He didn't speak up right away, so she thought maybe her intuition had failed her. She had to say something to let him off the hook. "I have so much to do, I'm not sure I have time."

"Same here," Pete said as he fidgeted with his napkin, looking as nervous as Bethany felt. "I mean, Bethany and I like each other and all, but I'm busy with my family business, and my dad needs my help getting started in his new venture."

Naomi glared through squinted eyes and groaned. "Don't let time get away from you."

Bethany forced a laugh. "I'm just doing what you've always wanted me to do. First I got rid of the clutter, and now I have an active social life with the garden club."

"True, that's what I wanted, but not at the expense of something even more important."

"There are only so many hours in the day." Bethany lifted her fork. "These enchiladas are excellent. What did you put in them besides chicken, sauce, and cheese?"

"Spinach and pureed carrots."

♡ ♡

So Pete's suspicion was correct. Bethany preferred her new social life to spending time with him. As much as he cared for her and wanted her to be happy, he had to admit he was disappointed. By now, he'd hoped they'd be more than just pals. But he didn't want to make her feel bad, so he went along with her. He'd deal with his own feelings later.

Naomi pushed her plate toward the center of the table and leaned back. "So tell us about your dad's new venture. I hear he was looking for business space on Main Street."

Fortunately, Pete's dad hadn't sworn him to secrecy. "He's always loved trains, and he found a really cool store that sells everything related to model trains."

Naomi nodded appreciatively. "I always say people should follow their passion. When do you think he'll be ready to open the doors?"

"He's narrowing down the locations to two, and then he wants me to help him decide." Pete didn't verbalize the real reason—that he had a much better business mind than his dad.

"Smart man, since it'll probably wind up being yours someday."

Pete shrugged. "I'm not all that much into trains. I actually like the plumbing business."

Naomi tilted her head toward Bethany. "It's always nice to have a plumber around when you need one."

"Mom." Bethany tried to give her mother a warning look, but Naomi wouldn't look her in the eye.

Instead, she tapped her chin with her index finger. "Say, Bethany, didn't you mention something about an old train set of Charlie's you found up in your attic?"

"Yes, it's still there."

Naomi grinned. "Why don't you get it down and give it to Frank for his new shop?"

"I don't think—" Pete looked at Bethany and then turned back to Naomi. "I don't think we should sell it since it belonged to Charlie."

"I'm not saying sell it," Naomi said. "Use it as a display. I bet your dad would appreciate that."

Pete looked at Bethany, but he didn't say anything. He was afraid to.

Bethany shrugged. "Sure, that's fine."

"I'll talk to Dad about it." Pete gave Bethany a questioning glance, but she didn't say a word. He wished he knew what she was thinking.

The rest of the time at Naomi's place was strained. Bethany gradually withdrew into her shell, while Naomi cast questioning glances at both of them. No doubt when the two of them were alone, Naomi would give Bethany the third degree. He wished he could do something to help, but he couldn't think of what that could be.

They engaged in more forced conversation, until Bethany finally said she needed to go home. "I'm having some of the garden club members over tomorrow for lunch."

Naomi squinted. "We're having a meeting at your place?"

Bethany slowly shook her head. "Not a meeting. Just a few people—Gina, Sherry, and Bailey are coming over."

"Oh, okay." Naomi nodded her understanding. "You young members want to get together to figure out a way to overthrow the old regime."

For the first time since they'd been there, Pete saw Bethany crack a smile. "Yes, that's totally it. Sorry you had to find out this way."

Naomi clicked her tongue and cackled. "Whatever it takes to make you happy, sweetie. You know I'd do anything for you, even if it means being kicked to the curb."

Bethany looked at Pete and rolled her eyes before hugging her mom. "I'd never kick you to the curb, and you know that. It's just that Gina thought it would be fun for the four of us to hang out more."

Naomi nodded. "I agree. You know I was just funnin' ya. I know you adore me and would never turn your back on your old mama."

Chapter 31

Pete's dad rubbed his chin. "Yes, I absolutely do remember that train set. I helped his dad pick it out. Charlie couldn't wait to show it to us." He chuckled. "Remember when he came running into our house without knocking that Christmas morning?"

"Now that you mention it, I do remember."

His dad chuckled. "When he realized he'd forgotten to bring the train, he burst into tears. Your mother was so worried something terrible had happened. She called his parents, and they told her they'd be right over with the train."

"Bethany found it in her attic, and she's offering to let you borrow it for your shop."

His dad's eyes bulged. "You're kidding. Does she realize what that thing's worth?"

Pete shrugged. "I think so, but that doesn't seem to matter to her."

"Was it her idea or yours?"

"Neither." Pete cleared his throat. "Naomi suggested it, and Bethany agreed. It's just sitting in her attic gathering dust, so if you want to use it, I say go for it."

"Sounds good. Now I have something to discuss with you." He gestured toward a chair in the empty space that would soon be his train hobby shop. "Sit down, son."

Pete obeyed, and his dad pulled up a folding chair and sat facing him. "Is something wrong?"

"Not with me, but there does seem to be a problem with you."

Pete tilted his head. "What are you talking about? Everything's fine with me." He thought for a few seconds. "If you're concerned about the business—"

"I'm not worried about that. It's in good hands now that you're there." His dad leaned forward with his elbows on his knees, buried his face in his hands, and let out a deep breath before finally straightening up and looking Pete in the eye. "But that's also part of the problem. I see how responsible you've become, but I also realize you've sorely neglected your personal life."

"My personal life is just fine."

"Is it?" His dad raised his eyebrows and stared at him. "I don't think so. You've been so involved in making sure the family plumbing business thrives you haven't taken the time to develop a relationship with a woman."

Pete shrugged. "I'm afraid it's too late for that." No point in mentioning Bethany since that was a hopeless cause.

"Oh, but I disagree. I take full responsibility for that not happening yet, so I've decided to help rectify the situation. Your mother and I have known for years how you've measured every woman you've dated against Bethany."

Pete started to deny it, but he knew his father could see right through him. His dad wasn't a good businessman, but his intuition in personal matters was always on the mark. "There wasn't anything I could do about that, was there?" He let out a nervous laugh. "I never wanted to settle for anything less than the best."

"And you don't have to." His dad stood, placed his hands on his hips, and looked down at Pete. "She's single again, so what's stopping you?"

"She's busy?"

His dad laughed. "I probably shouldn't tell you this, but your mother and Naomi have asked me to have a man-to-man chat with you about women. They think you've held back for so long you don't even know when the love bug has bitten."

"Love bug?" Pete joined his dad's laughter. "That sounds like Mom and Naomi."

"Maybe so, but I agree with them. It's pretty obvious to everyone you and Bethany have deep feelings for each other." He chuckled. "Even I've seen the scorching looks the two of you exchange."

Pete felt his face grow hot. "What am I supposed to do? She's so busy now with the garden club and her friends she doesn't have time for me."

"That's what you need to learn about women. If they have a void in their lives, they fill it with other things."

"Charlie's death sure did leave a void," Pete agreed. "And with Ashley gone, I'm sure she's pretty lonely."

"And that's where you come in. Let her know that not only are you there for her, you'd like her to be there for you."

"Isn't that selfish?" Pete asked.

His dad gave him a goofy grin and waved his arms around. "No, that's what you have wrong. Most women like to feel needed. If she thinks you're only there to console her about Charlie and Ashley, she'll go where she feels like she can do some good. But if she feels like she can help you, well . . ." His grin widened. "You'll both have what you want."

Pete frowned. "I don't know. It's not something I—"

"You're right. It's not something you'd normally do, but that's all the more reason for you to step up and do what's right. Your mother and I are fine. The business is fine. Stop worrying about everything and concentrate on your personal life. You've done such a good job with the plumbing company, it can run all by itself for a few months. Once you get your romantic life in order, you can find a balance."

Pete cleared his throat and stood. "I'll have to put some thought into this. It's not easy to change the way I do things."

"You'll do just fine. What's the worst that can happen?"

Pete grimaced. "She may never speak to me again."

"Trust me, she'll speak to you. I'm not saying it won't be awkward, but over time, both of you will be glad you spoke your mind." His dad gestured around the room. "So what do you think? Did I pick the best spot for a train shop or what?"

"It's perfect." Pete pointed. "And I think Charlie's train set should go right over there on that ledge."

"Good thinking, son. That's exactly where it'll go."

Bethany had only been up for an hour when she heard her doorbell. When she opened it, she saw her mother standing there, a big basket in her hand, and an expectant look on her face. "Mind if I come in?"

"Sure." After she closed the door behind her mother, she glanced down at the basket. "Whatcha got?"

"Food. Let me go put this in the kitchen." Naomi scurried off but stopped in her tracks. "Don't go anywhere. I'll be right back."

"Okay." Bethany wondered what her mother was up to now. "I'll be in the living room."

After Naomi left, Bethany walked toward the large picture window and looked outside. The bright sunshine cast a cheerful glow on the morning dew, bringing a glistening shine to her yard. She sighed. Naomi bearing food meant one of three things: a bribe, an apology, or a mother-daughter talk.

Naomi returned a moment later and pointed to the chair in Bethany's living room. "It's time for us to have a mother-daughter talk."

Bingo. "Haven't we had enough of those since I've been back?"

"Apparently not." Naomi put a fist on her hip and rolled her eyes. "So it's time for another one, like it or not."

"But—"

"Stop. Before you say another word, I want to let you know I love you with all my heart. In fact, I've always loved all my kids. That's why your father and I got so involved in the community. We wanted to make it a better place for our kids and grandkids." Her voice dropped as she added, "Too bad all of you moved away before you had a chance to enjoy it." Then her voice boomed. "But you're back, and I'm not about to let something as important as your future happiness slip away."

"What are you talking about?" Bethany said. "I'm happy."

"Not happy enough."

Bethany tilted her head and gave her mother a "you're kidding" look. "How happy am I supposed to be?"

"It's not a matter of *how* happy. It's more of *what kind* of happy."

"Now you're talking in riddles." Bethany smiled. "Want to explain?"

"Don't mind if I do." Naomi plopped down on the sofa and turned toward Bethany. "You and Pete are missing the boat. Everyone sees how you two look at each other. What's holding you back from loving him, girl?"

"I appreciate your concern, but I've told you over and over that Pete and I are just good friends."

"That's not all you are," her mother said. "There's a spark. Don't tell me you don't know about it because I'm sure you do."

"Well . . ." Bethany opened her hands. "Okay, so there's a spark. But he's a confirmed bachelor and very busy with his business."

"So that's why you're too busy for him. It's a crazy, vicious cycle fueled by silly pride." Naomi contorted her mouth. "I get it.

But you can't let that stop you. Lots of guys are confirmed bachelors, but that's only because they don't know what they want. It's up to us women to show them."

Bethany laughed. It was so like her mother to think she knew what everyone wanted.

"So here's what we do." Naomi spent the next half hour telling Bethany how to ramp up the relationship with Pete. She started to interject, but her mom shushed her every time. Finally, she just sat back and listened. And the amazing thing was she actually agreed with almost everything her mother said. By now she knew she and Pete both felt something, and it probably was time to see what it was or where it could go.

She only had one concern. "What if I'm assuming something that isn't there and ruin our friendship?"

Naomi rolled her eyes. "If your friendship can't withstand a simple misunderstanding, I'd say it's not much of one."

Bethany thought about it and nodded. "Good point."

Pete couldn't get his dad's words out of his mind. True, he did feel the burden of success for the family business, and he carried it around from the moment he first stepped foot behind the management desk. Not only did his parents rely on the profit, so did most of the plumbers in Bloomfield. Because of his diligence and determination, he'd been successful, so everyone involved with the business had a good life. He'd never thought about backing down a bit and testing how strong the business was, but he suspected his dad was right. It could run itself for a while—at least long enough to get his personal life in order.

He hadn't even tried to kid himself about loving Bethany, but it would be a risk to actively pursue her. After her marriage to someone like Charlie, how could he ever measure up? What if he made his move and Bethany rejected him? Would he ever be able to face her again? Maybe, but it would be a while. Then his dad's words popped into his head. *Over time, both of you will be glad you spoke your mind.* Maybe there was some truth in that.

He decided to take the chance and tell Bethany how he felt about her. Even if she laughed, at least it would be out in the open, and he could quit wishing things could be different. Before he lost his nerve, he pulled out his cell phone and called Bethany. She'd been so busy lately, he fully expected to leave a message, so he was surprised when she answered.

"Mind if I stop by a little later?" he asked.

"Um . . . that's fine."

"If it's not a good day, I understand—" Pete stopped himself, took a deep breath, and started over. "Good. How about after dinner?"

"Do you have plans for dinner?" she asked. "If not, why don't we eat together?"

His call totally wasn't going how he expected. "Okay. What time?"

"Will you be able to come over at six thirty?" Was that his imagination, or did she sound as nervous as he felt?

"Six thirty is perfect. I'll have time to go home and wash up first. See you then."

After he got off the phone, he leaned back in his chair and smiled. His nerves sat awfully close to the top of his skin, but at least he had taken action. Finally.

Bethany scurried around her house, straightening up for company. It wasn't like Pete hadn't seen the house in much worse condition, but she wanted it to look extra spiffy for him when she dropped the bomb and let him know how she felt. She didn't want him to look around and have to worry about escaping the mess. The very thought of that sent her mind reeling in another direction. What if he freaked out when she admitted her feelings?

After she vacuumed the carpet and dusted all the now clutter-free surfaces, she showered and changed into something a little softer . . . a little more feminine. Her flowing palazzo pants and gauzy peasant top were a little different for her, but Aunt Mary assured her it brought out her girly side. She finger-combed her hair, added some large hoop earrings, and stood back to see the overall effect. All she needed now was a smidge of mascara and some tinted lip gloss, and she'd be ready for Pete. She'd already made the salad, and the casserole would be ready at seven.

The big question now was whether Bethany should confess her feelings before or after dinner. She practiced a couple of times in front of the mirror and finally decided it would be best to wait until after dinner, but before the dessert her mother had dropped off right after she found out Pete was coming over.

She paced for the last few minutes until the doorbell finally rang. One last run of the fingers through her hair, and she went straight for the door, opened it, and motioned for Pete to come in.

"Can we talk first?" he asked. "Unless dinner is already ready, that is."

"No, if you really want to talk now, that's fine. Dinner won't be ready for a while."

His obvious nervousness made her uneasy as they went into the living room and sat down in adjacent chairs. He smiled, fidgeted, and finally blurted, "Bethany, I'm tired of the way things are between us."

"What?" Her heart sank.

"That didn't come out right." He gave her a sheepish look as he stood, walked over next to her, and knelt. "I've always liked you." He cleared his throat. "Quite a bit in fact. And I'd like to . . . um . . ." He looked away and then turned and met her gaze. "The fact is I'm in love with you and have been for a long time. I know saying this is dangerous and might even make you want to tell me to get lost, but I've kept it inside for so long."

Bethany couldn't believe what she was hearing. She reached over, placed her hand behind his head, pulled his face to hers, and kissed him right smack on the lips. He looked stunned.

"Okay," she said as she leaned back, feeling smug. "So what were you saying?"

He took her by the hands and pulled her to her feet. "I like what you were saying much better. Come here, you."

This time, he put his arms around her and slowly lowered his face to hers, feathering her face with kisses, and finally settling on her lips. When he finally pulled away, he smiled down at her.

She sighed. "That was nice. Do it again."

He laughed. "So all this time I've been worried for no reason?"

"If you were worried about what I'd do if you kissed me, I'm afraid so. I've wanted to do that for ages."

"Ages?" He pretended to frown.

"Well, at least several months." Then she remembered the biggest obstacle. "And I have to admit I'm worried about getting my heart broken since you've been so open about not wanting a relationship."

He grimaced. "Yes, I suppose I did say that once or twice."

"You've said it as long as I can remember. Anyway, I understand if you need space, but it sure does feel nice to kiss you."

"So you're saying you'd like to be involved . . . I mean . . . be my girlfriend?" He leaned back and laughed. "This sounds so juvenile, but I have to admit, I feel like a teenager."

She giggled. "If it makes you feel any better, I feel like a teenager too, and I've been married before, and I have a grown daughter." She took a step back but never broke their gaze. "I don't want you to feel like you can't have your space, but I sure did enjoy that kiss."

"Space is overrated." He grinned as he held his hands out toward hers. "I'm ready to be tied down."

He kissed her again, leaving her breathless. She opened her mouth but realized she didn't have anything to say. The kiss pretty much said everything she felt.

"So what does a guy have to do to get dinner around here?" Pete teased.

Bethany had lost her appetite for food, but she served dinner anyway. At least it gave them something to do as they talked about their new relationship.

Bethany awoke Sunday morning and looked around her bedroom. Everything seemed brighter, and when she got up and passed the mirror, she realized she was still smiling. After Pete had left last night, she resisted the urge to call her mother with the news. She and Pete had agreed to go to church together and tell their parents afterward. Together.

She sighed at the very thought of that word. *Together.* It had been a long time since she'd been half of together. What had floored her was Pete's confession that he didn't know what to do about his feelings for her. She'd always assumed he was in complete control in all situations.

By the time he picked her up for church, she'd rehashed the entire evening in her mind, and her smile had grown even wider. To her delight he looked as happy as she.

"I cannot believe this is happening," she said.

"Me neither." He pulled away from the curb. "All the way home last night I kept pinching myself to make sure it wasn't a dream."

Bethany laughed. "You sound like me."

As they pulled into the church parking lot, Bethany sighed. "I'm really nervous."

"Remember, we're in this together," he said.

There was that word again. She nodded. "I like the sound of that."

The second they reached the church steps, out popped Naomi and Gertie, and both of them had the biggest grins ever.

"It's about time you two came to your senses," Naomi said.

Pete glanced down at Bethany and smiled. "I don't think we have to say a word."

Gertie hugged Bethany. "What we see between the two of you speaks louder than words." She grinned at Naomi, and they fist-bumped. "Looks like our plan worked."

"So when's the wedding?" Naomi asked.

"Wedding?" Pete glanced back and forth between the two moms.

Naomi cackled. "Gertie, that boy of yours—"

Pete glanced at Bethany, who appeared mortified, so he squeezed her hand. "The wedding will happen when we're good and ready. Don't rush us or try to hold us back. This is between Bethany and me."

Naomi's eyebrows shot up. "I reckon you just told us."

He nodded. "Yes ma'am, no disrespect intended." He placed his hand in the small of Bethany's back. "Let's go find a seat."

She grinned up at him and nodded. As they left their mothers with their mouths hanging open, she giggled. "I think you just rendered them speechless."

"I hope so." He gestured toward a pew. "How's this?"

"Perfect." She'd barely sat down when she realized he was staring at her. "Do I have something on my face?"

"The look of love maybe. And speaking of love, how would you like to go look at rings later?"

Her heart pounded so hard, she was sure he could hear it. And when she opened her mouth, nothing came out, so she just nodded. He grinned and draped his arm around her shoulder.

"From now on, it's you and me, sweetie." He winked.

"Once you set your mind to something, you don't waste any time, do you?"

He shook his head. "No, the way I see it, there's no point. We've both been so slow, we have to make up for lost time."

If they hadn't been sitting in church, Bethany would have given him a big fat kiss. "Yes, I would love to go look at rings."

The organist started playing, so they turned to face the front. Throughout the sermon about the vastness of God's love, Bethany felt as though the pastor was speaking directly to her and Pete. Love . . . the greatest gift of all.

Dear Reader:

Thank you so much for choosing *For the Love of Pete* from the Bloomfield series. I brought back Murray the parrot to keep things interesting as Pete and Bethany's relationship grew. After all, Naomi and Pamela can't keep all the fun to themselves.

All the authors involved in this project have fallen in love with the quaint little town populated by quirky characters and an annoying bird with no filters. If you haven't had a chance to read some of the other stories, I would like to invite you to do so. My first Bloomfield story *Waiting for a View* is available in all digital formats. Gail Sattler's *Take the Trophy and Run* and *When Pigs Fly* are sure to elicit a few giggles. You'll also enjoy reading *Last Chance for Justice* by Kathi Macias and *Best Laid Plans* by Martha Rogers.

All the best to you and yours and God bless you all,

Debby Mayne

Discussion Questions

1. Pete remained a bachelor for many years because no girl or woman was as good as Bethany. Have you ever known someone who never married because no one matched up to his or her ideal? Do you think Pete could have been happy with someone else? Why or why not?

2. Why do you think Charlie wanted to leave Bloomfield right after he and Bethany got married?

3. Why do you think Bethany had a hard time getting rid of all her collectibles? Her mother-in-law's collectibles?

4. Have you ever held onto something long after you should have gotten rid of it?

5. Naomi obviously loves her children, and she did everything she could for them. Why do you think they all left town?

6. Naomi obviously likes to be in control of her environment. What are some of the ways Naomi controls things?

7. After Pete's dad took over the family business, it didn't do well, until Pete stepped in. What do you think made the difference?

8. Murray the parrot obviously says whatever he's thinking, very much like some children do. Have you ever been embarrassed by things children have said?

9. Pamela appears bossy, but occasionally we see a softer side of her. Why do you think she has such a crusty exterior?

10. Why do you think Andy clings to Murray after inheriting him from his sister?